The Lord's Oysters

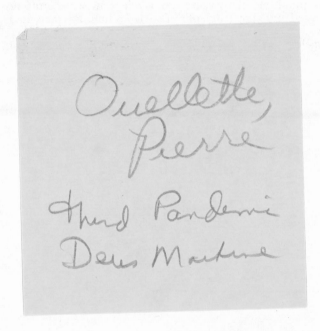

Publisher's Note

Works published as part of the Maryland Paperback Bookshelf are, we like to think, books that have stood the test of time. They are classics of a kind, so we reprint them today as they appeared when first published many years ago. While some social attitudes have changed and knowledge of our surroundings has increased, we believe that the value of these books as literature, as history, and as timeless perspectives on our region remains undiminished.

Also available in the series:

The Amiable Baltimoreans by Francis F. Beirne
The Potomac by Frederick Gutheim
The Bay by Gilbert C. Klingel
Tobacco Coast by Arthur Pierce Middleton
Watermen by Randall S. Peffer
Young Frederick Douglass by Dickson J. Preston

The Lord's Oysters

GILBERT BYRON

The Johns Hopkins University Press
Baltimore and London

Chapter 11, "To the Victor," appeared in the summer issue of *Prairie Schooner* for 1947 and is reprinted here with the permission of the editor of *Prairie Schooner* and its publisher, the University of Nebraska Press.

Printed in the United States of America

The Johns Hopkins University Press
701 West 40th Street
Baltimore, Maryland 21211-2190
The Johns Hopkins Press Ltd., London

Originally published by Atlantic/Little, Brown, 1957

Johns Hopkins Paperbacks edition, 1977
Maryland Paperback Bookshelf, 1986
Second Printing, 1991

The paper used in this publication meets the minimum requirements of American National Standard for Information Sciences—Permanence of Paper for Printed Library Materials, ANSI Z39.48-1984.

Library of Congress Catalog Card Number 57-6442
ISBN 0-8018-1959-8

This book is dedicated to my childhood playmates.

INTRODUCTION

Before I learned to read, my mother read to me; often Dad would come home from the river and stretch on the couch to listen. In the opening decade of the twentieth century, few people on the Eastern Shore possessed much wealth, but none of us was so poor that we did not have a few books, magazines, and newspapers scattered around the house. The absence of audio and video tubes gave us more time to read. Over the years, Aunt Carrie Byron, who lived in Baltimore, sent me a stream of books that included *Grimm's Fairy Tales, A Child's Garden of Verses,* by Robert Louis Stevenson, comic books that followed the antics of the Katzenjammer kids and Happy Hooligan, *Told by Uncle Remus,* by Joel Chandler Harris, *The Adventures of Robin Hood,* and *The Adventures of Tom Sawyer,* by Mark Twain. My thoughtful aunt also gave me a subscription to *Saint Nicholas* magazine, and this was renewed until I entered high school.

I began to read before entering the first grade, aided by my beloved nurse, Rose Mack, who must have been about fourteen years old when I was five. In elementary school, I was fortunate to have a number of dedicated teachers, maiden ladies who had a great respect for words and sentences. Their methods were simple and effective: either you learned while school was in session or you were detained and learned after school was dismissed, under the teacher's watchful eyes, until the shades of night began to fall.

One day a stranger sold Mama a set of *The Book of Knowledge* by exploiting her determination that her only son by a second marriage should have the best educational advantages. On rainy days, the children of the neighborhood often gathered in our parlor to explore the marvels of science and the legends of literature that are stored in this children's encyclopedia.

Each summer, Chautauqua pitched a hugh tent on a vacant lot in Chestertown and presented a week of culture. Sitting on my father's knee, I listened to the silver tongue of William Jennings Bryan and was entertained by a chorus of Swiss bell ringers. Every year, touring stock companies presented a week of plays, a different melodrama each night, with a special Saturday matinee for children. The floating theater pushed up the river and moored to the town wharf to offer another week of live theater. At an early age, I had seen *Uncle Tom's Cabin, East Lynne, The Girl of the Golden West, Ten Nights in the Barroom*, and *Peck's Bad Boy*—several times. Add to this fare: circuses and Wild West shows, touring minstrels and carnivals, the annual county fair, performances of local talent sponsored by church and civic organizations, and athletic contests that involved teams from the college, high school, and town. And a new medium, motion pictures, was beginning to attract large audiences.

Sunday was God's day. Guided and commanded by parents, the youth of our town attended church services regularly; I sang in the children's choir until my voice changed. During the long summers, on Sunday afternoons, the boys of different religious persuasions gathered for a game of baseball. Our elders warned us that the Sabbath was for meditation and rest, but fifty years ago on the Eastern Shore, baseball had already taken its place near a responsible God. Armed with a big bat, Homerun Baker led a host of earthy demigods.

Civic pride was the special province of the ladies. The Garden Club provided a fountain for the middle of the town square where streams of water poured from the mouths of griffins. A variety show was presented to raise money for the fountain; at a tender age, in company with a tiny, blonde ingenue, I sang a ballad that began: "Smarty, smarty, smarty, going to a party?"

One day when I came home from school, my mother, who was a skilled seamstress, had a new customer. Mrs. Dana, the wife of a young college professor, had commissioned Mama to make her a pair of the walking bloomers that were then fashionable in more urban areas. When Mama was uncertain whether she should contribute her talents to this view of things to come, Dad reassured her.

"She's the wife of Professor Richard Dana," he said. "His mother was Edith Longfellow, the Edith of golden hair in 'The Children's Hour'—remember?"

My father's formal education terminated in the fifth grade, but I was often surprised by the depth of his knowledge. Like most of the townsfolk, Dad had detailed information concerning the backgrounds of all newcomers to our bailiwick.

Some of my happiest hours were spent with Dad in his fifteen-foot bateau, which was powered with a noisy and unpredictable one-cylinder motor. On our river runs he often paused for a gam with oystermen and crabbers, or with the captains of the white schooners that sailed between the Chester River and Baltimore. Sometimes we visited my grandfather, who lived alone in a tiny ark pulled out on the bank of the river. The rich vernacular of these Chesapeake men must have touched my young ears and mind. Years later, some of these memories, augmented by the imagination, would become chapters in *The Lord's Oysters*.

My mother was determined that I should go to college; at the age of fourteen, I enrolled in the preparatory school that was then attached to Washington College. Many of the college professors also taught in the preparatory school; this was another fine part of my education. At sixteen, I entered the freshman class. That year, weighing in at 125 pounds, I played end on the football team, at least long enough to earn the varsity *W*. But my collegiate classwork suffered, as did my health, and for a time it appeared that I might withdraw from college. During this period our family moved to Baltimore, where Dad's leg was crushed in a shipyard accident. He never walked again, but I secured a scholarship that provided funds for almost all of my college expenses.

In the sophomore year, a young English prof came to the college who had recently graduated from Bates College in Maine. He had no advanced degrees but wrote poetry and book reviews for the literary supplement that Henry Seidel Canby edited for *The New York Evening Post*. This later became *The Saturday Review of Literature*. Lawrence Woodman guided me toward writing as a career. But after graduation, when a job on a Baltimore newspaper did not materialize, I turned to teaching. Over the years, I continued to write poetry, and in 1942, a small Vermont press brought out a collection of my verse, *These Chesapeake Men*.

In 1944, I wrote a short story that appeared in *The Educational Forum*. The setting was the river town of my childhood; it had the same characters and the boyish, colloquial style that would become a part of *The Lord's Oysters*. In May 1946, *The Canadian Forum* carried a second short story drawn from my childhood; it attracted the attention of a national publisher, who wondered if I were working on a novel.

By this time, I had written a dozen short stories and stopped teaching. That spring my mother died, and in the summer of 1946, I retired to a two-room cabin that I had built on a wooded Chesapeake cove to finish this book about boyhood in a tidewater town of fifty years ago. It took two years, and during this period, the interested publisher lost interest and I acquired an agent. The completed manuscript had forty-nine chapters and about 200,000 words.

In 1949, my schoolteacher wife of twenty-two years divorced me on the ground of desertion. With morale and cash at a new low, I aimed at the slicks, and in February 1950, *Collier's* bought a short short story, one about an old waterman and a giant soft crab that I had written in a single morning, for $750.00. But this was my only large sale, and that summer I worked on a neighboring farm as a hired man for 75¢ an hour.

In the fall I started to substitute in the public schools of Talbot County, and the next year returned to the fold as a full-time teacher. The novel continued the round of publishers until early in 1956 when it was entered in the annual book contest then conducted by Atlantic Monthly Press. In May, I learned that *The Lord's Oysters* was one of three finalists. On July 3, my agent telephoned to report that the judges had decided not to award any prize that year. Instead, Atlantic/ Little, Brown would publish all three finalists.

That summer I worked with Seymour Lawrence, director of Atlantic Monthly Press, preparing the book for publication. Twenty-one chapters were dropped. When the book appeared in February 1957, it was reviewed by many newspapers and a number of magazines. Some compared the book with Mark Twain's writings about his boyhood on the Mississippi. In December 1957, James H. Bready, book columnist for the Baltimore *Sunday Sun*, chose *The Lord's Oysters* for his annual "readability award" from some forty books about Maryland and by Marylanders that had been published that year.

With its publication I again left the classroom to write on a full-time basis. While a lot of words were lodged on paper, the sales were few, and in September 1961, Atlantic/Little, Brown allowed *The Lord's Oysters* to go out of print. By that time, I had completed several versions of another book with the same scene and characters, a children's novel that revolved around the first year in the life of a Chesapeake Bay retriever, which was published as *Chesapeake Duke.*

Folklore Associates, Inc., reprinted *The Lord's Oysters* in hardcover in 1967, in cooperation with the Maryland Affiliate, Reference Services Division of the American Library Association. I am grateful to the Johns Hopkins University Press for publishing this paperback edition, which makes the book available to a wider audience.

Gilbert Byron

Contents

The Lord's Oysters

Prologue

THE moon and tides were full; the summer southwest wind came up the river. It sighed through the
tall pines and rustled in the green marshes. Red-winged
blackbirds dipped the reeds. Schools of small fry, spawned
that spring, rumpled the quiet cove, dodged the watchful
kingfisher's eye. The soft crab hid in a mossy cell, waiting
for the day when its shell would harden to match the water moccasin's guile. Far out on the point, an old blue
heron fished the shallows of the sand bar. Methodically, he
plodded to and fro, pausing only when a slumbering minnow came within range of his marlinespike bill. Suddenly
he stopped and turned his yellow eyes toward the south.
In the distance, a huge white bird hovered close to the
water. It was far larger than the great swans which passed
his way each spring and fall, for it was a schooner, sailing
up the river, wing and wing. The old heron had seen it
many times and knew that the great white wings would
not harm him. He resumed his fishing. From the south
came sounds of explosions, riding the wind, and once more
the heron was tense. The popping became louder as a little bateau, propelled by a one-cylinder engine, creased the
river. Squawking nervously, the great bird took to the air,

chest puffed, long legs extended straight behind, and flew to the marshland where he was born.

In the yard of the house, a stone's throw from the river, a rat terrier was carefully examining an old chicken leg. He heard the pounding of the bateau's engine, and knowing it to be his man's boat, dropped the bone. On second thought, he hid it under the porch and trotted away toward the river.

Within the house, a woman heard the engine above the sound of her whirring sewing machine.

"Here comes your Daddy, Noah," she said to her thirteen-months-old baby, restless in his crib. She stopped sewing and listened. It was always thrilling to hear her man coming home. He really seemed more like a boy, for she was twelve years older than he, and as a young widow had reared six children before marrying again. Now, at forty-three, she had a young son and a young husband. She took the baby and went to meet him.

As she came to the cove, the bateau was approaching the bridge. For a moment, the boat was lost beneath the draw, the sound muffled. It emerged, the man stepped forward and shut off the engine, coasting across the cove until the stem of the boat crushed the soft sand.

"Hello, Mother," the young waterman said, jumping ashore and kissing his wife and son. He was a blue-eyed chap, with curly brown hair and a bronzed skin. Tall and thin, he was as tough as the hickory handle of his dip net. In contrast, his wife was short and pleasingly plump. Possessed by an ever-demanding energy, she was used to having her way.

"You've been drinking, George. I smell it on your breath."

"I haven't been drinking, Mother. I saw Captain Pete down the river and he gave me a couple of drinks, but that's not really drinking."

"What's that in the bottom of the boat?"

"I got us a mess of oysters. I sure would like to have my fill of oyster fritters for supper."

"You know you ain't supposed to take oysters before September," she said. "They'll put the law on you."

"They ain't never put the law on a person for taking enough to eat," he said. "Them's the Lord's oysters, the good Lord put them in the river for folks like us ones."

"You put them in that guano sack before somebody sees them," she said, treating him like one of her older sons.

"Tadde," the baby boy sang. "Tadde."

"Listen at him, electioneering for Teddy Roosevelt," his father said. "You suppose he's going to be one of them rich Republicans?"

"He's calling 'Daddy' for you, George," the wife said. "He knows you."

"Tadde," the baby cooed. "Tadde, oo, na, coo, was," and gurgled on in strange infant language.

"Listen to him," his mother said. "He's telling a story."

"Sure, let him tell his own story," his father said.

CHAPTER 1

Rose Mack and Miss Emma

THE earliest I can remember is Rose Mack coming to our house to be my nurse. I was sitting on Daddy's knee and we were watching Mama get supper. I was almost five years old.

"Oh, my poor head," Mama said. "I don't know what makes it hurt so."

"You must have strained your eyes threading needles," Daddy said. "Did you sew much today?"

"My head hurt so I had to stop in the middle of the afternoon and lay down. But I couldn't rest, wondering what the boy might be getting into, and I'm clear out of headache cologne."

"What you need is a black girl to play with Noah and help in the kitchen," Daddy said. "We could get a good girl for a dollar a week and her meals."

"If I could ease these headaches it would be money well spent."

"I'll ask around and see if I can find a girl."

The next day Mama was busy filling the bobbin on the sewing machine when we heard the screen door slam. It was Daddy with a colored girl. She had a white dress on and that made her seem even blacker. But she had a nice smile and pretty teeth.

"Here's your girl, Mother," Daddy said. "Her name is Rose Mack and her mother washes for Mrs. Unger. She'll come for a dollar a week and her meals." Daddy left Rose Mack with us.

"I want a colored girl to play with Noah and help me in the kitchen, Rose Mack," Mama said.

"Yes, ma'am," Rose Mack said, showing her pretty teeth.

"On nice days you can play with Noah in the yard, only you must never let him go in the road. A horse and wagon might run over him. You might think our street was a race track."

"Can we go out now, Mama?" I asked.

"Yes, but be careful, Rose Mack."

She took my hand and we walked out into the spring sun. Her hand was warm and the way she smiled made everything all right.

For a while we sat on the porch steps and watched the ants build a house.

"Those poor little ants work awful hard, don't they, honey?" she said. "And about the time they get their house all finished, along comes big feet and stamps it all to pieces."

"I'll stamp it all to pieces, like a giant," I said.

"You don't want to hurt the poor little ants. You ought to be a good giant."

"There ain't no good giants in the stories Mama reads to me."

"Those ants have slaves just like us colored people used to be," Rose Mack said. "My schoolteacher told me."

"I want you to be my slave," I said.

"I'll be your slave if you'll promise to always be a good giant."

"I promise, cross my heart and hope I die."

"Don't say that, honey. Did you ever find a four-leaf clover?"

"No, Rose Mack." I'd picked dandelions and daisies and buttercups but I'd never found a four-leaf clover.

"You'll have to help me, honey child," she said, so we found two four-leaf clovers before Mama called Rose Mack to help her with dinner.

"I want my Rose Mack to sit next to me, Mama."

"Rose Mack will eat her dinner in the kitchen."

"I want my Rose Mack to eat with me," I said. "Let me eat in the kitchen with her."

"She can't eat with us."

"Why can't she?"

"I'd just as leave eat in the kitchen where I belong, Mr. Noah," Rose Mack said. Her calling me "Mister" fixed things up but I still wondered why she couldn't eat with us.

On rainy days, Rose Mack helped me to build castles with my blocks. I liked to let her build a real tall castle and then I would knock it down. I made so much noise that Mama would stop her sewing machine.

"What's that noise, Rose Mack?" she would ask. "The boy didn't fall and hurt himself, did he?"

"No, ma'am," Rose Mack would answer. "He's just making out he's a good giant and knocking down the castles of the bad kings." Then she would build me another castle to knock down.

Even if she was only a little black girl, she had been to school and could read and write. She taught me to make my ABC's on an old slate and pretty soon I was reading the stories beneath the pictures in the big books Aunt Carrie sent me for Christmas.

We all liked Rose Mack except Rags, my little rat terrier. He was just as old as I was because Daddy got him to keep Mama company while he went sailing with Captain Pete. Rags used to sleep in my cradle. Anyway, Rags always barked and nipped at the heels of any colored person who came by our house. If they were carrying a package, Rags would bite them, too, or try hard. He knew they couldn't do anything about it and I guess he thought he was guarding the house.

Daddy said if you don't give a dog a job he'd pick one out for himself. And Rags wouldn't leave Rose Mack alone, even if she did work for us. He'd bark and try to take a piece out of her every morning. Rags was blacker than she was but it didn't seem to make any difference.

By the time she had been working for us a month, her legs began to show his teeth marks. One morning he drew blood.

"Rags has been pinching you again, hasn't he?" Mama asked.

"Yes, ma'am," Rose Mack said. "He's pinching harder every day."

"If you'd bring him a bone some morning, maybe he'd get to know you."

"He knows me all right," she said, but the next morning I saw her carrying a bag and figured she must have something for Rags. He was in the front yard, and when he saw that bag he dropped his bone and I knew he was going to bite her, or try hard. Rags started to snarl and turn up his lip. He looked awful fierce. Rose Mack took a nice bone out of the bag — it even had meat on it — and called to Rags. She'd never given him a bone before and I guess he figured that she was tricking him or maybe he thought she was going to chunk him. He wouldn't come and get it. Rose Mack cornered him against the house and at last he took the bone, growling and showing his teeth when he grabbed it. She turned to come in the back door and that was what Rags was waiting for. He dropped the bone and bit her, without even barking to let her know he was coming. We heard her yell.

"Oh, my," Mama said. "Rags has pinched Rose Mack again." She had to use peroxide. It was funny but Rose Mack's blood looked just like mine; it was red, too. That peroxide, fizzing and foaming, scared me worse than blood.

Rags never bit me but once — that was the time I tried to take his rag away from him. He had an old rag for a bed and used to chew and suck on it. If you said "Rags, Rags" to him, he would grab his old rag and shake it, growling and getting madder all the time. Daddy said it showed he was a good rat terrier. Only we didn't have any rats, just mice. Sometimes, at night, when everything was still, a little mouse would run out on the carpet, sit up and twirl his whiskers. That's what Mama said he was doing. Rags would look at the mouse but he didn't even bother to growl. I guess he figured the mouse was a part of our family. Anyway, Rags was sucking on his rag and I tried to grab it. He got so mad with the rag that he bit me. Mama cried and I almost did when she poured on the peroxide. Rags wasn't even sorry. He shook his rag and growled.

One morning I was so glad to see Rose Mack that I hugged her. She bent over and I kissed her and laughed. Mama saw me.

"Noah," she yelled, grabbing my arm and jerking me away. "You mustn't kiss her. Don't you ever kiss her again. And don't you let him, Rose Mack."

"No, ma'am," my nurse said. "He did it before I could stop him."

"I love my Rose Mack, Mama," I said. "Why can't I kiss her?"

"You just can't, and if you say anything more about it I'll get my hairbrush to you." She was mad and I knew she would.

When Mama's older children came to visit they always wanted to kiss me, but I wouldn't let them and turned my head away. If I couldn't kiss my Rose Mack, I wouldn't kiss anybody except maybe Mama or Daddy.

"What's the matter with your child, Mama?" sister Helen said one day. She almost squeezed me to death. "It's not natural for a youngun to refuse hugging and kissing."

"I don't know," Mama said. "He's always been that

way." I never told them, but I saw Rose Mack, standing off to one side, smiling. I guess she knew.

When the day came for me to start school, Mama left Rose Mack to take care of the house and took me herself.

"I hope Miss Emma won't think you are as bad as my other children," she said on the way. "You are such a good child compared to those others."

Miss Emma's room was crowded with parents and their children. We saw sister Helen with Rickard. He's a month older than I am but I'm his uncle. Ric looked mad and ornery.

"I had to carry him halfway," sister Helen said. "He don't want to go to school." She had a good grip on him or he would have run off.

Mama looked like she was going to cry when she handed me over to Miss Emma. "This is Noah, Emma," she said. "You'll find him a much better child than my first ones."

"I certainly hope so," Miss Emma said, looking at me through thick glasses. She was beginning to shrivel up like older teachers do.

"Good-by, Noah," Mama said. "Be a good boy. Rose Mack will come for you at dinnertime." She left and I could see tears in her eyes.

Most of the girls sniffled a little when their mothers left but only one boy cried, and he had long red curls which was reason enough. Ric yanked one of them and he really boohooed. Ric seemed to feel better and grinned at me.

"Let's ask Miss Emma if we can sit together," he said, "being's you are my uncle."

"All right," I said, "let's."

When she started seating us, Ric asked her.

"You might be a bad influence on each other," Miss Emma said.

"Noah can already read and write," Ric said. "He could help me."

Miss Emma looked right through me. "Can you read and write?"

"Yes, ma'am," I said. "Rose Mack showed me how."

"Who's Rose Mack?"

"My colored nurse."

"She's probably mixed you all up," Miss Emma said. "Especially if you are left-handed." Ric did get the seat right in back of me but that wasn't good for me. Every once in a while he would punch me when Miss Emma wasn't looking.

We spent most of the morning learning signals. If you held up one finger that meant you had to go to the toilet; if you held up two fingers you had to go, only this time you were in a hurry. Three fingers asked for a drink and four fingers meant you wanted to dip your slate sponge in the water.

"You might think we were deaf and dumb," Ric whispered to me, putting his thumb to his nose and wiggling his hand at Miss Emma when her back was turned.

"What does that mean, Ric?" I whispered.

"Why don't you try it on Miss Emma and find out?"

That seemed like a good idea, and when she turned toward us, I stood up, put my thumb to my nose, and wiggled all of my fingers at her. She turned red.

"Noah, how dare you? Come here this instant!"

I was feeling sort of smart as I walked up to her desk. I had a signal the others didn't have, except Ric. But when she glared at me through those glasses, I knew something was wrong. The rest of the kids were all quiet. I guess they felt it, too.

"You ought to be ashamed of yourself, Noah Marlin," she said. "Especially after your mother said you were such a good boy. I might have known. If you ever do that again, I'll whip you with my big ruler." She opened her top drawer and pulled out a big eighteen-inch ruler that was as heavy as a fence paling. It had holes in one end to blister you, and just to look at it made my lip quiver.

"I won't never do it again, Miss Emma," I said, my voice shaking.

She looked at me awhile and balanced the ruler in her hand before putting it in the drawer. "You stand in that corner facing the wall."

"Yes, ma'am," I said, and stood in the corner the rest of the morning. When the noon bell rang, I had to wait until all of the rest were let out. But Ric was waiting for me when I reached the steps.

"Did you tell her I told you to thumb your nose?" he said.

"No, Ric."

"You'd better not if you know what's good for you," he said, fierce-like.

I couldn't see Rose Mack anywhere. After standing in

the corner for so long I felt weak and was scared to go home by myself.

"Have you seen Rose Mack, Ric?" I asked.

"I saw her hanging around in the street. I guess she thought you had gone. Ain't you ashamed to have a nigger girl walk home with you?"

"Don't you call my Rose Mack a nigger," I said.

"That's all she is," Ric said.

"Anyway, she's a nice nigger girl," I said.

"Come on home with me and we can play in the boat my pop is building in the back yard. You can eat at my house."

"All right," I said and went to Ric's house. Sister Helen was surprised to see me.

"Your mother will be worried to death about you, Noah," she said. "I'll send Annie over to your house and ease Mama's mind." Annie is Ric's older sister.

After eating we played in the boat, only Ric had to be the captain. He made me do whatever he said and I was tired out by the time we got back to school. I was careful not to get into any more trouble. When Miss Emma let us out, Mama and Rose Mack were waiting at the door.

"You almost scared us to death, Noah," she said. "Don't you ever do a thing like that again."

"I couldn't find Rose Mack."

"You must have been late getting out and she thought she had missed you."

"Yes, ma'am."

"Miss Emma didn't keep you in, did she?"

"Sorta."

"Oh, my," Mama said, "I knew I shouldn't have bragged about you like I did. What did you do?"

"I just made a signal with my hand."

"You mean number one or number two?"

"No, ma'am."

"Show me what you did."

I put my thumb to my nose and wiggled my fingers. Mama slapped me. She'd threatened me before but this was the first time she had ever laid her hand on me, except with the hairbrush.

"I hope that'll put some sense in you," she said. "Who showed you how to do that?"

"A boy," I said, "but I don't even know what it means."

"I wouldn't be the one to tell you," she said. "Your father will take a hand when we get home. Rose Mack, did you ever see Noah do that before?"

"No, ma'am."

We walked the rest of the way home without saying anything. Daddy was resting on the couch.

"How do you like school?" he said, kissing me.

"All right," I said, "only Miss Emma got her big ruler out and made me stand in the corner."

"Good Lord," Mama said. "It's getting worse. Did she use it on you?" She began to look me over for marks. "She'd better not."

"She don't use the ruler, it's to scare them," Daddy said. "The law won't let her lay her hands on, except to shake."

"Noah made an awful sign at Miss Emma, George," Mama said.

"Show your Daddy, Noah," he said.

Before Mama could stop me, I put my thumb to my nose and wiggled my fingers. Daddy looked at me and started to laugh. He fell off the couch and rolled on the floor, still laughing.

"You did that to Miss Emma?" he said.

"He did that to Miss Emma but he doesn't know what it means," Mama said.

"I guess a lot of kids have wanted to do that to Miss Emma," he said.

"You'll have to tell him what it means, George," Mama said. She and Rose Mack went out into the kitchen.

"When you do that, sonny," Daddy said, "you cuss the person you are looking at. It's the same as telling them to kiss your backsides. Do you understand?"

"Yes, sir."

"If you want to double it, you use both your hands, like this," Daddy said, and he showed me how. "Don't ever do that to anybody who can catch you or lick you, like a teacher."

"No, sir," I said, thinking about how much I had learned my first day in school.

Mama saw what Daddy was teaching me. "You stop that this minute, George," she said. "How do you expect Noah to grow up right with you showing him things like that?"

"Give him time to grow up, Mother," Daddy said. "He's not much bigger than a bull minnow."

"Don't you start mixing him up with the river," Mama said. "He's never going to follow the river."

" 'Never' is a long time," Daddy said.

I wondered how long a time never was.

CHAPTER 2

A Breath of Fresh Air

THE next morning, Rose Mack took me to school and I was careful not to make any strange signals or do anything Ric told me to do.

All of the first month we didn't do much but draw on our slates and that suited me. Daddy was good at drawing and Mama said I had his talent. Anyway, I liked to draw pictures of schooners with their sails full, coming up the river. Daddy showed me how to make sea gulls flying and waves on the river. One day I drew such a pretty schooner on my slate that even Miss Emma was pleased.

"I want you to go to the principal's office and show him your nice drawing, Noah," she said, "and be sure and tell him that I sent you."

I didn't want to go to Mr. Manning's office because that's where most of the kids get licked. He's got a ruler twice as big as Miss Emma's, at least that's what Ric says, and he's been there. Only Mr. Manning just took it out and threatened him with it. But if Emma sent Ric again, he was going to get a whaling.

"Go ahead, Noah," Miss Emma said. "I'll give you a note so there can't be a mistake." She wrote something and folded it up before she gave it to me. The hall was empty and I could hear the big clock ticking, or it might have been my heart. I felt awful lonely and ran until I came to Mr. Manning's door. I rapped, not making much noise.

"Come in," a loud voice said, and I went inside just in time to see Mr. Manning put the big ruler in his closet. It was the size of a baseball bat. The boy he had been showing it to was sitting on the chair crying. Mr. Manning looked at me and I could see he was wondering if he had put it away too soon.

"Who sent you?" he said, sort of red in the face from fussing with the other boy.

I was so scared I couldn't say a word, but I did have enough sense to give him Miss Emma's note. He read it.

"Well, let's see your picture," he said, sitting down behind his big desk.

I gave it to him and sat down quick, my knees were weak.

He looked at the slate and he looked at me. "You drew this?"

"Yes, sir, only my father helps me to draw waves and gulls."

"What's your name?"

"Noah Marlin."

"You're the waterman's son?"

"Yes, sir."

Mr. Manning watched the boy in the chair — he was still crying — and examined my picture again. He gave me the slate.

"Thank you, Noah, for coming and showing me your

picture," he said. "Keep on drawing and doing whatever you really like to do, that's the important thing."

"Good-by," I said, and ran all the way back to Miss Emma's room.

When I got home from school, Mama asked me like she always does, "Did you have any trouble with Miss Emma today?"

"No, ma'am, but she sent me to the principal's office."

"Good Lord," she said, not giving me time to explain. "Sent to the office and you only in the first grade, and this only the first month of school. This never happened to my other children."

"I didn't do nothing wrong, Mama," I said, trying to tell her what happened, but she wouldn't let me.

"And you're not even remorseful," she said. "Maybe I ought to whip you with my hairbrush."

"Mama, I went to show Mr. Manning a picture I drew, a picture of a schooner." I shoved my slate into her hands.

"Well," she said, looking at the picture. "Why didn't you tell me? Ain't that nice."

One day in December, when I got to school, Miss Emma wasn't sitting at her desk. It felt queer not to have her there, just like it does when you get lost from your mother. Mr. Manning came in with a young girl about the age of my Rose Mack. We got real quiet because Mr. Manning is the principal and he's allowed to whip.

"Miss Emma is sick today, children," he said. "This is Miss Mary and she will teach you until Miss Emma is well."

Our new teacher was scared when Mr. Manning left

her. We looked at her and she looked at us. She smiled and she had the prettiest smile, even nicer than Rose Mack's.

She didn't teach us the way Miss Emma did. It seemed easier, so I guess she wasn't as good a teacher as Miss Emma. But when recess time came, she went outside and played with us. Miss Emma never did that, she bossed us from the window. Miss Mary played dodge ball with the girls first, then she came over to us boys.

"Come on, boys," she said, "all join hands and make a circle. We're going to play bull in the ring. Who wants to be the bull and break out?"

Ric was the first bull. He pawed and snorted before breaking out and ran around the school building twice before Erny tackled him and the rest of us piled on. It's a good game, almost as rough as football. Erny was the bull because he caught Ric. I would have liked to be the bull but I never caught any of the other bulls.

When I got home from school, Mama noticed my dirty clothes and one knee bleeding through my long black stocking. She got the peroxide and the stocking was stuck. It hurt.

"You've had a fight, Noah," she said. "Who have you been fighting with?"

"I ain't been fighting, Mama," I said. "Our teacher taught us a new game, bull in the ring."

"You know Miss Emma is too old to play with you. You've been fighting."

"No, ma'am. Miss Emma's sick and Miss Mary is our teacher. She's young and pretty."

"If what happened to you is playing, I'm going to take myself up to that school and see Mr. Manning. You look half killed."

"Aw, Mama, it's the first real fun I've had since school started. She's a pretty teacher and I like her."

"Pretty is as pretty does," Mama said. "She's probably one of them new normal-school teachers and only fooling around until she can catch a man. If you come home bloody again I'm going to see Mr. Manning."

Miss Emma was still sick the next day and it snowed all morning. We didn't do much work but kept looking at the flakes coming down. Miss Mary didn't know what to do with us until she got an idea.

"Do you children like snow ice cream?" she asked.

"Yes, ma'am," we all said.

"If all of you will behave yourselves and do your lessons, we will make vanilla snow ice cream just before dismissal this afternoon."

Even Ric was good and offered to wash the blackboards for Miss Mary. Miss Emma would have been surprised if she had seen us that day. About two o'clock, us boys put on our boots and went out with Miss Mary. We got a lot of nice clean snow in buckets and the girls put vanilla and sugar on it. It was good, only I almost froze on the way home.

"Well, did you play bull in the ring today?" Mama said, looking me over.

"No ma'am," I said, "we made snow ice cream instead."

"You mean you ate some of the snow?"

"Yes, ma'am, about a bucketful with vanilla and sugar."

"And you with such a weak stomach you almost died when you were a baby," she said. "Now I am going to see Mr. Manning. That young girl will have you sick with measles or worse. Don't she know the air is full of germs when it snows?" She came over and felt my forehead. "You feel cool enough. Are you all right?"

"Yes, ma'am, only I'm cold."

"I can see you're coming down with a chill and fever. Take off your clothes and get in bed. I'll get a hot iron."

"Aw, Mama, I'm not sick."

But she made me go to bed and stay there. Several times that night I woke up and Mama had her hand on my forehead.

I was all right in the morning but three of the other kids came down with the mumps and even the doctors blamed Miss Mary. Six of the second-grade kids got the mumps and they didn't eat snow ice cream.

Anyway, Miss Emma got well and we didn't see Miss Mary again. But for the rest of the year when we were dumb and made mistakes it was always Miss Mary's fault. She caused a lot of trouble during the few days she taught us. I'll always remember Miss Mary like the breath of fresh air you get as you run down the school steps on a spring day. I guess that isn't the way education should be.

I'll never forget Miss Mary for another reason. After she left, we were playing bull in the ring and I got to be the bull. I'm sort of small and it was hard for me to break out. I had to trick them, but once I did, they had a lot of trouble catching me. I'm small but I'm hard to catch, especially when there is a bunch chasing me. I ran around the schoolhouse four times, and I guess they never would have caught me if I hadn't tripped over a root and fallen down. The gang was right behind me and they were going so fast that they ran right on over me and one of them stepped on my nose. I felt something crack and my face was all bloody when I got up. It scared the rest of them and they took me in to Miss Emma. She washed the blood off my face.

"Your nose is bleeding," she said. "Sit down quietly and it will stop."

I sat down and kept real still but it wouldn't stop. I held a handkerchief to my nose, but it wouldn't stop.

"Seems like I've heard somewhere that if you drop a cold door key down your back it will stop nosebleed," she said. She took a key out of her desk drawer. "Rickard, take this key to the washroom and soak it in cold water."

By that time recess was over and all of the kids were watching my nose bleed. Ric brought the key back, dripping water, and Miss Emma dropped it down inside my long underwear. But my nose kept on bleeding.

"I think you had better go home, Noah," Miss Emma said. "The rest of the children won't get anything done as long as they can watch your nose bleed."

"Can I go with him and keep him company, Miss Emma?" Ric said. "He's my uncle."

"You may," she said. She acted like she was glad to get rid of both of us.

I bled all the way home and I was beginning to see spots in front of my eyes. Mama saw us coming and came out to meet us.

"What are you boys doing out of school this time of day?" she said. "Have you had trouble with Miss Emma?" She saw my nose bleeding. "You've been fighting."

"No, ma'am," Ric said. "We were playing bull in the ring and somebody stepped on his nose."

"Why didn't Miss Emma stop it? She knows a cold door key will stem nose bleed."

"We tried that."

They took me inside and Mama gave me a cold glass of water to drink. "If I only had a piece of ice — some folks fancy ice more than a cold door key," she said.

"I can go down to the cove and get a piece of ice," Ric said, and he did. Mama undid my long underwear and dropped the ice down my back. It felt worse than the wet door key. I started to shiver but my nose stopped bleeding.

"It's a good thing Miss Emma got well," Mama said. "If that young teacher had taught you much longer she'd figured out a way for all of you to kill yourselves."

I had a bad cold in the morning and Mama let me stay home.

One day, me and Rose Mack walked home from school another way. We had always gone down High Street, past the stores, and sometimes, if Mama had given Rose Mack a penny, I could stop at Mr. Billy Mac's and buy a stick of licorice or a coconut strip colored like a rainbow. The licorice lasts longer but the coconut is prettier.

"Let's go down Cannon Street, Mr. Noah," Rose Mack said. "It's closer to home."

Colored people live on Cannon Street and most of the kids were playing in the street or sitting and looking. The men were loafing on the steps in the sun, but the women were busy washing clothes or digging in their gardens. It was the last of March and time to get busy with your garden. They all spoke to me and Rose Mack.

"Good afternoon, Miss Rose," a young colored man said, "Ain't it nice to be spring again?"

"It sure is, Mr. Willie," Rose said, smiling and looking cute.

"How about me coming around to your house tonight?" Willie said.

Rose Mack looked down at her shoes and rubbed the toes together like her feet were itching. "You can come if you want to, I might be home and I mightn't."

"We might take a walk on the bridge," he said. "There might be a moon."

"I might go," she said, and we walked toward home.

After that we used to travel Cannon Street almost every day and Rose Mack would stop and talk with Willie. You could see that they were getting thicker and thicker. One day, Rose Mack didn't come to work and I had to walk to school by myself. It got so she was sick half the time, or that is what she said. Mama put up with it as long as she could and then she put her foot down.

"You've only been here two days this week," Mama said. "Have you been sick the rest of the time?"

"No, ma'am," Rose Mack said.

"Where have you been?"

Rose Mack grinned. "I've got myself a man and have to cook for him when he's home."

"Why didn't you tell me you were getting married?"

"We ain't married, we're just engaged."

"Are you living with him?"

"Yes, ma'am, when he's home. He's a steamboat man, and when that old horn blows he has to truck."

"That ain't respectable, Rose Mack, living with a man and not being married to him."

"No, ma'am, but it's nice."

Mama looked to see if I was listening. "'If you are going to live that way, you can't work here any more. You'd better get your things."

"Yes, ma'am," Rose Mack said. "I sort of need a change." When she went out the door she smiled for me. "Good-by, Mr. Noah."

"Good-by, Rose Mack," I said.

After she left, Mama talked to me. "I want you to grow up into a respectable man, Noah, like my father — you are named after him. Rose Mack started going bad the minute she met that steamboat man. The river ain't respectable. Lord knows I wish your father would leave it."

"Yes, ma'am," I said, but all the time I was listening for the sound of Daddy's bateau.

CHAPTER 3

Rags! Rags! Rags!

IT was funny but I didn't miss Rose Mack much, but I guess Rags missed her.

"I don't know what's come over Rags," Mama said. "He acts like he had a quarrel with the world."

"He's gone mean, all right," Daddy said. "I noticed him changing right after Rose Mack left."

"I guess he misses pinching Rose Mack," Mama said.

"He snapped at Old Man Wood yesterday," Daddy said. "He threatened to see Mr. Jester if Rags drew blood."

Old Man Wood is our next-door neighbor and Mr. Jester is the town constable.

"Did he draw blood, Daddy?" I said.

"No, he just tore his pants. But if Rags don't stop biting everybody, we'll have to get rid of him. Soon or late, he'll bite somebody who will sue me. Then where will I be?"

After Rags tried to bite him, Old Man Wood took a dislike to him. It seemed like Rags knew it, and he did everything he could, without going too far, to make Old Man Wood mad. The worst he did was to raise his leg against our neighbor's gatepost whenever he got a chance. Old Man Wood would sit in his parlor, fuming and peeping out the front window, trying to catch Rags in the act. But Rags always waited until Old Man Wood went uptown. And dogs being like they are, pretty soon Rags had all the dogs in the neighborhood hanging around Old Man Wood's gatepost, reading the news. My dog kept one eye on the corner, and as soon as his enemy rounded it, he would slip over in his own yard and gnaw on his bone.

One day, Old Man Wood came home and chunked the other dogs. He looked at Rags, peacefully studying his bone in our yard.

"You little devil," he said, sniffing and snorting, "you're the cause of all this."

Rags knew his rights, and when he was cussed he knew it too. He dropped his bone and ran to the fence that divides our yards. He snarled and showed his teeth, cussing with his looks.

"I'd like to get a hold on you once," Old Man Wood said, looking for a chunk.

Me and Daddy were watching from our front window. We went out on the porch.

"Don't you chunk Rags, Mr. Wood," Daddy said. "He was minding his own business until you cussed him."

"Do you call scenting my gatepost minding his own business?"

"You can't prove it," Daddy said. "You've had a grudge against Rags ever since he snapped at you."

Mama came out with us. "Why don't you and Rags make up, Mr. Wood?" she said. "He used to be such a nice little dog before he started feeling that everybody was down on him."

Old Man Wood was on one side of the fence and Rags was on the other side. They eyed each other.

"Go ahead and pat Rags, Mr. Wood," Daddy said, "and everything will be all right."

Mr. Wood thought about it. He edged closer to the fence and stuck his hand over in our yard. "Nice old Rags," he said, and reached down to pat him.

I guess Rags figured it was too good a chance to miss. He didn't growl or even snarl, but he jumped up and bit Mr. Wood's hand. And he drew blood.

"You treacherous little bastard!" Old Man Wood yelled, forgetting Mama. "That does it, George. I'm going to get Mr. Jester." He went off wrapping his handkerchief around the hand Rags had marked.

You could see Rags didn't think he had done anything wrong, being he was in his own yard and Old Man Wood had cussed him a few minutes before. But Daddy kicked at him and Rags fastened on his shoe just like a snapping turtle. He couldn't cut through the leather but he wouldn't let go and Daddy kicked so hard that his shoe flew off.

"You little devil," Daddy said, and Rags crept under the house. You could see he felt the world was down on him.

"You can't fight Rags," Mama said, "you have to reason with him."

Pretty soon Mr. Wood was back and he had Mr. Jester with him. And the constable had on his shiny badge.

"What's this I hear about you harboring a vicious dog, George?" he said.

Rags heard the new voice, and I saw him peeping at Mr. Jester from under the house, sort of measuring him before marking him. But he must have seen that shiny badge. Anyway, he came out, dragging his old rag, and walked up to Mr. Jester wagging his tail and looking cute like rat terriers can. He put his rag down at the constable's feet and drew back. I figured it might be his scheme to get a good bite at Mr. Jester if he dared to touch the rag, but it tickled the constable.

"Ain't he cute?" he said. "Mr. Wood, this dog ain't as vicious as you painted him."

"You touch that rag and you'll see how deceiving he is," Old Man Wood said.

We all held our breaths and watched Mr. Jester, and be doggone if Rags didn't let him pick up the rag.

"Well," Mr. Jester said. "What d'you say to that, Mr. Wood?"

"He's an ornery little devil but he knows which side his bread is buttered on," Old Man Wood said.

When Rags heard that cussword he snarled, and our neighbor jumped back.

"See that," he said. "He almost bit me again."

"You cussed him," Daddy said. "He'd bite me if I cussed him. You can't blame him for that."

"Where were you when the dog bit you, Mr. Wood?" Mr. Jester said.

"Standing in my yard."

"You reached your hand over the fence into our yard,"

Mama said. "Your hand was in our yard when Rags pinched you."

"You told me to pat him," Old Man Wood said.

"I did not," Mama said. "I only suggested that you make up with Rags. You ought to have talked it over with him first."

"The way I see it," Mr. Jester said, "the dog has some rights, as long as he is in his master's yard. If Rags was in his yard I can't do a thing. But if you let him out and he bites somebody, I'll have to shoot him."

"We'll keep him in," Daddy said.

Rags was listening close, especially when Mr. Jester said anything, and I knew he was figuring on how far he could go.

Old Man Wood started home mad and Rags followed him along the inside of our fence, growling and cussing, low-like, so nobody else could hear him.

After that Rags knew his rights and only bit folks who came to visit us. Every morning he lay in wait for the ice men and tore the cuffs off their pants as fast as their wives could put them on. But he was careful not to draw blood and he waited until they were inside our yard. It got so nobody would come to see us. Mama lost some of her sewing customers or had to go to their houses. Miss Louisa was the only stranger who could come into our yard and not get pinched. Her father is president of the school board. That didn't stop Rags. He tried, but she fooled him.

One day she started for our house to see Mama about making a dress. Rags saw her coming and crouched low, ready to scare her. Women scare easier than men and Rags knew it. Just as she put her hand on the gate, he leaped out of the tall grass growling and showing his teeth.

Miss Louisa was ready for him. "Whose little doggie are you?" she said, using baby talk and a Southern drawl. "You cute little sweetie-pie. You ought to be ashamed to bark at little me." She wasn't little, but Rags couldn't stand that baby talk. He started to wag his tail and he wagged all over. He would have opened the gate for her if he had been big enough to reach the latch. After that, Miss Louisa always used baby talk on him and he loved it, and her. But she was the only one he loved, for by that time he was down on me, and Daddy, and even Mama, except around mealtimes.

Rags could bluff all of the dogs on our street. The bigger they were, the tougher Rags was, and they all backed down when he showed his teeth. Even Ponto, Mrs. Steers's collie, who was about three times his size, was respectful when he passed Rags.

One day a pack of coon hounds were coming home after hunting all night and they happened to pass our house. They were creeping along, dragging their feet, and looking sad and worn out. Rags must have figured it was a good chance to make a big reputation. He cussed all of them and dared them to come into our yard, offering to open the gate. They were too weary to pay any attention. Rags took that as a slight, and slipping under the fence, darted out into the road and bit the hind leg of the leading hound.

"Kiyi," the poor old hound moaned, not even knowing what had him. "Kiyi," he howled, mournful-like, and loped off toward home. Rags bit all of them. He was so small he could run under their legs, and they all started to bay like the coons were after them — maybe that's what they really thought. They were so tired and their feet were so tender, they never even took up for themselves. By the time Rags had put his mark on all of them, they had passed the corner, and he let them go because that was out of his territory. He came strutting home and crawled back under the fence, through the same hole he used to get out. That shows you how much smarter a dog is than a chicken. An old hen can find a hole to get out of a yard, but just try to chase her back through the same hole. Ducks can, though, and that shows they're smarter than chickens. But ducks ain't as smart as dogs, at least not rat terriers like Rags.

Sometimes when I went to the store for Mama, Rags would slip under the fence and follow me. He would wait until I rounded the corner by Miss Lizzie's and then he would keep out of chunking range. He was afraid of the oyster shells I sailed at him.

"Go home, Rags," I would say as I picked up a shell. He would cringe and stretch on the ground or crawl on his stomach, begging to go. Sometimes I would give in, and he knew before I told him and would come running. Everything would be all right unless we met a strange dog or Mr. Brewster came along driving his horse and carriage. He's the richest man in town and Rags liked to nip at his horse more than anybody else's. Mr. Brewster would try to cut Rags with his buggy whip but my terrier was too fast for him.

One day in July the circus came to town, and I started toward High Street to see the parade. When I left our yard, I was careful to hook the gate. I didn't see Rags and figured he must be under the house, asleep. But when I reached the corner and looked back, there he was, creeping along Miss Lizzie's fence.

"Go on home, Rags," I said, and sailed an oyster shell in his direction. He turned and ran to our gate before stopping. Old Man Wood was standing beside his gate and they must have cussed each other.

I ran fast all the way to the next corner, where the iron fence is, and stopped to look back. Rags had rounded Miss Lizzie's corner, but when he saw me looking he stepped behind a tree. I started to walk toward him and he trotted toward home, disappearing around the corner. I turned and ran as fast as I could to Mr. Leary's store before looking back. Rags was creeping along the iron fence. It was then I heard the circus band playing as the parade went down High Street, and I knew if I didn't hurry they would be back inside the big tent before I saw them. I forgot all about Rags and ran the rest of the way to High Street. Ric was waiting for me. I got there just in time. The ringmaster was leading, riding on a white horse, and he was followed by the clowns. They were playing jokes and squirting water, like us boys do in school. I guess all of the kids in town were watching the clowns. One of them was rolling a big hoop, and having a lot of fun, when a little black terrier ran out and grabbed the seat of his pants. Everybody thought he was a circus dog and laughed — that is, everybody but me and the clown, because it was Rags.

He ran back into the crowd but I knew he wasn't through because the elephants were coming. Rags wouldn't miss the chance to bite an elephant. I looked for him but he must have been crouching low, waiting for the elephants. They came down the street, and us boys and everybody backed up to give them plenty of room, but not Rags. He darted out and bit the heel of the leading elephant, growling and snarling worse than I'd ever seen him before. The elephant rolled his eyes and swung his big trunk around. He was too late! Rags was working on the second elephant, and passed on to bite the tip of the third elephant's tail. You might not think that great big elephants would be scared of a little dog, but you didn't know Rags. He had them trumpeting and trotting down the street as fast as they could go. He was so busy with the elephants, he didn't see the calliope coming, and that was the end of Rags. The calliope was pulled by four black horses and wasn't playing when Rags stampeded the elephants. All of a sudden it started piping "The Blue Danube" and the sound scared Rags, or worried him anyway. He crouched, and before he could size up the situation, the horses and calliope ran over him. With all that, he ran home, but when I got there he was dead.

We buried Rags by the horseradish and sunflowers, where he liked to bury his bones. I guess most everybody was glad he was gone, but Miss Louisa missed him and so did Old Man Wood.

CHAPTER 4

Come Dogwood Time

I WAS sick a good bit that year I was in the second grade and stayed home from school off and on all winter.

Soon after Christmas, Daddy started mending his nets for spring fishing. It was too cold to work outside so he brought them into the kitchen. In a few days they reached into the dining room, but Mama put her foot down and wouldn't let him stretch them into the parlor.

"I can't hardly walk for fish nets," she said. "How do you expect me to get you anything to eat? Why can't you wait until it's warm enough to work outside? Ain't it almost time for the midwinter thaw?"

"I got to do something, Mother, I can't sit around all winter," he said, pausing to fill his seine needle with twine. "Besides, spring is going to be early this year and we got to have the nets ready when the run starts. Jesse says the dogwood buds are starting to swell already."

"I don't know why you don't leave the river and get yourself a decent job," Mama said. "It ain't right just catching fish and crabs for a living. You're setting a bad example for Noah."

Daddy started to get mad. "I guess we talked that all

over before," he said. "The river was good enough for my pappy and it's good enough for me. I ain't going to tie myself down like a slave for nobody. Folks have forgotten about 'life, liberty and the pursuit of happiness.' All they want is to make a pile of money."

"You sound like the Fourth of July," Mama said.

Somebody knocked on the back door and it was Mr. Jesse. He had his hip gum boots on, and must have come by way of the creek.

"Look what I picked up on the way over," he said, and pulled a diamondback terrapin from his pocket. Its feet were pulled inside and the shell was all closed up. "Spring ain't far off when Mr. Diamondback starts coming out of the mud."

"That turtle's dead," Mama said, sort of disgusted-like. "Don't you smell up my house with it either."

"It ain't dead, neither," Mr. Jesse said. "You open your oven and let me toast his toes for a minute or two. You'll see how dead he is."

"You're not going to put that mud turtle in my clean oven," Mama said, but she let him just the same, and when Mr. Jesse opened the oven a few minutes later the terrapin was almost sweating, his eyes bulging. He crawled out and dropped to the kitchen floor without being prodded.

"Just like going to Florida," Daddy said.

He and Mr. Jesse went to work mending the rotten places in the nets.

"First warm day we have, let's take what we got finished outside and tar it," Mr. Jesse said.

"You can't get them out of here too fast for me," Mama said.

"That old bateau ought to have a coat of red lead on her bottom before we put her overboard," Daddy said. "And the engine needs a lot of work on it."

Mama sort of snorted. "You might as well take the engine out of the boat, as much good as it is to you."

"Is that so? Well, this year she's really going to run. I've already ordered a new carburetor. Once you get her started that old Ferro always was a good engine."

"That's all you have to do, get it started," Mama said, sarcastic-like.

The last week in January it was right warm, and Daddy and Mr. Jesse got all the nets outside by the tar barrel. They built enough fire under the barrel to melt the tar and gave the nets a good coating. Ric came by and I chunked him with a ball of it. He didn't mind.

"Look, Noah," he said, "the dentist just pulled out four of my front teeth."

When he opened his mouth it looked that way but it was only a strip of tar.

I stuck a piece over my front teeth and went into the kitchen. "Look, Mama," I said, "I lost two front teeth," and I opened my mouth.

She took one look. "Good Lord, Noah, how did it happen?"

I pulled the tar off my teeth and opened up again. Mama saw the tar. "You get out of this house this minute," she said, "or I'll get the broom to you."

After Daddy and Mr. Jesse finished fixing the nets, they

went down to the river and started working on the
bateau. They scraped the bottom and poured tar into
the seams. Then they gave it a good coat of red lead.
That keeps the worms from boring it full of holes.

One day when I went down to the river after school,
they had the bateau turned over and were working on
the engine. Daddy had put in the new carburetor and had
finished tightening the spark plug in the one big cylinder.

"These two-cycle engines don't use much gasoline," he
said. "Just fill up that little tank and she'd take us to
Baltimore to get a pint of liquor." Our county voted last
year not to have alcohol and now all the men have to take
an empty suitcase to Baltimore when they want to get
liquor.

"I could stand a drink right now," Mr. Jesse said, looking in my direction, but Daddy shook his head. Mama
doesn't like him to drink around me.

"Let's see if you can start her, George," Mr. Jesse said,
sort of moving away from the gasoline tank.

"Aw, she'll go right off," Daddy said, and he knelt down
in front of the big iron wheel. Taking hold of it with
both hands, he turned it over several times, but nothing
happened.

"She must be a little cold," he said. "I'll prime her."

He opened a petcock on top of the cylinder and squirted
gasoline into it and turned the wheel once more. That
old Ferro sounded like it was choking to death, only
nothing else happened.

"Maybe you don't have enough juice in that battery to
fire her," Mr. Jesse said.

Daddy reached down and touched a wire. "Damn!" he cried, and jumped clear out of the boat. "I almost electrocuted myself. You try her awhile, Jesse."

"All you have to do is to get her started, Daddy," I said.

He looked at me. "You sound more like your mother every day," he said. "You go on home, we don't want no kids playing around this engine, you might get hurt."

I went on home, and I was already hurt, only nobody knew it.

Along toward the middle of March it started to get warm, so Daddy and Mr. Jesse loaded up the bateau and went on down the river to set their nets. Sometimes Mama would let me miss a day of school to go with Daddy, but she wouldn't that time.

"You're too young to be tempting the weather this early in the spring, Noah," she said.

After they had gone, before light, we heard the old one cylinder start off like a Gatling gun.

"She started, Mama," I said. "They ain't going to have to row."

"You just give it time," she said, "it'll stop again."

"Daddy says once you get it started, it'll run all day."

"Your father says lots of things," she said. But it didn't stop. I could hear it for a long time first loud and then getting softer and softer, going down the river. Then I ate my breakfast and went to school.

Late that afternoon I kept looking down the river and listening for that old two-cycle engine, and finally I saw them coming, only they were rowing. Daddy and Mr.

Jesse each rowing a pair of oars, standing up, facing the bow. They could really push that bateau along. Besides, the tide was flooding. They looked like two herons flying close to the water. Mama and I went down to the river to meet them.

"I thought that engine would run all day," she said.

"It did," Daddy said, "until we ran out of gasoline."

"More money," Mama said. "I don't know why you don't row. Rowing was good enough for your pappy."

"Pap can still row," Daddy said. "Me and Jesse stopped in to see him at the Cliffs this afternoon. He's snug as a bug in his little ark. Talking about getting a tow up the river and visiting us for a while."

"Don't you dare tow him. You let him stay down the river," Mama said. I guess she doesn't like Grandpappy because he lives in a little ark by himself. Daddy gives him some money now and then and he makes a little more at shoemaking.

"Pap's sight is failing," Daddy said.

"We don't have room for him," Mama said, and that settled it.

By that time it was getting dark and toward the west the sky had all kinds of color.

"I don't like the looks of that sky," Mr. Jesse said. "Today's been too good for this time of year, it's a weather breeder."

Mr. Jesse knew what he was talking about, because Mama woke me in the middle of the night putting another quilt on my bed, and when I got up in the morning, it was snowing.

"I guess we've got a March blizzard," she said.

Daddy was already up and I never saw him out of bed that early unless he was going fishing or crabbing or oystering.

"What's the matter, Daddy?" I said. "You ain't sick, are you?"

"I'm worried about them nets," he said. "If it turns real cold and the river freezes over, we'll lose them all. The ice will cut them to pieces."

The kitchen door opened and Mr. Jesse came in. He had on his oilskins, sou'wester and hip gum boots and was carrying a can of gasoline. The snow had frozen on the oilskins.

"It was a weather breeder like I told you, weren't it?" he said. "Somebody's Jonahing us."

"We got to go down the river and take them nets up before the cove freezes over," Daddy said. "If it freezes hard, our nets will be ruined."

"You're not going down the river in this here snow blizzard, George," Mama said, and you could see she was getting scared.

"I don't want to go any more than you want me to," he said, "but we can't let our nets go."

"We'll be real careful," Mr. Jesse said, looking out of the window and watching the wind blow the snow across the back yard. "You don't need to worry over us."

Daddy put on an extra sweater and then slipped on his oilskins and boots. "If we don't come home by dark, you'll know we're staying over at the shanty." He and Mr. Jesse had built a shanty in the woods by the cove where they fished. They had a stove there with a couple of bunks and blankets.

"You might starve down there at the shanty," Mama said.

"We got flour and beans and coffee," Daddy said. "And Jesse can really cook good flapjacks. Maybe we'll shoot a snow goose." He looked at the snow swirling past the window.

"Here's something that might help to keep you warm," Mama said, and going to the closet she reached in back of some boxes and pulled out a pint bottle of whisky. Mama always kept it for medicine in case somebody got sick and she couldn't get the doctor quick enough.

"I could stand a drink now, George," said Mr. Jesse. So they both took a long swallow.

"I guess we'd better get along," Daddy said, and he kissed Mama and me good-by. He smelled good.

"Don't let nothing happen to you and Jesse," Mama said.

"Don't nothing ever happen to us river men," Daddy said. "Our old bateau will take care of us." They both took another drink and went out, shutting the door quick before the snow could blow in.

I put on my overcoat and boots and went out in the back yard in the shelter of the willow tree. After what seemed like a long while I heard that old engine backfire. A minute later it started and I could tell they were going down the river, for the hammering was fainter and fainter. Then I couldn't hear them.

It was snowing so hard Mama said that I could stay

home from school. I think she wanted me for company. It kept on snowing all that day and night and we didn't expect Daddy and Mr. Jesse to come home. They didn't. Mama didn't know what to do. The roads were all blocked and a lot of the telephone lines were down. There wasn't nothing we could do but wait. We sat up late in case something should happen, and every time I looked out the window, the snow was deeper. When we did finally go to bed, the wind whined around the corner of the house and I wished that my Daddy was home. I tried to imagine him and Mr. Jesse snug in that little shack with the pot-bellied stove red hot, playing cards on the table, with the bottle of liquor almost empty.

"I guess they're as snug as Grandpappy in his ark," I thought. Then I must have gone off to sleep.

The next morning when I woke up everything was still. The wind had stopped blowing and the snow wasn't coming down any more. But there was plenty of snow outside and the biggest drifts came up to the top of my gum boots. In the crotch of the willow tree a robin redbreast was crouched with his head stuck under his wing, trying to keep warm. I walked down to the river and saw that Brewster's Cove was frozen over but the middle of the river was open. I threw a stone across the ice and it went booming and ringing until it slipped into the channel. "I guess Daddy and Mr. Jesse can come home if they get that old engine started," I thought. I went home and got some breakfast.

Mama kept opening the door and listening and I knew she was hoping she would hear that old engine hammering, coming up the river. She'd listen awhile and then go back to the rocking chair and rock.

"If they're not here by noon," she said, "we'll have to notify the sheriff and he can send a searching party down the river."

That was nine o'clock. Well, ten o'clock came and I went down to see if they might be rowing home, but I couldn't see anything, nothing but the river with an ice border on each side. When I got back home Mama was almost crying.

"If he comes home this time, I'll never fuss with him again," she said.

"Aw, Mama," I said, "they're all right. You know how Daddy likes to stay in bed late in the mornings and that old engine is awful hard to start. Maybe they blew out a gasket going down the river." But I was getting scared, too.

When the twelve-o'clock whistle blew, you could see that Mama had made up her mind. She put on her winter overcoat and rubbers and tied a shawl over her head.

"We'll have to go and notify the sheriff, Noah," she said. "You come along and walk with me."

We went out the front gate and I sort of broke the way for Mama and picked where the snow was the shallowest. We were almost up to the corner when she stopped and listened like she heard something. Then I turned toward the river and listened.

Put, put, put, the old engine sounded way down the river. *Put, put, put.* Then silence. *Put, put.*

"Mama, it's them, it's the old Ferro, did you hear it miss? Daddy says it needs a new timer."

We hurried down to the river. By the time we got there, the bateau could just be seen a couple of miles down the river.

"Can you see how many's in it, Noah?" Mama said.

She was still worried and expecting the worst. I climbed a tree and I could see Daddy at the tiller and Mr. Jesse sitting up near the bow. I could see that they had the nets, too. The river colors were so pretty. The water was a bright blue; the riverbanks were all white; and the bridge was a tinsel strip. In ten more minutes they were breaking the ice in Brewster's Cove with their oars and soon they were on the beach.

"Are you all right, George?" Mama said, hurrying down to the beach.

"Me and Jesse are all right," he said, sort of tired-like, "but look at them nets."

The nets had been cut by the ice. They looked pretty bad.

"Don't worry about the nets, George," Mama said. "I'll help you and Jesse fix them and so will Noah. It can't be much different from crocheting. As long as you are all right, nothing else matters."

"We ain't going to set them nets again until it comes dogwood time," Mr. Jesse said.

"We're all right," Daddy said. "Nothing ever happens to a riverman as long as he stays on the river where he belongs."

CHAPTER 5

Frogs and Turtles and
Puppy Dog Tails

IT seems like the river does keep Daddy well and happy, but I was sick again. Mama called Dr. Salmons. After he had given me calomel powders and pink medicine, Daddy came home and dropped a tobacco bag on the bedspread. When I picked up the bag, it jingled. I dumped it out and had a dozen of the new buffalo nickels. All were just as shiny as the day they were made, with an Indian on one side and a buffalo on the other. Seemed like those new nickels spruced me up more than the calomel.

Another time, before Election Day, he brought me a handful of election buttons. Daddy was a good Democrat but the buttons were from the Republicans too. I sort of fancied Teddy Roosevelt myself, because the Christmas before Aunt Carrie had given me a Rough Rider suit. But Teddy Roosevelt let Mr. Taft win the nomination — anyway that's what Daddy said.

I guess Mama would rather have Daddy bring home a pay envelope than anything else.

"Things will never be right until you get a steady job,

George," she used to say. "Noah ought to have a college education, and it ain't too soon to start saving for it."

Daddy would nod his head but he never did anything about it — I guess the river was in his blood.

Mama didn't always like the things Daddy brought home. One evening he came toting a guano sack and dropped it on the kitchen floor.

"What have you got in that bag, George?" she asked.

"Croak," said something in the bag before he could answer, and Mama jumped.

"You get them frogs out of this house," she said, and he took them out in the side yard where they could be cool and comfortable. We didn't hear any more from the frogs until we went to bed. It was a warm night in late April and all of the windows were raised. Just as I was getting to sleep, one of the frogs opened up.

"Bay rum," he said, sort of clearing his throat, "bay rum."

"What's that, George?" Mama said, and I could hear her getting out of bed. Then she remembered. "Oh, it's them frogs."

That one big frog started the whole sackful complaining and muttering. One whose voice hadn't changed yet started off right shrill, "Knee-deep, knee-deep," just like they do in the Uncle Remus stories.

"He thinks he's in the creek," Daddy said. "Don't they sing pretty-like?"

"They don't sound pretty to me," Mama said. "We ain't going to get a wink of sleep tonight, and I've got a big washing to do tomorrow."

"Let's keep real quiet," Daddy said. "Maybe they'll shut up when they see there ain't no competition."

We kept still and the frogs got quiet but not for long. That same big fellow started it again.

"Lemme out," he groaned, "lemme out." At least that is what it sounded like. The whole chorus joined him.

"That big bass one sounds like Eben Pauley singing in the church choir," Daddy said, laughing.

"How do you know?" Mama said. "You ain't been to church in ten years."

"I heard him rehearsing when I was playing poker in Lawyers' Row the other night."

"Don't be sacrilegious, George."

I heard the screen door slam next door, and I knew it was Old Man Wood. He only slammed it like that when he was mad.

"If you don't put them frogs somewhere so I can sleep, I'm going to have a warrant sworn out for you, George," he said. "You're disturbing the peace."

Mr. Wood is like that. Always threatening to go to the law. Daddy is scared of the law, so he got up and took the frogs down to the creek and hid the bag in the marsh. The next day, when he went to get them, they were all gone.

Daddy really caused a commotion the time he brought home the snapping turtles. It was a spring day, and he and Mr. Jesse had been down the river to fish their nets. I heard that old engine pounding and went to meet them. They didn't have many fish, but in the boat were two of the biggest snapping turtles I had ever seen.

"Where'd you get the turtles, Daddy?" I asked.

"They were in the nets and almost tore them up," he said. "That's why we ain't got many fish."

They packed the fish in ice and Daddy said, "Which one of the snapping turtles you want, Jesse?"

"The missus would be scared to death if I took one of them creatures home," Mr. Jesse said. "You keep them both, George." So Daddy carried them up to the house and dropped them on the kitchen floor. One of them crawled under the stove just like a hound dog.

"Look what I got, Mother," he called.

Mama was stitching on the sewing machine but she stopped and came to look.

"My Lord, George," she said, "what are you going to bring home next? You can't keep them monsters in this house. Look at their evil eyes." The turtles were scratching around on the floor, darting their eyes here and there.

'I'll keep them in the woodshed," he said. "Remember, Noah, don't you play with them. If they once get a hold on you, they won't let go until the sun goes down, even if you chop their heads off."

Snapping turtles are more fun to play with than hard crabs. If you nudge them with a long stick, they will snap at it like a bulldog, and once they grab something a turtle really holds on. After Daddy walked uptown, I went out to the woodshed and opened the door a crack. I heard someone coming and closed the door, but it was Ric.

"I caught you," he said. "What you been doing, smoking cornsilks?"

I opened the door again. At first we couldn't see the snapping turtles. Then we saw them back in the corner with their flippers and heads drawn into their shells. They looked like a couple of wood slabs. But when the ray of light hit the corner, their heads popped out and they began to stir around. We took a bean pole and nudged them. They got all mad but they couldn't do nothing.

That night I had a nightmare and dreamed that those snapping turtles had a grip on me, one on each ear, and they wouldn't let go until the sun went down. Only it was *night time*. I must have yelled, because Mama came in the room and stood at the foot of my bed.

"What's the matter, Noah?" she said. "Are you sick?"

"No, ma'am," I said. "I just had a bad dream and it scared me."

The next morning was Saturday, and after breakfast I went out to the woodshed to prod the snapping turtles for a while. When I opened the door, I couldn't see them anywhere. "I guess they must have hid," I thought, and poked all around with a long pole. But they were gone, and in one corner I saw a chink of light. They had dug under the sills and got out. I ran to the house.

"Mama," I said, "the turtles have gotten out of the woodshed."

"Oh, my," she said and called upstairs to Daddy. "George, get up, the turtles have gotten away." She turned to me. "You keep out of the tall grass until he catches them. They might snap you."

Daddy came downstairs and went out in the back yard. "They don't travel very fast," he said. "We'll find them right here." We poked all around with two bean poles, but we didn't see hide or hair of them.

Mrs. Steers, who lives next door, on the side toward the river, saw us progging around. "What are you hunting for?"

"Two big snapping turtles that belonged to Daddy have got out of our woodshed," I said. "Maybe they crawled over in your yard."

"Good Lord," she said, "to think they might have grabbed me. And they won't let go until the sun goes down. You'd better come over here and poke around."

We went over in Mrs. Steers's yard and looked all around in the tall grass but they weren't there. By that time the whole neighborhood knew that Daddy had lost his two big snapping turtles. The men and boys were looking for the turtles but the women and girls wouldn't leave the house.

Just then a dog gave a great howl and came crawling out from under Mrs. Steers's house. Our renting-houses don't have cellars. They are just set on cement blocks. It was Ponto, the Steerses' dog, and the tip of his tail was bloody.

"One of them monsters has bitten my poor Ponto's tail," Mrs. Steers said. "Somebody will have to crawl under the house and catch it."

"We can't go under there," Daddy said. "Anybody who crawls under these old houses will get cut up with broken glass and tin cans. Maybe we can catch them if they crawl out."

All that day we watched Mrs. Steers's house. If the snapping turtles were under there, they didn't come out. Mr. Jesse came over that afternoon and heard the news.

"Why don't you set muskrat traps for them?" he said.

"If you bait them with old stinking meat, you're liable to catch them."

That sounded like a good idea and Daddy set five muskrat traps around the edge of Mrs. Steers's house, chaining them to the cement blocks. He baited them with tripe he used for crabs. We didn't have to wait very long.

"Yeow! Yeow!" a creature yelled, and we had caught Mrs. Unger's yellow tomcat.

"Ain't no telling what lurks under your house," Daddy said, letting the cat go.

"Maybe you ought to see the sheriff and have him organize a posse," Mr. Jesse said. "If one of them critters clamps on somebody, there's really going to be trouble. They might sue you, George."

At the mention of being sued Daddy turned pale. "I didn't let them loose."

"No, you were just harboring them," Old Man Wood said. "Maybe I'd better go and get Mr. Jester."

"They probably crawled right back to the river," Daddy said. "I expect they're ten miles down the river by now, tearing somebody's fish nets."

"My poor dog's tail don't look like they're down the river," Mrs. Steers said. You could see she was mad and scared. I guess everybody was scared, especially after it got dark. Soon as the sun started to get low, I could hear all the mothers calling their children. Those big snapping turtles might take hold in the dark — you'd never know until it was too late, and twenty-four hours would be a long time to wait for the sun to go down. Nobody on our street stirred out of the house after it got dark.

Next morning, even though it was Sunday, me and Daddy were up early. We went out in the yard cautious-like and looked at the muskrat traps. We hadn't caught a thing and by that time the bait was really advertising. We poked all around in the tall grass but there wasn't any sign of the snapping turtles. Sunday ain't a time for folks to work in their yards, but when the people on our street did go out that Sunday they stepped mighty gingerly. And by the time the sun went down everything was closed up tight again.

On Monday things were getting serious, for none of the women would do their week's washing because they were afraid to go out in the yard to hang up their clothes. When I came home from school, Daddy was lying on the couch, all worn out from worrying so much about the turtles.

"I don't know what to do," he said. "It's just like we'd had a flood, or invasion, or something."

But I knew what to do, because if things worry me too much I always take my fishing pole and go down to the brick wall. I had baited the hook and was fishing by the big sewer pipe when I saw them. Daddy's two big snapping turtles were just laying back, floating on top of the water, enjoying themselves catching bull minnows. I threw a couple of oyster shells at them and they dived. I never saw them again.

I ran up to the house and told Daddy and he told Mama and she told Mrs. Steers and I guess she told everybody else. Anyway, the women hung up their wash, and the children came out and played, and after it got dark we caught lightning bugs and put them in a green glass bottle.

CHAPTER 6

Puss! Puss! Puss!

WITH those two snapping turtles at large, I was half scared of going in the river all summer. I was playing two-batter-two when Mama called for me to go to the store. It was my next bat, but it sounded like she meant business, so I went home.

"Noah," she said, "go up to Mr. Leary's and get me fifteen cents' worth of chipped beef and a loaf of bread. And you be sure to come right back. You can spend a cent from the change."

I started out on a trot just like Doc Beller's mare Emily, and by the time I reached the store I almost had the heaves. Mr. Leary sliced the beef on his new machine and wrapped it in a piece of brown paper. I didn't know whether to buy a stick of licorice so I could spit tobacco juice or two whisky drops with my cent. But there was a tray of new penny-prize boxes and I took one of them. It had a picture of Ty Cobb with the popcorn. Not bad.

On the way home I was galloping along, munching the popcorn, when I dropped the chipped beef in front of Mrs. Duncan's. As I picked it up, I heard a weak "Meow, meow," and looking up, saw a little bobtailed kitten in the fork of the big monkeynut tree. He was scared and couldn't get down. I couldn't reach him, either, but I found a long branch and held it up to the crotch. The kitten looked for a minute, tried to climb down the branch, slipped, and turned over two times before he landed on his feet. He crept over and smelled the chipped beef. "Poor little thing is hungry," I thought. "Maybe Mama will let me keep him." I picked up the packages and the kitten and ran the rest of the way home.

"Look, Mama," I said. "Here's a poor little kitten I found. He's hungry. Can I keep him?"

"You cannot," she said. "You take him right back where you found him, and where's the change?"

"Aw, Mama," I said, but I gave her the food and the change. I took the little bobtail and left him in front of Mrs. Duncan's. "Good-by, little kitty," I said. Then I ran home.

When I reached the front gate I looked back, and dog-gone if that little kitten wasn't coming down the road like a streak. By the time I got to the porch he had caught up with me. Mama was rocking and sewing.

"Noah, I thought I told you to take that kitten back."

"I did, Mama, but he followed me home. Can I keep him?"

"Can you keep him," she said. "It looks like a female to me and that bobbed tail ain't hardly respectable."

"Please, Mama," I said. "I ain't had an animal since Rags was killed."

"All right," she said, "you can keep him. Go get a box of dirt."

Puss — that was what I called the bobtail — turned

out to be a little tomcat, which was a good thing, because
Mama didn't want any more females in the house. He was
awful rough with his claws until he found out I wasn't
going to hurt him. Whenever I would call "Puss! Puss!
Puss!" you could hear him coming over the fences, a long
ways off. When he reached me, he would roll on his back
and purr. Puss used to go fishing with me, and he would
sit and wait until I caught him a white perch or a yellow
ned. Once I gave him a big hard crab but he couldn't
figure that out. By the time school started in the fall he
was large enough to take care of himself, but whenever I
called, "Puss! Puss! Puss!" he would come home. I liked to
hear the scratching he made when he struck Miss Lizzie
Wallace's high board fence.

School kept me pretty busy and I didn't see much of
Puss. After the nights got cool, and we were all in bed,
sometimes Puss would meow sort of mournful-like, especially if there was a moon.

"Damn that cat," Daddy said one night. "I wish he
would do his courting somewheres else."

Then Mama said, "He's too young for that, he's just
practicing for next spring."

"What's going to happen next spring, Mama?" I asked
from the next room.

"Noah, you go right to sleep."

"Mama, let me put Puss on the back porch, then he
won't meow and keep us awake."

Daddy chimed in, "That's a good idea."

"You keep out of this, George," Mama said. But from
then on Puss always slept on the back porch.

By the time the river froze over, Puss was full-grown and real pretty. He was gentle with me but he could lick any of the cats in the neighborhood. He liked to stretch out under the kitchen stove. Then, all of a sudden, he would go to the door and meow to be let out. But he always came home when I called, "Puss! Puss! Puss!"

One warm day in March, I saw the old fish hawk that lives in the rotten tree on Brewster's Cove hovering high above the river and I knew it must be spring.

"Mama," I said, "can I go barefoot?"

"You want to catch your death of cold?" she said. "Don't you dare take your shoes off before the first of May."

That same day, Puss didn't come home when I called him about sundown. I lay awake wondering if anything had happened to him and all of a sudden I heard him singing. When I looked out the front window, he was sitting on the gatepost. Close by was a strange cat, spitting in his face. After that Puss stayed out nights, and one week he was gone for three days, visiting. But he came home again.

The weather got warmer and Miss Lizzie Wallace's hens began to take their little biddies out in the pasture where we played ball. Those old hens acted crazy. Every time a ball landed in their neighborhood, they would run over and peck it. One old hen even set on it like it was an egg. While I was getting the ball, I looked over in the tall grass and there was my Puss, crouched and watching the little chickens.

On the way home from school the next afternoon, Miss Lizzie was standing by her gate.

"Noah," she said, "something happened to two of my little Dominickers yesterday. I think a creature caught them. Does that tomcat of yours bother chickens?"

"No, ma'am, Puss ain't never caught any chickens. He gets plenty to eat at home. I bet it was an old chicken hawk."

"You'd better watch that cat of yours," she said. "If I catch him eating my chickens, I'll have him killed."

"Yes, ma'am," I said, and as I walked on home I thought of Puss crouching in the tall grass.

Mama was planting flowers when I got home. I told her what Miss Lizzie had said.

"Lizzie better not touch your Puss," she said, seeing I was worried. "Noah, Puss ain't been eating much at home lately. Do you suppose he has been catching those young fryers? Those Dominickers look mighty tempting."

After that, while I was playing ball in the lot, I kept looking in the tall grass for Puss but I never saw him there again. Those Dominickers were growing fast. Soon they would be too big even for my tomcat to tackle. Then one day when I was taking my turn at bat, there was a loud squawk out in the field. It looked like a cat carrying something that might have been feathers. It went over the back fence in a hurry.

Ric, who was playing the field, came running in. "Noah, your cat just carried off one of Miss Lizzie's chickens."

And I couldn't make him change his mind. "If you know what's good for you, you better not tell Miss Lizzie," I said. He swore he wouldn't and we all said we wouldn't mention it to nobody.

That night, at supper, I decided to tell Mama and Daddy. "Puss carried off one of Miss Lizzie's Dominickers today while I was playing ball."

"Lizzie came over to see me today," Mama said. "She's lost ten of her best fryers. If you tell her about Puss, she will want us to pay for all of them."

"Maybe I ought to take that tomcat and drop him somewhere," Daddy said.

"That won't do any good, George," Mama said. "The last time you dropped a cat, he beat you home."

"Suppose I drop him in the river?"

"Aw, Daddy," I said and started to sniffle, but I knew he wouldn't do anything to Puss.

"There's nothing to do but wait and see," Mama said.

When I came home from school the next day, Miss Lizzie was sitting on our front porch talking to Mama. She must have just got there for she was still puffed up and flustered.

"Mr. Jester saw that bobtailed cat of Noah's make off with one of my Dominickers, less than an hour ago," she was saying. "He's ruining my flock, taking the fat ones and leaving the scrawny Dominickers. You've got to do something about that thieving cat!" She saw me. "Well, Noah," she continued, "we've got the evidence on your cat. Mr. Jester saw him catch one of my chickens."

That sent a chill running down my backbone.

"Aw, Miss Lizzie, my Puss is a nice cat, he wouldn't touch your chickens," I said because I was so scared. Just then I heard something stirring under the porch, and Puss came out to stretch himself. His belly was full and anyone

could see that he had just had a good meal. As he licked
his chops, a small black and white feather dropped from
his whiskers.

Miss Lizzie let out a squawk that sounded a lot like one
of her setting hens and ran off toward her chicken yard.

"Now look what's happened," Mama said. "Maybe it
would have been better if Puss had been a female. What
are we going to do?"

When Daddy came home from the river, we talked it
over.

"George," said Mama, "you'll have to get rid of that
cat, and Noah can shake enough money out of his piggy
bank to pay Miss Lizzie for those two fryers that Puss
ate."

"I ain't never killed a cat and I ain't never going to,"
said Daddy. "It's ten years' bad luck."

"What would happen to a colored man who stole a
chicken, Mama?" I asked. "They wouldn't kill him, would
they?"

"No," she said, "they'd put him in jail and feed him a
little beans and corn bread, but that's different — a colored
person is human."

"Mama, let me keep Puss and put him in the woodshed.
That would be the same as jail for him. And I'll pay
Miss Lizzie with money from my piggy bank."

That didn't satisfy her but Daddy wouldn't do anything,
so I shut Puss up in the woodshed. I shook my piggy bank
until I got enough pennies and nickels to pay for the
fryers.

It was awful hard for me to go over to Miss Lizzie's but

Mama made me go by myself. She took the money and counted it.

"What did you do with that thieving cat?"

"He'll never bother you again, Miss Lizzie," I said.

"Not if I ever catch him," she said. Then I went home.

The woodshed didn't have but one small window, and as the days went by I could see that Puss was unhappy. His fur got sort of mildewy and he began to look gawky. But I gave him milk and caught fish for him. When I went to see him, I would close the door tight and sit down on a chunk of wood. Puss would climb up in my lap and look into my eyes. He knew he was in jail but he didn't know why.

After about three weeks of jail, Miss Lizzie's Dominickers were so big that not even my Puss would have dared to tackle them. One day Mama said I could let him out. I never realized before how much a cat loves the sun. He stretched in it for an hour or two, then he walked sort of lazy-like over to the roots of a tree and sharpened his claws. A grasshopper jumped from the rose bush and Puss made a great leap for it, tossed it away, shied at a butterfly, and the next thing I knew he was gone and I could hear him scratching and clawing, climbing the fences.

That evening I called, "Puss! Puss! Puss!" but he didn't come. I called again but there wasn't a sound except Mrs. Duncan's old hound sort of groaning. I couldn't sleep that night and lay awake hoping that I would hear Puss singing and courting on the front fence, but he wasn't there.

The next morning, real early, I went out and looked all

around, calling, "Puss! Puss! Puss!" but he didn't come. Mama said for me not to worry, he was probably off visiting his girl, but I couldn't help worrying. That evening I called, "Puss! Puss! Puss!" for a long time, but he never came.

When Daddy walked up from the river I told him. He was quiet for a while and then he put his hand around my shoulders. "Son," he said, "while I was running my trot-line yesterday, I saw Mr. Jester row out to the middle of the river and drop something in a guano sack. It never came up."

CHAPTER 7

Mr. Greenley's Ghost

ME and Ric were talking about Hallowe'en. It was only two weeks off.

"Let's dress like Indians, Ric," I said.

"Don't bring that up," he said. "Anyway, it's easier to dress like a nigger. All you have to do is burn a cork stopper and put on old clothes."

"Mama says you oughten to call them niggers, Ric."

"What does she want me to call them, colored gentlemen?"

"Are you going to dress like a colored person this year?" I asked.

"Did I say that?" Ric answered. "You're my best friend but I wouldn't tell you how I'm going to disguise myself."

"Burnt cork is awful hard to get off. Last year I used one of Mama's stockings with holes punched in it."

"That's sissy," Ric said. "Burnt cork or black shoe polish is the thing to use."

"Let's both of us disguise the same way this year. Let's dress like Charlie Chaplin."

"That ain't a bad idea if we could find a couple of derbies," Ric said, "but it's hard to get around corners with that hop Charlie has."

"Last year Billy Unger dressed like a girl."

"You can dress like a girl if you want to, but I ain't putting on no dress," Ric said.

"Let's dress like two ghosts and scare people," I said. "We could rap on Miss Lizzie's door and scare her good."

"Maybe we could scare her into giving some of our baseballs back," Ric said. Miss Lizzie used to keep our balls if we knocked them into her chicken yard.

"Maybe we could be two ghosts and have a haunted house to scare people," I said. "You know, rattle chains and make the doors creak."

"You're just dreaming again, Noah," Ric said. "How could we build a haunted house in two weeks?"

"I didn't mean to build one. How about that old house across the street from Miss Lizzie's? Nobody has lived there since Old Man Greenley died." Old Man Greenley used to keep the livery stable.

"He was mean enough to come back and haunt it," Ric said. "How could we get anybody to come to the house?"

"We might make up a few stories about seeing lights in the old house and hearing strange noises. When the people came to see what it was, we could scare them."

"I tell you what we need," Ric said. "We need an accomplice."

"What's that?"

"An accomplice is somebody to work with us and bring the kids for us to scare. Of course if they get caught, it means jail for them."

"Why?"

"I don't know, but the accomplice always goes to jail, even if the main ones are freed."

"Billy Unger would be a good accomplice," I said. "He's got a lot of mouth and can persuade you to do most anything, even if it's wrong."

"Billy would be all right if he wouldn't get talking and give it away," Ric said.

"Boy, wouldn't that be great. Me and you would be hiding in the haunted house, dressed like ghosts, and Billy would lure them to us. He could bring a lot of girls and when they opened the doors we could groan and rattle chains."

"I'd like to throw a bucket of water on the girls," Ric said.

"Ghosts can't throw water. They just complain and rattle their bones."

"Maybe I could throw flour."

"You got the wrong idea," I said. "Ghosts don't throw things. They can't, being dead and mostly spirit."

"If I can't throw something, I ain't going to be a ghost," Ric said, and I knew how stubborn he was.

"You could drop a sheet on them from the second floor."

"Dropping ain't throwing," Ric said, getting more stubborn all the time.

"All right. If you want to be a throwing ghost, go ahead."

"How do you know ghosts don't throw things?" he said, grumbling. "Suppose the ghost was a great ball player, like Christy Mathewson. You mean to tell me that when Christy Mathewson becomes a ghost, he's going to stop throwing? I don't believe it."

"I never thought of that," I said. "I was going by what I read."

"You read too much," Ric said, "and believe too much of what you read."

"I guess you're right," I said, soothing-like.

"Let's talk to Billy Unger about it."

"Suppose he won't do it? Then he'll tell everybody else how we are dressing."

"He won't tell nobody if he knows what is good for him," Ric said, and I knew he was right. Ric can look fierce when he wants to and he can back it up.

Billy was sitting on the brick wall watching the minnows.

"Hello, Billy," Ric said. "How are you going to disguise for Hallowe'en?"

"You think I'd tell you?" Billy said.

"Me and Noah have got an idea and we thought you might like to work with us."

"That all depends," Billy said. "What is it?"

"We ain't telling you until you promise not to tell any-body," Ric said.

"I promise," Billy said.

"That ain't binding," Ric said. "Cross your heart and hope you die if you tell."

Billy said the words after Ric and we were satisfied.

"We're going to haunt a house Hallowe'en night," Ric said, "and we want you to help us."

"Gee, who thougnt of that?" said Billy. "That's a great idea."

"Do you want to help us?" Ric said.

"Can I be a ghost?" Billy asked.

"Sure," Ric said, "you can be a messenger ghost."

"A messenger ghost?"

"You bring the people to the haunted house and me and Noah scare them."

"I knew there was something funny," Billy said. "If I can't haunt the house, count me out."

"Somebody's got to bring the kids to the house," said Ric.

"Yeah, if anything happens, I'd get all the blame," Billy said. "Why don't you be the one to bring them, Noah?"

"I'd rather rattle the chains and scream."

"You could be the ghost of one of the great wilderness guides," Ric said, "like Daniel Boone, and carry a gun."

"Nothing doing," Billy said. "I've got another disguise almost ready anyway."

"Maybe we could take turns luring them, Ric," I said. "That would be fair."

"That's an idea," Ric said, "but Billy would have to bring them first, being's we are letting him in on it. What about that, Billy?"

"I'll do it for the first hour if you let me see how you're fixing the house," said Billy. "We got about a ton of old chain in the cellar."

"We ought to have a skeleton," Ric said, "a real one that would rattle."

"How about the one in the science room at the high school?" I said. "Do you suppose Old Lady Gordon would lend Oscar to us?"

"You know she wouldn't," Ric said. "She won't even let anybody touch Oscar." Us boys called it Oscar only some said it was a female.

"We could wait until Old Lady Gordon went home on Hallowe'en and borrow Oscar without saying anything," Billy said. "We could take him back early the next day."

"That would be stealing," I said.

"Not on Hallowe'en it wouldn't be stealing," said Ric. "Look at all the gates and wagons that people take. Nobody calls that stealing."

"That's right," I said.

"We could hang Oscar right beside the door and rig it so he could raise his hand when the door opened," Ric said. He's good about fixing things because his father is a carpenter.

We went and rummaged around in Billy's cellar. "Here's an old telephone set," Ric said. "You can make an electric shock by cranking the handle."

"Can you fix it so as to give shocks in the haunted house?" I said.

"Ghosts don't know nothing about electricity," Billy said.

"We could be up-to-date ghosts," I said.

"Take a hold of this wire a minute," Ric said. "I want to see if this works." He cranked the telephone and I almost jumped out of my shoes. But it didn't hurt me.

"It works," Ric said. We took the telephone and chain

over to the house where Old Man Greenley used to live. It looked like nobody had been there since the undertaker had hauled him away. The yard was like a jungle and the front door was locked. But a window on the porch was open and a couple of black tomcats jumped out when they heard us coming.

"Maybe the cats will hang around on Hallowe'en night and get in a fight," Ric said. "They've got big yellow eyes on a dark night."

We climbed through the window and there was so much dirt on the floor that our feet made a trail. I opened a door and it creaked. All of the doors creaked, which was the way we wanted it.

"Let's put the chain upstairs," Ric said. "Ghosts always rattle chains on the second floor."

"I thought they rattled them in the cellar," Billy said.

We started up the stairs, Ric leading the way.

Ric stopped. "Somebody's up there. I hear them breathing." All I could hear was my heart pounding against my chest.

"Whoo!" something sighed upstairs, just like a man drawing his last breath, and we heard a flopping. Then everything was quiet except my heart.

Ric laughed. "Pigeons," he said, "it was pigeons." We went upstairs and he was right. The pigeons had been living on the second floor and the cats on the first floor. It doesn't sound right but that's the way it was. We put the chains on an old bed that still had sheets on it.

"I guess this is where Old Man Greenley died," Ric said, sitting down on the bed. It creaked — everything in the old house creaked, like it might have been already haunted. The place still smelled of horses. Old Man Greenley's boots were standing at the foot of the bed.

"Do you think there really might be ghosts?" Billy said as we watched a spider working on his web.

"There's been plenty of talk about them," said Ric. "Where there's so much smoke there's bound to be a fire."

A pigeon sailed through the broken window and almost took my hat off.

"Let's get out of here," Billy said, "and if you fellows want me to, I'll be the messenger ghost all the time. You two can do the haunting."

"That's all right with me and Noah," Ric said, "and remember, Billy, don't you tell nobody."

"Cross my heart and hope I die if I tell a soul," said Billy. We were out of the house by that time and I walked along the oyster-shell road toward home. Mama was waiting at the gate.

"Did I see you coming off the old Greenley property a minute ago?" she said.

"Yes, ma'am. Is supper ready?"

"Don't try to change the subject," she said. "What were you and Rickard and Billy doing dragging those heavy chains down the road about an hour ago?"

"We were taking them somewhere."

"Why?" she asked.

"It's a secret, Mama, we all promised not to tell."

"That wouldn't apply to your mother," she said. "Anyway supper ain't going to be served until I know what's going on. Whenever I see you and Rickard moving things I know devilment is afoot."

"All right, Mama, I'll tell you," I said, "if you cross your heart and hope to die if you tell anybody."

"I do," she said, but I wondered if she had her fingers crossed under her apron. It's hard for women to keep anything a secret for long.

"We're going to haunt Old Man Greenley's house on Hallowe'en night," I said. "Me and Ric are going to dress as ghosts and rattle chains and moan. Billy is going to bring the sissy boys and girls to the house and we're going to scare them almost to death."

"Ain't you ashamed of yourself, scaring poor little girls and boys like that?" she said, but I heard her sort of snicker to herself.

"It won't hurt them to be scared for a minute and they can always run away."

"How would you like to be scared like that?"

"They couldn't scare me. I ain't scared of ghosts."

"You're not?"

"No, ma'am," I said. "Me and Ric ain't scared of the supernatural."

"That's a big word you just used," she said. "I guess you know what it means."

"Remember you promised not to tell anybody, Mama," I said, hearing Daddy whistling as he walked up from the cove.

By the time Hallowe'en came, we had Old Man Greenley's house fixed up like a chamber of horrors. All we needed was Oscar, the skeleton. After school that day, me and Ric hung around and it seemed like Old Lady Gordon would never go home. But she did and we saw her go out the front door carrying her umbrella and books. She had left her classroom unlocked. We opened the door and there was Oscar hanging from a hook on the closet door.

"Hello, Oscar," Ric said. "You're going visiting." He shook hands with the skeleton but I wouldn't touch it.

"How are you going to carry Oscar so people won't see him?"

It had rained that morning and Ric still had his black gum coat. "Oscar can wear my raincoat," he said, "and we'll put a paper bag over his head." That covered him up, all but his feet, and maybe nobody would notice them. We got out of the school building without any trouble and walked down High Street. It was the time of day when most people were busy at home. We didn't pass a soul until we reached the corner where the Voshell House is. Simon, the old colored man who is porter for the hotel, had to be coming our way. He was about ten feet away when the paper bag Oscar was wearing over his head dropped off. Old Simon saw the skeleton's head and his face turned pale. He sort of froze. He used to pump the church organ on Sunday but that didn't help him.

"Get going, feet," he said to himself, but he was so scared he just stood and stared. "Carry me away, legs," he said, and this time they answered. Simon turned and ran off in the opposite direction faster than you would have thought an old man could run.

Ric laughed. "Maybe we ought to stop and introduce

Oscar to Miss Lizzie before we leave him at Old Man Greenley's house."

"Let's take Oscar to see Miss Lizzie after it gets dark," I said. "She'll scare easier."

"I guess you're right," he said. "We'll take the short cut across the field to Old Man Greenley's."

With the skeleton hanging inside the door and fixed so he would raise his hand when you opened the door, we were ready for Hallowe'en.

"I'll knock on your door about seven o'clock, Noah," Ric said. "Don't let me scare you too much."

"All right," I said. "I've got to get my sheet fixed. I think I'll use a pillow case to go over my head."

After supper I asked Mama to help me with a sheet and a pillow case.

"I don't want you ruining any of my good sheets," she said. "Like as not it won't be good for anything when you get through with it."

"Give me an old, torn one," I said. "That'll be all right."

She pinned me up and cut holes in the raggedy pillow case so I could see and breathe.

"Boo!" I yelled and jumped at her.

"You go scare somebody else," she said, "and don't you put any tick-tacks on people's windows. They might have weak hearts."

There was a knock at the door and I let Mama go. She opened it and backed up quick. 'Course it was Ric, and he let out a groan. We went out together and I pulled a stick along Old Man Wood's fence. That makes a racket and he always gets mad, only it ain't no use to get mad on Hallowe'en.

"Let's get Oscar and take him over to see Miss Lizzie," Ric said. We walked careful going into the haunted house, but those same black cats jumped off the porch and made an awful noise going through the grass. We had a lantern inside and lit it.

"Hello, Oscar," Ric said, "we're taking you to meet an old friend." Ric carried him without any clothes on and even a skeleton looks naked that way.

We rapped on Miss Lizzie's front door and Ric tucked Oscar under his sheet. I saw her raise the curtain in her parlor and peep out, then she opened the door a crack.

"You boys go away," she said. "I saw you both come out of Noah's house a while ago. I know who you are."

"We've got a friend we want you to meet, Miss Lizzie," Ric said, secret-like.

"A friend?" Miss Lizzie said, getting curious and opening the door. "Who is it? I don't see nobody."

"Here he is," Ric said and brought Oscar into view, sticking his bony hand in Miss Lizzie's direction. She took one look, screamed, and closed the door.

"Do you suppose she's fainted?" I said, but we heard footsteps and figured it would be a good time to get moving.

"Let's introduce Oscar to somebody else," Ric said. "It's as much fun as haunting a house."

"How about Miss Fannie?" I said. She lived up the street a little ways.

"She might know where Oscar came from and tell Old Lady Gordon," Ric said.

"That's right," I said.

"It's getting late, anyway," Ric said. "We'd better get to our haunting before Billy brings the first bunch for us to scare."

He tucked Oscar under his sheet and we glided along to Old Man Greenley's place. Ric opened the door and we went inside. It was awful quiet while Ric was lighting the lantern, but when he turned the wick up things started to happen.

Sitting on the two chairs in Old Man Greenley's parlor were two ghosts. They looked like they were the real thing and belonged there. One of them had riding boots on and was holding a buggy whip.

"My Lord," Ric whispered, "it's Old Man Greenley and his wife," only he spoke loud enough for them to hear.

"I heard you," the ghost of Old Man Greenley said, "and what, may I ask, are you two members of the Ku Klux Klan doing in my house?"

Ric's teeth chattered but he got out an answer. "We ain't Ku Kluxers," he said. "We're just two ghosts come to do a little haunting."

"You're trespassing," Old Man Greenley's ghost said. "Me and my wife are the proper ones to haunt our house."

"Yes, sir," Ric said, "we'll be going right away."

"Oh, no, you won't," the ghost said, and slid over in front of the door, cracking his whip close to Ric's shins. "Look at all this mess you've made in my house, rigging chains and other junk. You're going to clean that up first."

"Yes, sir," Ric said, "we will, right away."

The ghost of Old Man Greenley's wife hadn't said a thing, but now she spoke. "How do you know they're really ghosts, Mr. Greenley?" she said. "They might be deceiving us."

The ghost of Old Man Greenley pulled out a long knife. "I might cut an artery or two," he said. "If they bleed we know they ain't ghosts."

Me and Ric were ready to plead for our lives. "We ain't ghosts, Mr. Greenley," Ric said, "we're just two boys trying to play a trick on Hallowe'en."

"Why didn't you tell me it was Hallowe'en?" the ghost said. "I'd lost all track of time. In that case, I think we'll let you go."

"But don't you boys ever plan to scare little girls again," the female ghost said, and all of a sudden I knew I'd heard that ghost's voice somewhere before.

"Mama," I said, and when the ghost took her pillow case off, it was Mama. And Old Man Greenley's ghost was Daddy, laughing so much he shook. About the time we got calmed down there was a noise outside and a knock on the door. Mama almost jumped out of her sheet.

"It's Billy and the girls," Ric said.

"Being's we're here, let's all four of us scare them this once," Daddy said.

And even Mama helped us.

CHAPTER 8

On the Lower Deck

AFTER Hallowe'en, we started counting the days until Christmas.

"Next week," Mama said, "we're going to Baltimore on the *B. S. Ford*. I've just got to do my Christmas shopping."

I could hardly wait, the days passed so slowly. The night before I didn't sleep a wink; then early morning on the river, a quick breakfast, and we were off to the steamboat wharf.

Daddy never went to Baltimore with us — I think he must have been afraid of the city.

Mama took advantage of how he felt. "If you're such a sailor, why don't you cross the bay with Noah and me?" she would say. "You must be scared."

"I'm a riverman," Daddy would say. "As long as I stay on the Chester River nothing can't ever happen to me."

"As long as you stay on the river we'll be as poor as church mice," Mama said. "The river is like a fancy woman."

Dad smiled because he could see that Mama was jealous. "She's right pretty today. Wouldn't you rather go in the bateau than the *B. S. Ford*, Noah?"

Mama took my arm. "He's going with me. Noah's not going to follow the river."

Daddy shrugged his shoulders. I often wonder if Mama can feel the pull of the river. I guess not — her father was a dirt farmer.

While Daddy was saying good-by, the *B. S. Ford* began to shake and gave a warning blast.

"Hurry, George," Mama said, and with a quick kiss that smelled of liquor, he ran for the gangplank. Daddy didn't want to get caught on the *B. S. Ford*.

We went on deck and waved good-by to him. The gang-plank and mooring lines were pulled aboard, and with a loud blast and shake, the steamboat was off down the river, bound for Baltimore.

It was December and cold, so Mama kept me inside, close to the stove. I kneed all of the empty chairs and shinnied up the brass columns.

Mama grabbed me. "Sit down and keep quiet for a while."

I sat down on one of the big chairs, and the steady shaking of the boat almost put me to sleep. Just as I was dozing off, the *B. S. Ford* let out a great blast.

"She's a-blowing for Quaker Neck, Noah."

"Can I go out on deck and watch them dock the boat?"

"If you promise not to climb on the rail."

"All right," I said, and sliding the cabin door open I went out on the bow deck.

Up in the wheelhouse, Captain Wordhull was steering the boat, and if he wanted to tell the engineer something, he pulled a cord, "Ding, ding!" When we got close to the wharf, a couple of deckhands tossed the mooring lines ashore, where they were slipped over big cleats. They pulled the boat until it rested against the wharf and put out the gangplank. The first man to go ashore was a tall thin man who carried a little black box. He was the purser and it was his job to sell tickets to anybody who wanted to go to Baltimore. The deckhands began to bring the freight aboard, mostly fish, packed in ice, on two-wheeled trucks. They strutted and sang as they worked, just like they enjoyed it. When the boat was loaded and the lines pulled aboard, they settled down to play high-low-jack-and-the-game. Captain Wordhull wouldn't let them shoot crap on the boat. But they slapped the cards on the deck like they were dice and talked to those pasteboards like they were made of ivory.

"Hit 'em, ace, show 'em what a big boy can do," sang out one black man.

"Come on, little twosie trump, take big acey," said the next player as he took the trick in. They could really slap those cards on the deck.

I must have been sort of hanging on the rail watching the game when Mama came out and grabbed me.

"What are you doing?" she asked, and then she saw the Negroes gambling. "Watching those colored men gaming — ain't you ashamed? Blood will tell, I guess, blood will tell."

What she meant was that Daddy liked to play poker and sometimes lost. Nobody said anything when Daddy won, but when he lost and she found it out, Mama really fussed. I guess blood is thicker than water — anyway, gambling seems to be a lot of fun. Down on the lower deck, towards the stern, there was a bar with sawdust on the floor, and most of the men spent their time there while the *B. S. Ford* was pushing her way to Baltimore. They drank, and talked, and played poker.

I stood by the rail and counted the bateaus of tongers working the oyster bars in the river's mouth. I stopped after counting one hundred; in the distance the men looked like they were walking on stilts.

After we left Love Point and started across the bay, we ate the lunch Mama had packed in a shoe box. Then she dozed off and almost everybody was asleep but me. When I went to the men's room, there was Captain Pete. He sails the *Kessie Price* and drinks too much, at least that's what Mama says. I guess he'd had a few drinks.

"Good afternoon, Master Noah," he said. "How would you like to accompany me to the bar, or would your good mother object?"

"I'd like to go, Captain Pete," I said, "but we can't ask Mama. She's asleep and we better not wake her."

So I took hold of his hand and we went down the steps. It was crowded and a lot of men were leaning against the bar. Over by the stove a couple of games of poker were going on. I never saw so many brass spittoons in my life. The smell was warm and comfortable like a feather quilt.

"I didn't know you had a boy that age, Captain," said one of the men at the bar.

"This is George Marlin's boy," Captain Pete said.

"Hello, son," said the strange man. "Want a chaw of tobacco?" And he stuck out a plug of Brown's Mule.

"No, thank you, sir," I said. "I only chaw in my old clothes when I'm working."

The man laughed. "The boy is right flip, Cap'n. Maybe he'd like a cigar. Here, son, take a cigar. It's a lot better than that cornsilk I'll bet you smoke in the woodshed." He gave me a long cigar wrapped in tinsel paper.

"Thank you, kindly, sir." I put it in my inside coat pocket.

It was getting rough and I knew we must be in the bay when the purser brought out the gambling wheel and placed it on the bar. He put the paddles beside it and, reaching below, brought up an armful of doll babies without much clothes on and with big goo-goo eyes. They cried when he bent them over.

"Here you are, boys," said the purser. "Win yourself a kewpie doll before you get to Baltimore." He gave the wheel a turn that sent it whirling. " 'Round and round the wheel goes and where she stops nobody knows.' Step up, gents, who'll be the first to win a baby doll?"

The paddles were a nickel apiece and soon all forty were sold. The wheel went round making a sound like when you run and hold a stick against a picket fence.

"Number three wins a baby doll, who has number three? The gentleman with the derby hat wins a baby doll for his best girl. What color dress would you like, sir?"

There was something exciting about that clicking sound the wheel made when it turned. Me and Captain Pete stood and watched the wheel go round and the men carry off the baby dolls. Captain Pete stepped over and bought two paddles, looked them over carefully and gave

me number seven. He kept number eleven. The wheel
went round and round.

"Seven come eleven!" shouted the captain. Only it came
out the other way, for the wheel stopped on my number.

"What gentleman has number seven?" cried the purser.
"Number seven wins a baby doll."

"Here he is," said Captain Pete. "It's the boy."

The wheel turner looked at me and handed over the
kewpie doll. "The young man wins a baby doll," he said
and snickered when he said it.

Jerusalem! I hadn't handled a doll baby since I gave
up my teddy bear and got out my cap pistol. It sort of
squawked and I guess everybody looked at me. Captain
Pete laughed.

"Take it up and show it to your mother, Noah, only
don't tell her you were with me."

The boat was rolling as I carried the doll baby up the
steps to the main cabin. I had to brace myself and swagger
to keep from falling. When I reached the top of the stairs,
I stopped. There was a bunch of women sitting and talking. They looked at me and I almost dropped the doll
baby. It let out a loud squawk.

"Land sakes," said one of the women, "look at that big
boy carrying a baby doll."

"That's Evaline's boy, ain't it?" another one said.
" 'Pears like he's never going to grow up!" They all
laughed.

That laughing did something to me. Putting the doll
baby on an empty seat, I pulled out the cigar, and taking
the tinsel off, bit the end of it. There was a man standing

beside me looking out of the window and I asked him for a match. He was so surprised, he gave me one, and I lit up. That first puff was awful strong.

"Thank you, sir," I said, and picking up the doll baby I staggered away.

"Good Lord," I heard one of the women say, "I believe he's drunk, too."

Mama must have been dozing when I came abreast of her.

"Mama," I called. She opened her eyes and they almost popped out of her head.

"Oh! Oh!" she said. "Liquor, tobacco and gaming, and he not even nine!" She got up and took me by the hand. "You come out on deck."

The fresh air felt good.

"Now you throw that cigar overboard."

I walked over to the rail and threw the cigar into the bay. Then, before she could stop me, I pitched the doll baby after it. As it floated away toward the stern, one of its hands clutched the air above the waves. It let out a faint squawk.

"Mercy!" Mama said. "It's bordering on infanticide."

"What's that mean?" I asked.

"Don't you worry about that," she said. "Come on inside, maybe you can rest awhile before we get to Baltimore."

I settled down in the big chair and must have gone to sleep. The next thing I knew, the *B. S. Ford* let out a big blast and Mama said, "She's a-blowing for Baltimore. Come on, Noah, get your things ready."

I put on my overcoat and hat. "Who's meeting us?" I asked.

"Paul's wife. I'd better call a porter to carry the suitcase."

Soon we were down the steps and across the gangplank. The porter led the way in a white coat.

"There she is," Mama said, waving to her daughter-in-law. She gave the porter a dime.

"Gee," I thought, "I'd rather spend that dime on the lower deck."

CHAPTER 9

The Hunter Is a Sissy

EARLY in December, when I was looking in the kitchen drawer for my singing top, I noticed that Mama's soap coupons were gone. She had been saving them for the mission table on page thirty-five of the premium book.

"Mama, are you going to get that parlor table for Christmas?" I asked.

She sighed and smiled. "Noah, I'm going to get something for you instead, something you have been wanting for a long time." But she wouldn't tell me what it was.

"Aw, Mama," I said, "will you tell me if I guess?"

She wouldn't even do that so I got out the premium book and looked at all of the things I would have liked to have. On page forty-one there was a sled with steel runners; on page forty-two, I liked the erector set with the electric motor; but on page forty-five was what I really wanted, a big blue steel air rifle, a real pump gun, with a magazine that held fifty beebees. I had been wanting that air rifle for more than two years now. Slingshots and bows and arrows are all right, but when a fellow is eight years old, he needs an air rifle.

"Mama, I betcha it's this air rifle," I said hopefully.

"You know your father wouldn't let you have an air rifle," she replied. "They're too dangerous. You might shoot your eyes out."

"Ric got an air rifle for Christmas last year," I argued. "He's still got both eyes, and the Meekins boys have got cat rifles."

At the mention of the Meekins boys, Mama snorted. "Don't you compare yourself with those Meekins boys. They're no-count and their people let them run wild!"

"Aw, Mama," I said, and turned back to look at the big blue steel air rifle on page forty-five.

By Christmas Eve I just about knew what I was going to get for Christmas. Aunt Carrie had bought me a sled that was hid under Mama's bed; Mama was going to give me two dollars to buy more of the Rover Boys series and Daddy was going to buy me candy and firecrackers. He liked to set off the crackers as much as I did. But I still couldn't figure out what all of those soap coupons were being used for. "Maybe Mama has changed her mind," I thought. "She has a strong hankering for that mission parlor table finished in golden oak." I didn't even dare to hope for that air rifle.

Christmas Eve did finally come, and I helped to decorate the tree. Santa Claus didn't come to our house any more but I did hang up one of Mama's long black stockings. I went to bed so that I could be up early and fire the first firecracker on our street.

It wasn't even starting to get light when I slipped out into the front yard on Christmas morning. Just as I was sticking a big five-center in the gate, *Wham! wham!*

wham! doggone if Froggy Duncan hadn't beat me to it.
They sounded like ten-centers. I went inside and lit the
nickel lamp in the parlor. Everything was real pretty, the
tree all green with red ornaments, Mama's stocking lopsided with oranges, my sled, and Jerusalem! leaning against
the mantel piece all shining, was that air rifle from page
forty-five of the premium book! Gee! I could feel my heart
coming up in my throat. I was almost afraid to touch it. I
let out a yell and grabbed the rifle, swinging it to my
shoulder. Through those long range sights I could see the
tinsel star shining on the topmost branch of the tree.
"Bing, bing, bing!" I wondered where the beebees were.

Daddy opened the stairway door and called, "Noah, you
come back to bed, it's only ten minutes after six."

I didn't want to go back to bed but it was Christmas
morning and besides, Daddy probably had the beebees.
Anyway, I just slipped off my shoes and jumped in. I sank
down deep in the feather bed with my rifle beside me. I
felt like I was floating on a cloud. Boy! wouldn't Ric turn
green when he saw it. Ric only had a single-shot rifle,
which meant he had to carry part of his beebees in his
mouth so that he could load quick. I must have gone back
to sleep again for the next thing I knew, Mama was moving around the kitchen and I could smell sausage and buck-
wheat cakes cooking.

"I must have dreamed about that rifle," I thought. But
when I reached for it, it was there!

Mama called, "George, Noah, Merry Christmas, and
come on down and get your breakfast."

After breakfast Daddy said, "Noah, I want to talk to you

about that air gun. Your mother and I decided that you ought to have one like the other boys, but I want you to promise me that you won't ever point it at nobody."

"Suppose it ain't loaded, Daddy?"

"That don't make no difference," he said. "Every day you can read in the paper where somebody gets killed by a gun that ain't loaded."

"All right, Daddy, I won't ever point at nobody," I promised.

"Here's your beebees, then," Daddy said, and handed over a little paper bag heavy with lead. "Do you know how to load it?"

Daddy read the card that came with it and showed me how to load it. We went out in the back yard and he hit a tin can three times in a row.

"Gee, Daddy," I said, "I didn't know you were such a good shot."

"Sometime I'll buy you a real one, a ten-gauge shotgun," he said. "That will kick you flat. It takes a real man to shoot a ten gauger." He shot three more times at the can. "Now you're old enough to have a gun, you'd better start calling me Dad instead of Daddy, Noah," he said.

"O.K., give me a shot, Dad."

And doggone if I didn't miss that tin can!

Dad laughed and went back into the house. I crept along the street, cautious and ready for anything.

Down by the river I came across Ric and Erny. Sister Helen had given Ric a pair of high-top shoes for Christmas so he broke some ice and waded out to test them. Erny had some new ice skates. His feet were wet, too. Both of

them had their rifles along. Boy, you should have seen their
eyes bulge when they saw my new rifle. Erny threw a glass
bottle out on the ice and we all tried my new gun. We shot
tin cans. We shot at the glass knobs on the telephone poles.
We made a shooting gallery out of oyster shells and shot
for prizes. We went over to Cullen's barn to shoot sparrows
but it was even too cold for the sparrows so we all went
home.

Winter wasn't the time for hunting. There wasn't
enough wild life around. When spring came there was always something to shoot at along the river. Water snakes
were good hunting and so were frogs. There were mud
turtles, plenty of birds, and then there was Fannie the
shitepoke. We named Fannie after our third grade teacher,
Miss Fannie, and she had been flying up and down
the river for a long time. In the summer when we were
hauling seine, old Fannie would fly past and if you called,
"Hi, Fannie," sometimes she would say "Auk" right back
at you, just like a schoolteacher with a sore throat. Nobody
wanted to shoot Fannie, though, she belonged to the river.

One warm Sunday afternoon in late March, a bunch of
us boys was fooling around the river, playing in the boats,
when Fannie came flying by, right important-like, and lit in
a cherry tree that was just breaking out its white blossoms.
There she sat, with her long neck stretched out, trying to
spy a school of minnows for her supper. And I had to be the
only one to have my rifle along.

"Say, Noah, let me take a shot at Fannie," Ric said.

"Aw, you don't want to shoot Fannie."

Ric got mad when I wouldn't let him use my rifle.

"You're a sissy," he said. "And you're a scared-cat, too, if you don't take a shot at Fannie. What are you carrying that gun for if you are afraid to use it?"

The other boys sort of looked at me and snickered.

"All right," I said, thinking I would miss.

I took a careless aim and pulled the trigger. Fannie squawked and dropped to the ground, rolled her yellow eyes at me and died, shot right through her long neck with that one little beebee. She had such pretty, soft feathers.

CHAPTER 10

Birds of a Feather

SPRING came to the river again. Mr. Jesse had been poorly all winter — something was swelling inside his ear — and I helped Dad to fix the bateau. He had to send to the factory for a new timer, and by the time we had it, the shadbush had blown and the shad run was over. But the locust trees were spreading their white blossoms along the riverbanks and the peepies were singing — it was time to go soft-crabbing. I waited until Mama was in her best mood, after supper on Friday.

"Can I go soft-crabbing with Dad tomorrow, Mama?" I asked. "He'll need somebody on the other end of the seine."

"It's not June yet," she said. "You might catch your death of cold."

"We've had a warm spring," Dad said. "It won't hurt him."

Mama turned on Dad. "The boy isn't big enough to haul seine, he won't be nine until July."

"I hauled seine a couple of times last summer, Mama."

"It's a good thing I didn't know about it. Who's going to beat the biscuit dough? If you want beaten biscuit somebody's got to beat the dough."

"I'll beat them tonight, Mama."

You could see that she was about to give in. "If you get sick, remember what I told you. It's getting so that the pair of you team up on me."

"Aw, Mama," I said, "wouldn't you like to have a mess of fried soft crabs?"

"I don't want anything that comes from the river. Sometimes I wish we lived on a desert."

But she mixed the flour and I beat the dough for almost an hour. That was harder work than hauling seine. We had a biscuit block and I used a wooden maul that must have weighed all of ten pounds. By that time I was ready for bed; we were getting up at dawn.

Me and Dad ate by ourselves and left the dishes for Mama. We walked along the oyster-shell path, listening to the birds waking in the trees. There was a light air from the south'ard and I knew that we had picked a good day. When we reached the cove, an old heron flew out of the marshy fringe with a loud squawk, just like he might have been clearing the mist from his throat.

Dad spoke soft-like. "It's going to be a nice day."

I nodded and helped him push the bateau into the water. The seine was in the boat and we were away in a couple of minutes. The new timer made all the difference, the engine started quick and ran regularly. It pushed us faster, too.

Before we reached the bend in the river, the sun came out of the woods. It was as red as the buoy. Dad studied the buoy, it was leaning slightly down the river.

He yelled so as to be heard above the pounding of the engine. "The tide has started to fall."

Dad began to look for a likely cove. The first of the ebb tide is the best time to go soft-crabbing — if you wait too long the crabs swim out to deeper water. Dad pointed the bateau toward a sandy beach. I watched a great heron take to the air.

"He knows where the crabs are," Dad yelled.

The pounding of the bateau had frightened the heron. The woods echoed. I watched a watersnake wriggle into the marsh.

When Dad cut the engine, the silence was as clear as the sunshine. Our bateau coasted until its prow crushed the sand, only a few yards from where the heron had been crabbing.

I jumped into the shallow water and pushed the boat higher before carrying the anchor ashore and setting its flukes.

"Be careful with that grapnel, Noah," Dad said. "Ira Patchett, he was your second cousin on your grandpappy's side, fell on a grapnel and it gutted him, slit him just like you clean a roe shad."

I picked up an oyster shell and sent it skipping. The beach was wet with the falling tide.

Dad stirred and slipped over the side. He sat on the gunwale and pressed his toes through the moss and sand. He smiled sort of gentle-like. "Makes me feel like a lad again, coming down the river in the spring to haul seine. Seems like I shed my winter shell every spring."

"How long you reckon you will live, Dad?" I asked, still thinking about my second cousin Ira Patchett.

"It don't pay to think too far ahead, son," he said, reaching for the seine.

We spread it on the beach. "Time was when we-un was a boy, the crabs sloughed later, on the last of the ebbing tide. Now everything is civilized and faster," Dad said.

We found a gaping hole and Dad grunted. He closed the break with a piece of the twine he used for a belt. "Time to mend a net is after you use it."

"Jim Meekins used it last." I said. "He borrowed it last September."

"When you borrow something you ought to return it better than you got it," Dad said.

The seine was about the size of a tennis net with a line of lead sinkers on the bottom and a row of corks to float the top. The ends were laced to poles.

I took the shallow end and Dad took the deep end, looping the bateau's painter over his shoulder. It trailed us.

Schools of minnows and shrimp broke the water. They scooted away from the seine — they knew about being caught, without having to read and write. When the seine got heavy, Dad brought his end shoreward and we dragged our catch out on the beach. Minnows and sunfish jumped on the moss but we weren't interested in them. Most of them flopped their way back to the river; even a little fish knows which way to flip. We were careful with the soft crabs — six of them, not counting the hard jimmies and two peelers.

Dad was happy. "We're going to catch them today, we're right in the middle of the spring slough. The moon was full last night."

He was right. By the time the sun was overhead, we had taken six dozen soft crabs. They were a pretty sight, resting on wet moss in the shade of the bow deck. We had worked our way downriver, the water was saltier and colder. We were approaching the bay and the river was wider.

I was hungry and tired. "Let's go home," I said to Dad.

He had a different idea. "It's only a couple of miles to the Cliffs. Let's run over and have a bite with Pap. He knows how to cook a soft crab."

I sat on the bow deck, away from the engine's fumes, and looked for the bush stake that marked the channel across the bar. If we followed the regular channel, like the *B. S. Ford*, it would take us twice as long.

I saw the bush stake and sang out. It was dead ahead — Dad must have known it was there. Far down the river, I saw a schooner. She was coming our way, riding the southerly, and I knew by her topsail that she was the *Kessie Price*.

Dad rounded the bush stake and turned the bateau shoreward. The Cliffs are the tallest clay banks on the river. I began to look for Grandpappy's ark. I didn't have to search for long; it was beside the pier, just where I saw it when we passed it on the *B. S. Ford* last December.

As I watched, the ark door opened and Grandpappy came out on deck. I wondered if he would know the sound of our bateau — maybe the new timer would fool him. I wondered if he could see us.

Dad cut the engine. "Hello, there," he called.

I could see that Grandpappy wasn't sure who we were. He looked like Dad, only shorter and older, and he was smoking a white clay pipe. Dad chews except around election times, when he smokes cigars. A couple of cats, big toms, were rubbing against Grandpappy's legs.

"Is that you, George?" he asked.

"It's me and Noah."

"Come on in," Grandpappy said. "What's the matter, your wife drive you out?"

Dad ignored that. "Come here, Pap, and look what we caught."

Grandpappy wasn't sure of himself. Instead of walking down the steps, he sat on the edge of the deck and slid to the beach. "I never saw so much foggy weather for this time of the year," he said. "I can hardly see you, George."

"It's your eyes, Pap. You ought to see a doctor."

"Sometimes they do pain me, but I don't fancy having no doctor fooling with my eyes. They're the only ones I'll ever have."

Dad guided Grandpappy's hands along the gunwale. He must have heard the crabs, stirring and bubbling like crabs do, or maybe he smelled them.

He reached over the gunwale and ran his hand over the crabs. Maybe if you can't see, then you can feel things better. Anyway, Grandpappy picked the best crab, one that must have backed out of its shell just before we caught it, the crab was that soft and fat.

Grandpappy handled it easy-like. "You're a pretty thing, honey," he said, kind of to himself. "Didn't your mama tell you to keep in the channel?"

He laid the crab on the moss.

"How many did you seine, George?"

"Six dozen. The sloughs were everywhere."

Grandpappy whistled. "Why didn't you keep after them? You won't get another day like this all summer."

"The boy and I was getting hungry. We thought we might share a mess of soft crabs with you."

"Why don't you say you're just plain lazy?" Grandpappy said. "This is the first time you've been to see me since last November. I might have been dead for all you cared."

"Don't say that, Pap. I'd like to take you home for a visit, but you know how Evaline is."

Grandpappy got his dander up. "Who asked to go home with you? I just hate to see a son of mine let a woman boss him." He turned to me. "So this is my grandson."

His old hands strayed to my shoulders. I could smell the soft crab, mixed with tobacco and whisky.

"How old are you, boy?"

"I'll be nine in July, Grandpappy."

"Grandpappy," he muttered. "That's the first time anybody ever called me Grandpappy. I sort of feel older."

His face was so close to mine. It was lined like a seine, and his eyes were traced with red. He was fierce-looking, and kind, too, if that makes sense.

His hands pinched my arms. "He's sort of puny, ain't he, George?"

"He's small but he's strong," Dad said, "and he's smart.

Evaline is already talking about sending him to the college
on the hill."

Grandpappy snorted. "College," he said. "What would
that give him that he can't get by himself? He'd probably
end up one of them educated fools. Come on in and let's
eat before you get more damn-fool ideas."

Dad eyed the soft crabs. "I figure I can eat a dozen by
myself."

"You always was a pig, George," Grandpappy said, "but
if you'll pick a dozen of the best ones, we might make a
meal. Don't let your eyes run away with you. Remember
the smallest are the sweetest."

While Dad was cleaning the crabs, Grandpappy got a
basin and they washed the crabs in river water. A soft crab
is easy to clean — just pinch the hard eyes and mouth away,
take out the devil's fingers from under the shell, slip off the
saddle, and the crab is ready to fry.

Inside the ark, Grandpappy dropped some paper and
kindling in the little pot-bellied stove and soon it was
roaring. "I hate to build a fire after the first of May," he
said.

He took a large skillet from the wall and put it on top of
the stove. He put a half cup of water in the skillet before
adding the crabs.

"Where's the lard?" asked Dad. "Ain't you going to fry
them?"

"It's something new I learned," Grandpappy said.
"You're never really old as long as you can learn something
new. I steam them a little first, then the lard finishes the
job. That makes them more tender besides saving lard."

He lifted the lid and added salt and pepper and lard, then he filled the coffee pot.

My eyes had been traveling. In one corner of the ark, Grandpappy had a bunk that reminded me of a ship's bunk, and by the window there was a table and two chairs. Grandpappy's clothes and shoemaking tools were spread everywhere. Mama wouldn't like the way Grandpappy left odds and ends all over the place. Bread and butter and a can of evaporated milk were on the table. But the thing that took my eye was a pretty blue jar that had a picture of a man fishing.

Dad watched me.

"That jar belonged to your Grandpappy's brother John. That's a ginger jar and came all the way from China."

"Gee! Did Uncle John sail a clipper ship?" I asked.

Grandpappy snorted. "Don't let your dreams get the best of you, boy. John was a Chesapeake pilot and took ships from Norfolk to Baltimore. Used to come home wearing kid gloves and a derby hat, thought he was a gentleman. Damn fool let himself get killed in Baltimore harbor. Got hit on the head by a cargo boom."

Dad shivered. "How you feel these days, Pap?"

"Me? Outside my eyes I feel like a boy. Guess I'm going to live to be one hundred and three and be hanged for rape."

I don't think Dad liked Grandpappy to talk like that around me.

The coffee started to boil and Grandpappy lifted the lid off the crabs — they were ready.

"Pour yourself some coffee and set up, George. Noah, use that chest."

Dad found the plates and poured three cups of coffee. Grandpappy served the crabs. He filled the skillet before sitting down.

I don't like to eat hard crabs — by the time I pick one, my appetite is gone — but soft crabs are something else. I love them.

We didn't talk, we ate. Dad ate half a dozen while me and Grandpappy finished the rest. The coffee was strong.

Grandpappy was the first to clean his plate. He poured himself another mug of coffee. When he finished, he scraped the plates and fed the cats.

He and Dad leaned back in their chairs and Grandpappy lit his pipe. "So Noah is going to college. Next thing you know he won't be seeing people when he meets them on the street, folks like us."

Dad was spruced up by the food. "You was always pretty quick with figures, Pap. Don't you think it would be good for the boy to learn how to calculate things with x's and y's?"

"I never saw a problem that I couldn't figure in my head," Grandpappy said. "Arithmetic is powerful enough."

"Noah is good at arithmetic," Dad said.

"Is he?" Grandpappy said. "We'll see. How much is one-fourth divided by one-fourth, son? Quick, how much?" He almost stuck his finger in my eye.

"One," I said.

"That's right — then how much is one-half divided by one-half?"

I smiled. "One."

"Quick," he said, "how much is one-sixteenth divided by one-sixteenth?"

"One."

Grandpappy slapped me on the back. "The boy is sharp, George. But let me try him once more. Now tell me, grandson, what's the difference in size between one mile square and one square mile?"

I took my time. "They're the same."

"That's right," Grandpappy said. "Now I'll ask you one more easy one, that's all."

I knew by the way he talked that I'd better be careful.

"What's the difference between two square miles and two miles square?"

That was one to draw, so I drew it with my finger in the air.

Grandpappy made out he didn't like that. "You ought to be able to figure that one in your head."

"Two miles square is twice the size of two square miles." I even used the right grammar for him.

Grandpappy clapped his hands together. "I wish I could really see you," he said. "Are his eyes blue, George?"

"Blue as the river," Dad said. "Maybe you think he ought to go to college?"

"He's already got a better mind than most of the professors. Let him teach and pace himself — you shouldn't touch a good mind 'less it wants to be touched. He'll just get bored."

"Maybe you'd better explain that to Evaline."

"Women don't have balance enough to understand such

things. They're either all heart or the scheming kind."

I wondered if Grandpappy was right.

"How you fixed for money, Pap?" Dad asked.

"I ain't doing much shoemaking these days, keep hitting my fingers."

Dad dug into his pocket and found a dollar bill. "Maybe this will help you a bit, Pap." He dropped the bill into the blue jar.

"I guess it ain't wrong for a son to help his poor old pappy," Grandpappy said. I thought he was going to cry.

Dad was getting restless, so was I. "We'll lose the crabs if we don't get going," Dad said.

"You never stay," Grandpappy said. "Nobody stays put no more."

"I'll come to see you again soon, Pap, and bring Noah."

"That's what you always say."

Dad kissed Grandpappy's cheek and then Grandpappy kissed me. It was like having a crab kiss you, the smell and all.

Grandpappy didn't go down to the bateau with us. The last I could see of him, he was still standing on the deck of his little ark.

We sold the crabs for seven dollars and Dad gave Mama a five-dollar bill. That pleased her. He didn't tell her that we had been to see Grandpappy. Neither did I.

CHAPTER 11

To the Victor

DAD came home one night smoking a cigar and smelling of liquor. He was excited.

"Well, Mother," he said, "soon I'm going to have what you are always talking about."

"You talk like you were half drunk, George."

"Yes, sir," Dad went on, his tongue running free and easy, "after next November, I'm going to have a steady job."

"I guess you're more than half drunk," she said, "but why wait until next November?"

"That's when the election is. I'm going to have a political job."

"Political job," Mama said. "You'd better leave politics to the lawyers and them that are born to it. What kind of a job are you talking about?"

"Bridge tender of the Chester River bridge. Outside of dog catcher, there ain't a job in the county that pays more for less work. In the wintertime, you never have to open the draw at all."

"How much money is there in it?"

"Thirty dollars a month and the bridge house to live in. With that cash rolling in and the money I can pick up selling bait, we can live like kings. You might even have a colored girl to help you in the kitchen, Mother.''

"I can go fishing right off the front porch at the bridge house, Dad," I said.

"I'll take you fishing with me under the draw."

"Well, it's better than nothing," Mama said, "but how do you get the job? Such things don't come for nothing."

"All I have to do is to get the watermen to vote for the organization in the June primaries. After we win the primaries and the general election in November the county commissioners will appoint me bridge tender."

"There's many a slip between the cup and the lip," she said. "What's the organization?"

"We're one bunch of Democrats who believe in working together. After we lick the anti-organization in the primaries we're bound to win the election. The Democrats ain't lost the election in our county since the Civil War."

"How are you going to get the watermen to vote for the organization?" I asked.

Dad laughed. "That's easy," he said. "I'll go up and down the river in my bateau giving them all cigars and drinks of liquor, and telling them what the organization is going to do for the watermen, like oyster beds set aside for the tongers, and a longer season for the pound net fishermen. Then I'll ply them with more liquor."

"Ain't that awful," Mama said. "Men will do anything for tobacco or whisky. It'll be pretty, though, living on the river. But suppose the anti-organization wins?"

"You would think of that," he said. "Always looking on

the dark side of things. But they can't win because we've got more and better liquor."

"Who pays for the liquor and cigars, Dad?"

"That I can't tell you," he said, "but if it'll make your mother feel any better, they're the same men who put silver dollars in the collection plate on Sundays."

"Why do they want to win bad enough for that?" I asked.

"So they can run things and get the money the people who run things always get. Like selling the lumber to fix the bridge or the oyster shells to put on the road."

"Now that you're a politician, I don't suppose you could be asked to chop us some wood," Mama said. "These spring days are chilly."

But Dad felt so good he went out and cut enough wood to last the rest of the week.

The Democratic primary was the third week of June, so he had to get busy with his politicking. I would have liked to go with him on Saturdays, but I was working for Mr. Leary, the grocer. Then, one Sunday afternoon, all of the Sunday school teachers were away attending a convention and I saw my chance. Dinner was over and Dad was sitting back resting. After a while, he pulled out one of those big cigars and lit up.

"Certainly is a nice afternoon," he said. "I think I'll take a little run up the river to Buckingham." Some of the watermen lived at Buckingham Wharf in little arks.

"Can I go, Dad?"

"It's all right with me if it's all right with your mother."

"What's all right?" Mama called from the kitchen, hearing him mention her name.

"Can I go up the river with Dad?"

"Can't he even stop politicking on the Lord's Day? If he'll leave that jug of liquor home, you can go with him."

"You don't want me to get a steady job, do you, Mother?"

"Will you leave that jug of liquor home?" she asked, looking towards the closet where Dad kept it.

"All right," he said, with a sigh. "I'll take some extra cigars instead," and he filled his coat pocket from a box in the kitchen. "Come on, Noah," and we went down to the river. On the way he patted his hip pocket and smiled. "Mother didn't know I had a pint in my hip pocket," he said. "I guess we can oil a few votes with that."

It was a nice day — wind from the southwest coming up the river, the sky blue and the river blue. A fish hawk hovered over the cove, looking for his dinner, and the king-fishers were fishing, too. Dad was careful not to flood the engine, and we were away in a twinkling. I sat on the bow deck and he steered from the stern. The old heron on the point took time out from his fishing to look us over but he didn't bother to fly off to the marsh. I guess by this time he knew Dad was one of his partners and wouldn't hurt him. Pretty soon we were abreast of Buckingham and Dad turned the engine off.

Two of the Cable boys, who were about my age, were stretched out on the wharf. They didn't even have any shoes on and seemed interested in fishing. By the arks, the fishermen were working on their seines and the women were sitting on the ark steps. One of them was nursing a baby.

"Hello, boys," Dad said. "How's tricks?" They mumbled and he walked up to where the men were. I followed.

"Getting ready for crabs already, Med?" Dad said to a man who only had one arm.

"Yep," Mr. Med said and threw another knot from the seine needle. For a one-armed man he was quick.

"You going to vote in the Democratic primaries?" Dad asked.

Mr. Med stopped to fill his needle. "Maybe."

"I guess you know about us organization Democrats," Dad said. "When the old organization wins in November, the Chester River is going to be a paradise for us watermen. Longer fishing seasons and less meddling from the state inspectors."

"Maybe you won't win," Mr. Med said.

"We can't lose," Dad said. "Here's a couple of cigars the organization sent you, Med." He looked at me and watched the women sitting on the steps. I wandered down to the wharf, but over my shoulder I saw him hand Mr. Med the bottle. They were standing in back of a tree where the women couldn't see them. That oiled things and pretty soon I heard Dad and the other men laughing and talking.

"Ain't you got some licorice for us, Noah?" one of the boys on the wharf said.

"You boys ain't old enough to vote," I said.

"I'll hook one of those cigars your dad gave my old man," the smallest boy said. "He wouldn't do nothing but chew it."

"Do you ever sneak a nip from your pop's bottle, Noah?" the bigger one asked.

"Naw," I said, "I just signed the temperance pledge in church. I can't touch a drop as long as I live."

"Suppose you get sick and your ma can't get the doctor?" the big boy said.

Dad and the other men came down to the wharf and we stepped into the bateau.

"I'll be seeing you at the primary in June and I'll have a bigger bottle then," Dad said.

"We'll be there, George," they said, laughing and puffing on the cigars. The old two-cycle started like a Gatling gun and we ran toward home.

Dad burned up plenty of gasoline and cigars in May and had to get the big jug filled about twice a week. He never said who filled it, but I saw him come out of the drugstore carrying it and a box of cigars. It must have been good stuff. As the day for the primaries came nearer he got more and more excited.

"All of the watermen from Buckingham's to Cliff City are going to support us, Mother," he said.

"How do you know they will?" she said. "Nobody knows what goes on behind that curtain. Like as not they are taking cigars and whisky from the anti's, too, and promising to vote for them."

"Depend on you to look on the dark side," Dad said, "just when I'm trying so hard to get a steady job."

Two days before the primary, Dad turned up wearing a new suit of clothes, new shoes and a straw hat with a gay band. He had a haircut and his mustache was trimmed. I guess Mama liked to see him looking so prosperous even if he did have liquor on his breath. He had a different walk, something like Mr. Eben Pauley, who is a county commissioner and the president of the bank, only easier and free-like. But I never saw him again until the day of the primary. That was when I walked around by the firemen's hall, where they did the voting. Seems like I never saw so many mustaches and beards before. Most of the men were at least half drunk and some had given up and were sitting down on the curb. Only the officials seemed sober. If they had been drinking they carried it so you couldn't notice it. There was Dad, and his new suit was all rumpled up like he had been sleeping in it. He saw me.

"Don't hang around here, Noah," he said. "You might hear some language your good mother would not approve of. Go home and tell your good mother not to wait supper for me. I'm dining out tonight." So I went home.

Mama was frying crullers. She knew me and Dad were mighty fond of crullers. "Did you see your father on the way home?"

"Yes, ma'am. He was around by the firemen's hall, where the voting is going on."

"Was he drunk?"

"No, ma'am, not full drunk."

"What do you mean, not full drunk?"

"He was still on his feet," I said. "He told me to tell you not to wait supper for him. He said he was dining out."

"Dining out," she said. "He's talking mighty fine lately, and just when I'm frying these crullers he likes so much."

"I don't think we will see much of him until they've finished counting the votes."

Sometime early in the morning I woke up to singing. First I thought I must be dreaming, but then I knew it was Dad coming home and singing in that tenor voice he had at certain times. "I guess the organization must have won," I thought and went back to sleep.

He was still asleep when I ate my breakfast, but I walked by the firemen's hall on the way to school and the results were tacked on the door. Sure enough, the organization had carried the county and I knew that Dad would have a steady job after next November, but that was a long time to wait.

That summer was a hot one, and Dad seemed to suffer from the heat more than usual. He didn't do much hard-crabbing and he and Mr. Jesse only hauled seine for a couple of weeks. Mama doesn't do much sewing in the summer and we would have been hard up if Mr. Leary hadn't let us run up a bill at his grocery. Dad was trading on his steady job even before he got it. That summer he spent most of his time hanging around the bridge. He acted like he owned at least a part of it. On the hot days he would crawl down beneath the draw and stretch out in the cool shade.

"This is the coolest place in Maryland," he said one day when I had climbed down and joined him. "Look at the cool green water, just like an eye shade." We stuck our feet in the water and it felt wonderful. But a schooner captain blew three long blasts, which means that the bridge better open. "I guess we don't want to get caught in the gears,"

Dad said, so we climbed back to the top of the draw and helped the bridge tender to turn the big key. He didn't seem to mind losing his job even though he had been opening the bridge for more than ten years.

"I'll be glad to get back to farming, George," he said. "You're going to find this bridge tending is awful confining. You never know when some fool captain is going to toot his horn, night or day, rain or shine, and then you have to run like a trick monkey." But what he said didn't ruffle Dad.

Before I knew it the summer was over and I was in school again. One night I heard the geese honking on their way south and I knew it wouldn't be long before Dad had a steady job. We would live in a house on the river like the rich folks. The Democrats were so sure to win that they always held a torchlight parade on election night, even before all of the votes were counted. The election wasn't as exciting as the primaries and not as many cigars or liquor traded hands. I guess the Republicans spent some money trying to get the colored people to vote, but most of them didn't bother to register. They hadn't forgotten the Civil War and there were still stories about men who dressed in sheets and rode on dark nights, always stopping at the doors of the colored people who voted. I don't think it was true but most of the colored people believed it and that is what counted.

Mama took me to the movies on election night. We saw a newsreel with Teddy Roosevelt and the other candidates for President. There was a Keystone Cop reel that I fancied better. Those cops can really speed and they never get hurt. After the movies we stood around waiting for the Democrats to parade. It was cold and I was glad when they came marching down the street led by the volunteer firemen's band playing "There'll Be a Hot Time in the Old Town Tonight." All of the Democrats were carrying lighted torches, the kind that burn in different colors.

"There's Dad," I said, pointing to a group of rivermen.

"What's he carrying in his hand?" Mama said.

"A torch like the rest."

"I mean the other hand," she said.

I looked close and saw he was carrying a bottle, only a good many of the men were carrying bottles, and some of them were using them.

"Where are they going, Mama?"

"Going?" she said. "They ain't going anywhere. They'll walk around until their legs or the liquor gives out. Let's go home."

I didn't hear Dad singing that night, but the next morning the papers said the Democrats had won the local elections in Maryland and that Woodrow Wilson was President. The Democrats had won every office in Kent County and Dad would be the bridge tender after the first of January.

Even Mama got excited while we were moving. The bridge house wasn't very far, so we carried all of our furniture except the stoves and beds in my little express wagon. On New Year's Eve, Dad got the coalman to move the stoves in his big wagon. I was so excited with the moving that Christmas vacation didn't seem the same. I didn't feel right until we got a coal fire started in the kitchen stove.

The second week of January, the river froze solid and it was that way for a month, with skating every day until the snow came. The men raced their sleighs along High Street and us boys coasted with our sleds and built snow forts. Dad sat by the fire and looked at the frozen river.

"This is the longest cold spell we've had since I was a boy," he said. "Back in the Eighties we sleighed right over the fences, the snow was that deep." He moved closer to the stove. "I could sleep all winter like old Mr. Diamondback and not crawl out until the warm spring sun shines. I'll bet I'd feel rested." But Dad didn't sit much longer.

Early in February, Mr. Eben Pauley knocked on the bridge house door. Mama let him in and he came right to the point.

"Taking it easy, eh?" he said to Dad. "Well, last week the county commissioners voted that now would be a good time to repair the bridge. Tomorrow, if it's a good day, I will come down and we'll look the bridge over. Every time I cross she rattles so I don't know whether I'm going to make it or not. She hasn't been repaired in five years. I'll mark the bad boards and you can replace them."

"I'm not much of a carpenter," Dad said in a weak voice.

"It's rough work, sawing and nailing," Mr. Pauley said. "Any able-bodied man can do it. When you signed the bridge tender's papers it included repairs for the bridge. Didn't you know that?"

"No," said Dad, "I didn't know that."

"You should always read before you sign," Mr. Pauley said, laughing.

"Yes, sir," Dad said. "I'll be ready tomorrow."

"You'd better get your saw sharpened," Mr. Pauley said as he went out the door. "Those oak boards are really tough. They'll be good for your circulation." I saw Dad wince.

After Mr. Pauley had gone, Dad sat for a long while, watching the flames through the isinglass door of the stove. Then he went to the kitchen drawer and got out his copy of the bridge tender's papers. He read and read.

"Here it is," he finally said, "under 'Maintenance.' It says, 'The bridge tender shall grease the draw's gears once every three months or on shorter intervals if necessary. He shall also replace all weak boards, as decided by the county commissioners, that body to furnish the lumber and nails.' "

"I told you people didn't get something for nothing," Mama said. "I told you."

"You're always telling me," Dad said. "Oh, my, what have I bargained for? I never did like carpentering, it's such violent exercise." But he got out the saw from the tool chest and took it up to the hardware store for sharpening.

The next day was a sunny one and Mr. Pauley knocked on the bridge house door before Dad was out of bed.

"Where's George?" he said.

"He must not be feeling very good this morning," Mama said. "I'll call him."

Mr. Pauley sat down in the parlor and you could see that he wasn't used to waiting. He did fiddle around with the stereopticon, but he wasn't interested. He took himself awful serious. Dad swallowed his oatmeal and coffee.

"You've wasted almost an hour of my time, George," Mr. Pauley said, and he was provoked.

"Yes, sir," Dad said, putting on his coat and gloves.

"We'll walk across the bridge and mark all of the weak boards with this heavy crayon," Mr. Pauley said as they went out the door. From the parlor window I could see them walking and kneeling and marking the boards. It seemed like they were marking a lot of them, but that old bridge did rattle when a two-horse wagon crossed it. They finally finished and Mr. Pauley talked to Dad a long while before getting into his carriage and driving off. Dad came in and sat down close to the stove.

"Thirty-five boards," he said, "thirty-five boards, oak boards, two inches thick and eighteen feet long." He shivered.

The next day he went up to the lumber yard and when he came back he was feeling better.

"There won't be any sawing, anyway," he said.

"Didn't Mr. Pauley tell you to sharpen your saw?" Mama said.

"I bargained with the lumberyard man and he is going to cut the boards to the right length with his buzz saw."

"Bargained," Mama said. "What did you bargain with?"

"He likes to fish off the bridge and I'm going to furnish him with peelers next summer."

"You don't mind mortgaging the future," Mama said. "First the grocery store bill and now fish bait." But I believe she was half proud of his bargain.

When the lumberyard wagon brought the boards, Dad got a colored man to help him and he had them all in place in less than a week. He never said what he gave the colored man.

On Valentine's Day somebody pushed an envelope under the bridge house door with my name on it. It had a funny picture and said I was only a fisherman's son. I guess Ric did it. The same day Captain Cable knocked on the bridge house door and wanted to see Dad.

"I'm bringing the *Bohemia* down the river the first of next week, George," he said. "You want to be ready to let me through because I want to carry the ebb tide to Annapolis."

"Where you bound, Captain?" Dad said.

"I'm sailing her down to Solomons," the captain said. "We're hauling out at Davis's. Her centerboard well leaked all last summer and kept us busy with the pumps. Like as not they'll find more trouble when they start tearing her apart. She's an old boat."

"What time does the ebb make at Buckingham's next Monday?" Dad asked.

"I figure about two in the morning," Captain Cable said. "There's a good moon and with the yawl boat kicking her, we ought to be ready to go through about three o'clock."

"I'll be ready to let you through," Dad said.

"Can I help you turn the draw, Dad?"

"That's too early for you to be up," Mama said.

"It's too early for anybody but the chickens," Dad said.

"I got to have the tide to help me until I pick up the breeze around Love Point," Captain Cable said on the way out.

The *Bohemia* would be Dad's first boat, and he wanted everything to be right. He greased the gears and squirted oil all around, even if it didn't need it, cleaned the lights on the draw, and trimmed the wicks so that they would burn brightly. Sunday night he wouldn't go to bed and rested on the couch in the parlor. I went to bed but not to sleep, and soon after the town clock struck one, I got up and went downstairs. Mama was up making a pot of coffee.

"Can I have a cup of coffee too, being's it's so cold, Mama?"

"You're not old enough to need coffee," she said.

"Why don't you give the boy a cup, mostly milk and sugar?" Dad said. Mama gave in to him.

"Let's go," Dad said, and putting on all of our clothes we went outside. It was a clear night with about three-quarters of a moon making a path up the river toward Buckingham.

"Do you see her, Noah?" Dad said, looking up the river.

"I can't see her yet," I said, straining my eyes on the moonlight, "but I can hear her yawl boat." Dad cupped his hands to his ears and listened. *Put, put, put,* we could hear the little yawl boat pushing the big schooner down the river.

"I guess we'd better get ready," he said, and slid the big bolts which held the draw to the rest of the bridge. While he was doing that, I took down the large key and lugged it over to the hole in the boards. Dad lowered it down into the slot and we were ready to turn the draw.

"I'd better shut the gates too," Dad said. "Some fool might be traveling at this time of night." The gates close off the open ends of the bridge when the draw is opened. He put a red lantern on each gate.

Dad had just finished when the captain blew his horn, three long blasts, like a knight in one of the King Arthur stories. It carried a long way on the cold winter night. We couldn't see the *Bohemia* in spite of the moonlight.

"She's off Morgneck Creek," Dad said. "Let's open the draw so we will be all set for her." He moved to one end of the bar on the key and I took the other end. We both pushed but nothing happened.

Captain Cable blew his horn again, and looking up the moonlight path, we could see the tall masts of the *Bohemia*. He didn't have her sails raised, but the yawl boat and the tide were bringing her down the river at a fast clip.

"Let's try once more," Dad said. "I don't mind you riding on the bar but don't drag your feet." We both pushed, but it was like trying to shove your way through the side of a hill.

"I'll swing a red lantern and stop her," Dad said, running over and getting one of the lanterns on the gates. He climbed the side of the draw and started swinging the lantern to and fro. The *Bohemia* slowed her speed, swung broadside to the current. By this time she was in hailing distance.

"What's the matter, George?" Captain Cable called. "Ain't you strong enough to open her?"

"Something is stuck!" Dad yelled. "I guess the grease is frozen."

"I've got to get through." Captain Cable called. "I'll

bump the end of the draw with my bowsprit and break her loose."

"All right," Dad said, "but take it easy. It's a cold night to swim." He looked at me and we both shivered.

The *Bohemia* straightened out and came on right at us, getting larger and larger. Captain Cable had cut off the engine in the yawl boat but the current was bringing her fast enough.

"Watch the key and don't let it hit you, Noah," Dad said, just in time, for when the *Bohemia*'s bowsprit hit the draw, it started to turn and the key with the bar flew faster and faster around. I hopped back and felt the wind as the bar grazed me. The big schooner slid by, making a sigh as she passed.

"You're one hell of a bridge tender," Captain Cable said, "and if you don't have her open when we come back in the spring, I'm going to report you to the county commissioners."

We closed the draw and went home but Dad didn't say anything.

The trouble that Dad had opening the bridge changed him. He had always been so free and easygoing, but now his forehead was wrinkled half the time and he went around looking like he had something on his mind. He must have been thinking about what might happen when Captain Cable brought the *Bohemia* up the river in April. Like as not there wouldn't be another boat through the bridge before the *Bohemia*, but he was awful jumpy. Every time a fish horn blew on Water Street, he would jump up and look down the river.

March came, and toward the end of the month, Dad got up in the middle of the night in a hurry.

"Come on, Noah, I heard the *Bohemia* blow," he called. We dressed and ran out on the bridge. It was blowing half a gale and the wind went right through my clothes.

"Captain Cable said he was coming in April," I said, trying hard not to let my teeth chatter.

"He must have changed his mind," Dad said. "Anyway, I heard something blow. Listen, there it is again."

We listened. "Honk, honk, honk."

"Well, I'll be damned," Dad said. "It's the geese flying north again. Don't you tell anybody about this, Noah."

"I won't," I said, and we went to bed again.

After that Dad sort of resigned himself and didn't worry.

"What's going to be will be," he used to say, "and you can't change it."

He started catching up on his sleep, day and night. The wrinkles on his forehead disappeared. But one night changed all of that.

I woke up and heard Mama calling him. "George, wake up," she said. "I heard a boat blowing for the bridge to open."

"Huh?" he grunted. "You must have heard the geese honking. Why don't you let me sleep?"

I heard it and that honking wasn't geese. It was a boat horn and it was awful close. I jumped out of bed and so did Dad. We had our clothes on and were out of the house in a minute, but we were too late. When my feet hit the bridge, I felt it shake, and there was a terrible crash followed by a ripping sound and two thuds.

"There go the masts," Dad said. "Good Lord!"

After that everything was quiet until we heard a man cussing, and he cussed worse than I'd ever heard before.

"I guess the captain is all right, anyhow," Dad said. "They won't book me for murder."

"Dare we go out to the draw, Dad?"

"I don't dare but I've got to," he said, and we ran out to the draw or to where the draw had been. The *Bohemia* must have been coming up the river with the southwest wind in back of her and she had sailed right on through the bridge. The draw had carried away her masts. I never realized that a schooner had so much rigging and most of it was wrapped around the bridge. Captain Cable saw us.

"You're going to pay for this, damn you," he called to Dad.

Dad spruced up. "You can't get blood out of a turnip."

"I'll take it out of your lazy hide," Captain Cable said.

"If you touch me, I'll have you arrested for attacking an official," Dad said. He'd learned a lot about the law while playing poker with the lawyers.

Captain Cable's two boys were with him and they were cussing to themselves but they weren't hurt.

"Why didn't you open the bridge?" Captain Cable said.

"I didn't hear you," Dad said. "The county commissioners are liable to sue you for carrying away the draw. There'll have to be a ferry until the bridge is fixed."

"Sue me!" the captain said. "I'd like to see them try."

"Can I help you any?" Dad asked.

"Damn you, you've done enough," the captain said.

"All right," Dad said, but we closed the gates and hung red lanterns before going back to the bridge house.

Early the next morning, Dad went uptown to tell the county commissioners. Mama hadn't said a word, she was too flabbergasted. It was Saturday and I hung around the bridge stopping all of the teams on our end. About noon Dad came home with a relieved look on his face.

"What are we having for dinner, Mother?" he said.

"Anybody that's going to get discharged like you are ought to lose their appetite, too," she said.

"They can't discharge me," Dad said, right uppity-like.

"What do you mean, Dad?" I said.

"Who do you think you are, talking like that?" Mama said.

"They can't discharge me," he said. "I already resigned this morning."

"Resigned," Mama said. "Well, you'd better walk over to the basket factory and get a steady job."

"I can't ever get a steady job no more," he said.

"Good Lord," she said. "Hear the man talk. Has it affected your head, George?"

"If I get a steady job, Captain Cable is going to attach my wages for the damages done his schooner," Dad said. "I can't ever afford to work steady again. Maybe I'd better go down the river and live with Pap on his ark."

"Maybe you'd better march yourself down to the basket factory this instant," Mama said.

Dad winced.

CHAPTER 12

The Birth of Hypochondria

ONE warm November day, when we were all restless waiting for the dismissal bell to ring, Miss Bertie rapped on her desk.

"Boys and girls," she said, "I have a surprise for you. Tomorrow you are going to see a motion picture, here in our schoolroom. There will be four reels and a gentleman will accompany the picture with a lecture."

The three o'clock bell rang, and we stood up to be dismissed by rows. All except the ones who already knew they had to stay in. They sat still.

As we were going out the front door, Erny punched the football Ric was carrying under his arm. It bounded down the steps and rolled out on the lawn. Ric cussed and ran out on the grass in spite of the sign that said KEEP OFF THE GRASS. Mr. Manning came down the hall in time to hear Ric cuss and see him step on the grass.

"Ah! I've caught you this time, Master Rickard, swearing and walking on the grass," he said, taking Ric by the collar.

"Ain't I got the right to get my football?" asked Ric. "Why don't you catch the fellow who knocked it out of my arm?"

"Don't you know better than to carry a football like a loaf of bread?" said Mr. Manning. He had been a football player in his college days. Then he remembered who he was. "Don't you tell me what to do," he said, getting red in the face. "You're going to stay in my office until five o'clock."

"I want a lawyer," Ric yelled, smart-like, but he went back in the building carrying the only football we had.

We played with Erny's hat for a while but that wasn't much fun, so we wandered down to the river and sat on the old sewer pipe. It was Indian summer. The trees were bare now but the marsh grass was yellow and dotted with clumps of red coonberries. We watched a schooner sailing up the river, sailing wing and wing.

"Hey, Erny, do you think Miss Bertie's going to show us 'The Clutching Hand' tomorrow?" I asked, holding up my hand and clutching the air. We always used to do that like the fiend in the movies.

"Naw," Erny said. "I guess it'll be old stuff like 'The Perils of Pauline.' Maybe she'll have one of those Keystone Cop films. I could see them ten times. They last twenty minutes."

"That lecture stuff don't sound like much to me," Billy said.

"Well, we have to take that to get the pictures," Micky said. His father owned the town movie theater. "Anyway, that's better than listening to Miss Bertie talk all of the time."

After resting awhile on the sewer pipe, we went over to Brewster's Cove and skipped oyster shells until Old Man

Brewster came along in his horse and buggy and chased us. He's never caught nobody, but being a lawyer he can really fuss. When he threatened to get Mr. Jester, we all went home.

The next morning I was up before Mama.

"What's the matter with you, Noah?" she said. "Are you running a fever?" Mama is awful scared of fevers.

"No, ma'am," I said. "I got up early so I can be sure to get to school on time. Miss Bertie is going to show us a movie today."

"Did I hear you right?" she said. "You're going to have a moving picture in school? Things are coming to a great state. Can't you learn enough from all them books they give you? I only had three books when I went to school, and my father had to buy them, now you even have moving pictures. Pretty soon school children won't have to read, all they'll have to do is look and listen and play games. Next time I see Miss Bertie, I'll give her a piece of my mind."

I heard Dad stirring upstairs. "Why do you have to have all that arguing early in the morning?" he said. "I can't sleep at all."

"Yes, sir," I said, then I ate my breakfast and went to school.

It was a good thing I got there early, for Miss Bertie had two sheets to put on the wall, and she needed somebody who could climb the stepladder. There were blankets to fasten over the windows. It was lucky for us that the electricity had been hooked up to the school during the summer; we had two places where the movie machine could be plugged in. The gentleman who was going to run it had already arrived, and he showed us how to fit the film into the little sprockets so it wouldn't jump. Ric said he thought he might be a movie operator when he grew up. Then he could see all of the pictures without having to pay anything. It was right nice having a man in our schoolroom. The only time that happened was when Mr. Manning came in and he usually visited us when something was wrong.

The last bell rang, and we all went to our desks without having to be told. Miss Bertie unlocked a drawer and got out the little red book she used to take attendance. For the first time all year everyone was in school on time. There wasn't even anyone sick.

"Boys and girls," she said, "I am very proud to announce that we are the very first classroom in Kent County to use moving pictures as a means of instruction. This treat comes largely through the courtesy of Mr. Francis E. Bonestreet, of the U. S. Public Health Service. When I turn out the light, the picture and the lecture will begin. I expect everyone to be quiet and orderly." She went over to the wall and turned the lights out.

Being in a schoolroom is bad enough any time, but being in one that is pitch black is even worse. We all started to whistle and stamp our feet like we do in the town movies. One of the girls screamed and Miss Bertie turned on the lights. But she didn't catch anybody. She said something to Mr. Bonestreet, and he threw a spotlight on the sheet. Then she switched off the lights again. While he was trying to find the starter switch in the back, Micky stuck up his hand and made a big clutching hand on the screen. Somebody else waggled two fingers, and you know what that means. The lights came on again just in time to catch Alvin thumbing his nose with both hands in hopes of getting a big shadow. He got sent to the principal's office instead, and the rest of us settled down.

"Young people," the lecturer said in sort of a sissy voice, "the first thing that I am going to show you is a film on what happens to your breakfast after you swallow it."

The machine started to buzz, and a picture of the human body flashed on the screen. The mouth opened, and the food slipped down the gullet into a little bag that looked like the pig bladders we get from the slaughter-houses, only the film called it the stomach. Ric, who was sitting beside me, let out a big belch, but nobody said anything. We could see the bile getting to work before the blood stream took over. Breakfast was pretty close to most of us, and I could feel my innards quivering and speeding up like they were trying to catch up with the insides that were working so fast on the sheet.

Ric leaned over and whispered, "Ain't we got a lot of things inside of us to get out of whack?" He belched, only louder than before.

The second film was about the eye, and it showed one that was fixed up like a camera. Mr. Bonestreet hadn't said anything since he started, but now he began to talk, trying hard to be interesting.

"Can any of you young people name the three parts of the eye?" he asked while he was changing reels. Erny held up his hand.

"All right, son, name them."

"Pupil, adult, and larva," Erny answered.

That sounded correct to me, but there must have been something wrong, because Mr. Bonestreet didn't ask us any more questions.

The third film showed the heart, made something like a pump, only you couldn't prime it like the pump we have in our back yard.

But the last film was the one that really scared us. It was about germs. I never knew there were so many of those little critters lurking around, waiting for a chance to send me to bed. Only they weren't little on the sheet. They were big monsters, squirming and riding on the feet of a fly the size of one of those old dinosaurs. Just let somebody cough and millions of those tuberculosis germs flew through the air, lighting on everybody. Then those old germs would go to work, and soon it was too late to do anything about it. Too late for anybody but the undertaker.

When the lights went on, I never saw such a sickly-looking bunch of kids in my life. Miss Bertie thanked Mr. Bonestreet, but she looked pale, too. The lecturer was the only one who looked well. He was smiling and seemed to like those germs. Mama says you can get used to anything if you have to do it long enough.

After school, me and Ric went over to Bosy Robertson's to see if he would let us pick up a few fall apples. Bosy told us to help ourselves, and we soon had our pockets and blouses full, besides the ones we ate.

"Let's go over and play in Bosy's straw stack," Ric said.

"Maybe he wouldn't want us to."

"Aw, it's all settled," Ric said. "Besides he can't see us."

Ric climbed to the top of the stack and wouldn't let me up, but I grabbed his legs and we both went down. We played mountain climbing and jumping until we were all worn out. We covered up in the straw and tried to sleep. But it was getting late, so we loaded our blouses and ran home with the apples bumping against our ribs. I was awful tired and went to bed pretty soon after supper.

When the sun woke me up the next morning, I knew something was wrong. First, I thought it was a sore throat. My voice was sort of husky, and if I tried to take a deep breath something in my throat and lungs felt different than it ever had before. I didn't tell Mama because she would put me to bed and send for Dr. Salmons. He would come and after sticking a thermometer and spoon in my mouth, write something in Latin. Then I would be sick.

On the way to school, I felt like I was smothering. But I got there and spent most of the day sitting at my desk. It seemed like every breath might be my last one and I was starting to cough. All of a sudden I knew what was wrong. I had met up with some of those tuberculosis germs Mr. Bonestreet showed us the day before and they were going to work on me. But I did go out on the school grounds at noon and met Ric.

"I'm sick, Ric," I said, in a hoarse voice. "Do I look as bad as I feel?"

Ric took a look just as I coughed and spat. "You look awful, Noah," he said. "But you're not the only one, I'm in terrible shape, too." And he coughed and spat, stopping to look.

"No blood yet," he said.

"What do you mean, no blood, Ric?" I asked.

"Don't you know what's wrong with us?" Ric said. "That old tuberculosis germ has got us. When you start to spit blood, it's got you for keeps."

"Ric, let's take our lunches down to the river and not go to school this afternoon," I said. "We might give it to somebody else, even to Miss Bertie."

He coughed and nodded.

So we took our lunches and went down to where Brewster's Creek makes into the river. It was right warm for November, what we call Indian summer.

"Can you still eat, Ric?" I asked, unwrapping a ham sandwich and taking a bite. It tasted all right.

"I don't have much of an appetite," he said, "but I guess I ought to try to eat to keep up my strength." He finished up a hard-boiled egg in a couple of swallows.

"When did you first notice the germ, Ric?"

"As soon as I got up this morning," he said. "I could hardly get to school."

"That's when it struck me, Ric. How does it make you feel?"

"It's hard to breathe."

"Do you suppose we have the galloping kind?"

"I don't know, Noah. Let's spit again."

Ric spat and looked it over. "My Lord, Noah, look!" he said. I bent over and could see some dark streaks. Then I had to snicker.

"Aw, Ric, that's the piece of chocolate cake you just ate."

He washed his mouth out with river water and spat again. It was clear.

"Maybe we shouldn't go to school tomorrow," I said. "We might give it to one of the others."

"Naw," he said, "it wouldn't be right. Let's leave home with our lunches like we were going to school, and meet here. And bring your fishing line. I saw a school of rock yesterday."

"Dad always says that nothing ever happens to a river-man as long as he stays on the river," I said.

"Well, we're river boys," Ric said. "I feel safer here."

Before I went to bed that night, I said my prayers for the first time since last Christmas. I said a little prayer for Ric, too.

Early the next morning I stretched and took a deep breath. That same queer feeling was there but it seemed like I was getting used to it. I spat. "Well, at least I ain't in the last stages," I thought. While Mama was getting breakfast, I sneaked a hand fishing line off the back porch.

"Breakfast certainly tastes good this morning, Mama," I said.

"Breakfast always tastes good," she replied. "They say a condemned man, about to be hanged, enjoys his breakfast before he goes to the gallows."

"Does he?" I said, and coughed.

"Have you got a cold, Noah?" she asked. "Your brow is right hot."

"Aw, Mama, I'm all right," I said. "It's the sunburn I got yesterday."

"How'd you get sunburned in school?"

"I guess I'd better be going before we wake Dad," I said, and grabbing my lunch I ran out of the door and headed up the street in the direction of school. When I was out of her sight, I cut across the field to the creek and followed it to the river. Ric was waiting for me.

"I was worried about you, Noah," he said. "I was afraid something might have happened. Any blood this morning?"

"Not yet, Ric, how about you?"

"My condition is about the same," Ric said, right fancylike.

"Which one of us do you think will last the longest?"

"You've got the most meat on your bones, they say it helps."

"Ric, since neither one of us is going to be here very long, let's make the most of it. Let's go fishing every day."

So we caught some minnows in the tin cans along the creek and baited our hooks for the fish that fed in the deeper water at the creek's mouth. Soon we had a nice string of pan-size rock. We cleaned them with our penknives and made a fire in the stone oven we had built a long while before. Soon they were sizzling. It seemed awfully hot so we took off most of our clothes.

"Are you hot, Ric?"

"I'm burning up with the fever, Noah. Soon it will sap our strength. We've got to eat plenty to keep it up."

We ate all of the fish and took a quick swim after rubbing our stomachs with cold water so we wouldn't get cramps. We hunted frogs and snakes along the creek. When the twelve o'clock whistle blew, we dressed and ate our lunches, only neither one of us was hungry.

During the afternoon, me and Ric made our wills leaving each other our possessions. When we heard the school dismissal bell ring, we took our books and lunch boxes and started for home.

"You don't look so well, Noah," Ric said. "I'd better walk home with you."

I felt right sad, walking along under the maples. Most of their yellow leaves had fallen. "I guess the fall is a good time to die, Ric," I said. "Everything else is dying, too."

Ric didn't say anything but he looked sad. When we reached my gate, there was sister Helen sitting on the porch, talking to Mama.

"You, Rickard," she shouted, "where have you been all day?"

Ric looked at me and I looked at him. Then he examined his books. "Didn't you hear the school bell ringing, Mama? School just got out."

"Miss Bertie sent notes to me and Mama," sister Helen said. "You two boys haven't been in school all day. Where have you been hiding?"

"And you, Noah!" Mama said. "Where have you been? You come here right away!"

Me and Ric went and sat down on the porch steps and Dad came out from the front room where he'd been resting on the couch.

"Well, boys," he said, "you might as well tell the whole truth."

By that time we both were sniffling.

"Me and Ric have got a contagious disease and don't want to give it to anybody in school," I said.

"I don't believe it," Mama said, but she came over and put her hand on my forehead.

"Yes, ma'am, we have," Ric said, and he had a terrible spell of coughing. "We both got tuberculosis."

"Tuberculosis," sister Helen said. "How do you know?"

"There was a man who showed us moving pictures of the germ in school, two days ago, and he told us all about the symptoms. We got it." Ric spat and looked.

"Where could you boys ever pick up tuberculosis?" Dad said. "Where have you been lately?"

"We ain't been nowhere," I said.

"When did you first feel the symptoms?" Mama asked, scared-like.

"Yesterday morning, when we got up," Ric said.

"Where were you day before yesterday?" asked Dad.

"We went to school," I said.

"Where else?" Dad asked.

"After school me and Ric went over to Bosy Robertson's and picked up apples."

"We played in the straw stack, too," Ric said.

Dad was quiet for a while, then he started to laugh. I never heard him laugh so hard before.

Mama got mad. "George, here these two boys are sick with a deadly disease and you start laughing. Are you crazy?"

Dad only laughed louder. "Deadly disease! There ain't nothing wrong with them except they got straw seeds in their throats. Give them a cup of sassafras tea. That'll fix them up."

CHAPTER 13

Izzy Comes to Town

S OME folks say that it's sissy to like poetry, but in the
spring I like to recite verses and other stuff. "How
much wood would a woodchuck chuck if a woodchuck
could chuck wood? He would chuck as much wood as the
woodchuck would if the woodchuck could chuck wood."
I said it over again faster and didn't miss a word I
matched it to my pace down the cement walk, being sure
to miss all of the cracks for good luck. Somebody whistled
behind me and when I looked around it was the new boy,
Izzy Zeller.

"What was that you were saying about a woodchuck,
Noah?" he asked. "That's one I never heard in New York
City." Izzy's father had worked there before opening a
clothing store in our town.

I said the piece about the woodchuck as fast as I could,
hoping he wouldn't be able to catch it, but it didn't take
him long to learn it.

"Do you know the one about the woodpecker?" he asked.

"No."

"A woodpecker pecked on the woodhouse door, he
pecked and pecked until his pecker was sore," Izzy said,
and he laughed right smart-like. "Ain't that slick?" I

laughed too, but I didn't think it was as good as the one about the woodchuck.

"How'd you know about a woodpecker, living in the city?"

"We've had stores in a lot of places besides New York," Izzy said, and that is all he would say. He lived on the same street as I did, only three houses away.

"So long," he said. "You want to get wise to things, Noah."

When I got to our gate Mama was sitting on the front porch.

"What did you learn in school today?" she said, and before I could answer, "Is Miss Bertie still having trouble teaching you fractions?" Miss Bertie is our fifth-grade teacher and since she's just out of normal school, she doesn't know as much as the older teachers.

"She's got a new way of dividing fractions," I said. "It's different from the way Miss Laura taught us. Miss Bertie says it's easier but the only one who agrees with her is Izzy, the new boy from the city."

"Being a Jew, he would," she said.

"What's that got to do with it?"

"They always know which side their bread is buttered on," she said. "Did I see you walking and talking with that boy just now? I don't want you mixing with him."

"He told me a rhyme about a woodpecker," I said.

"What was it?"

"A woodpecker pecked on the woodhouse door; he pecked and pecked until his pecker was sore."

"Oh," she said. "Oh, my, don't ever say that again." She

looked me over carefully. "You don't even know what you are saying. That city boy is tricking you."

"What's wrong with it?" I asked. "Maybe it should be woodshed, I never heard of a woodhouse."

"If you don't know, I won't be the one to tell you," she said. "Promise me not to say it again."

"Yes, ma'am."

Dad came up from the river carrying a guano sack.

"You take those boots off before you come in the house, George," Mama said. "That Jew boy who lives up the street has just taught Noah a dirty rhyme."

"What was it?" Dad said, pricking up his ears.

"I'll tell him, Mama," I said.

"You will not," she said, and she called Dad over and whispered in his ear.

He laughed real loud. "That's pretty good," he said. "I'll have to remember that."

Mama snorted. "How is Noah ever going to grow up respectable with you like you are?"

"Aw, Mother," Dad said. "He's going to hear a lot worse than that. The new boy is a smart one and Noah might learn how to fend for himself from him."

"He's already learned enough," she said. "I don't want Noah to have anything to do with that boy and that's that."

"Love thy neighbor as thyself," Dad said.

Mama ought to have known she couldn't argue with Dad. "Anyway, I don't want you playing with that Jew boy, Noah," she said. "Do you hear me?"

"Yes, ma'am."

Izzy was in the fifth grade along with me and Ric so I

couldn't help but mix with him every day. He never seemed to study but he got most of the answers right and he knew other things that weren't in the book. Since Miss Bertie was a new teacher, she didn't know too much and let him recite even if it wasn't in the book. He knew a lot of funny stories and was always catching somebody.

"Say, Ric," he said, one day, "do you know why George Washington wore red, white and blue suspenders?"

"No," he said, "why?"

"To keep his pants up," Izzy said, laughing right out. Bessie sits in back of me and Ric. She heard it and laughed. It sort of spread down the desk row and Ric's face got red. He glared at Izzy. "The next time I catch you out of this room I'll take your pants off," he whispered threateningly. And he did, in the washroom, two days later. Izzy never tricked Ric after that. He treated him respectful, like he was a preacher or teacher.

That same day, the principal came into our room and Izzy poked me. "Why don't you try that one about the suspenders on Mr. Manning?" he said.

"I would," I said, "but I don't know him well enough."

Mr. Manning came over and stook in back of us. "What are you boys studying about?" he said.

"George Washington," Izzy said, poking me under the desk.

"What are you learning, Noah?" the principal said, placing his hand on my shoulder.

"Do you know why George Washington wore suspenders?" I asked him.

He looked at me for a moment and smiled. The room

was so quiet and everybody was listening for the answer.

"I thought George Washington wore a belt," he said, and walked away.

"Yes, sir," I said, thinking it over.

Izzy giggled. "We really got a slick principal," he said, and I could see that next to Ric, he respected Mr. Manning the most.

He got along with Miss Bertie, too. One day we were singing or trying to sing the songs in the Blue Book. We had just finished the one about seeing Nellie home when Izzy held up his hand.

"Yes, Isadore," Miss Bertie said.

"Why do we have to sing these old songs about quilting parties when there are new songs we could sing?"

"They're in the book," Miss Bertie said, for even she was catching on to that answer. "What songs are you thinking about, Isadore?"

"Popular songs like 'On the Trail of the Lonesome Pine' or 'Always Tell a Girl Named Daisy.'"

"The first one would be all right," Miss Bertie said, "but where would we get the words?"

Bessie held up her hand. She's learning to play the piano. "I have the song at home," she said. "If you want me to I could bring it to school and write it on the blackboard."

"That would be fine," Miss Bertie said, "and be careful to write so we can all read it."

"I don't see why we can't sing the one about Daisy," Izzy said. "There ain't nothing wrong with it."

"Isn't, Isadore," Miss Bertie said.

"Well, if you agree with me, why can't I bring it to school?" he said. Izzy never gave up.

Miss Bertie thought it over. "All right, Isadore, you may bring it to school and if I approve it, we will sing it."

The next morning, everybody was at school early but Bessie had already written the words to "The Trail of the Lonesome Pine" on the board. I never knew she could write so well and as Miss Bertie said later, it was better than she could do. And to make matters more interesting, Izzy had showed Miss Bertie the song about Daisy and she had said it was all right. He was putting it on the board and though his writing wasn't as perfect as Bessie's, we could all read it.

"Doesn't anybody know the tune of the 'Trail of the Lonesome Pine'?" Miss Bertie asked. Most of the girls knew it and she let the girls sing it with Bessie leading. "You boys can whistle it to learn the tune," our teacher said. Most of us kept quiet because somehow it seemed as wrong to whistle in school as in church. She had a hard time getting us boys to sing but we finally let go. While Izzy was leading the song about Daisy I happened to look toward the door and there was Miss Laura, the fourth-grade teacher, looking through the glass. Her room is next to ours and I guess we must have disturbed her. She rapped and Miss Bertie answered the door.

"Don't you know it's past nine o'clock and time to have lessons?" I heard Miss Laura say. "Mr. Manning will hear about this."

"Oh, I'm sorry," Miss Bertie said, "we were all so interested that I forgot. I'll stop right away."

The next day we went back to singing in the Blue Books. Somehow most everybody said that Izzy was more to blame than Miss Bertie. He was so flip.

Dad said the real reason why people didn't like the Zellers was because Mr. Zeller was taking business away from the other stores. I guess he was more right than wrong. Anyway, I heard Mr. Leary and Mr. Stokes saying about the same thing.

"I don't know how he does it," Mr. Stokes said. "He's selling merchandise cheaper than I can buy it. If something doesn't happen, I'll have to go out of business."

"He's going to Baltimore about once a week," Mr. Leary said. "I'll bet he gets a lot of his goods from the damaged freight sales and buys up odd lots of bargains."

"Yes, I suppose that's what he does," Mr. Stokes said. "It's unethical, that's what it is."

"Why don't you do the same thing?" Mr. Leary said.

"I couldn't change my business methods now," Mr. Stokes said. "I'm getting too old for all that traveling. It's too much trouble." I could see his face getting red. "Us American businessmen ought to get together and chase that dirty Jew out of town. The next thing you know one will come in and open a grocery store. You'll feel the way I do then."

"Maybe he'll move away after making some money," Mr. Leary said, soothing-like. "Them Jews are great on moving. Like as not he'll have a fire and collect the insurance before he goes."

I could see hope rising in Mr. Stokes's eyes. "Yes, that's about the only thing that would save me."

I was loading my express wagon with groceries and listening close. Mr. Leary turned to me. "You'd better hurry that delivery, Noah," he said. "Mrs. Unger wants the bread and soup for dinner."

"Yes, sir," I said and pulled the wagon out the side door. But all the way to Mrs. Unger's I wondered what else Mr. Stokes said to Mr. Leary. I guess I took an interest in the Zellers because they lived on our street. That first winter was a hard one for them. I used to see Izzy carrying in wood to start the fire in the stove early in the mornings. You are really poor in our town if you can't burn coal in the kitchen stove and bank the fire at night. And the Zeller's next-door neighbor told Mrs. Steers and she told Mama that they lived mostly on potatoes and cheese that first winter. In the spring, Izzy used to come to school smelling of garlic so strong nobody wanted to sit close to him. Some of the boys would look at Izzy and put their fingers over their noses only he never seemed to see them.

But after they had been in town only a little while, Mr. Zeller bought a house on High Street, and anybody could see he was getting richer every day. He was generous with it, too, and always gave money to organizations like the volunteer fire company; leastwise, that's what I heard. On the way home from school, I would see him standing in the door of his store, smiling and nodding to passers-by. He had two clerks to help him with the sales and even Mama said you could get the best bargains at Zeller's Department Store. The way she felt about Jews didn't keep her from going there to trade.

I guess I would have forgotten all about what Mr. Stokes

said to Mr. Leary only for what happened. One Saturday morning, I was working in Mr. Leary's store when Mr. Stokes's colored man, Old Pokey, came in and bought five gallons of coal oil. I noticed Mr. Leary looking at me while he filled the can. I couldn't help remembering that Stokes's was the first store in town to put in electric lights the summer before.

"I guess Old Pokey is going to clean some paint brushes for Mr. Stokes," I thought.

That night after we had finished supper and Mama was clearing off the dishes, the fire whistle blew.

"Oh my," she said, "that always scares me so. Do you suppose it's close?"

Dad reached over and put his hand on the wall. "No danger yet," he said, and sat back to finish his cup of coffee.

"I'm going out on the porch to see if I can smell the smoke," Mama said.

I followed her. All of the people on our street were out on their porches, smelling and looking. The volunteer firemen had already run off in their boots and pretty soon we heard the bell of the fire engine ringing. Dad came out and listened.

"Sounds like it's on High Street," he said.

"Let me go up to the corner and look, Mama," I said.

She was getting ready to say "No" when Dad started up the street and I went with him. From the corner you could see smoke rising up from the center of town.

"Let's go," he said, and we ran up the street. When we reached the corner of Queen and High Streets I could see that it was Zeller's Department Store. The fire was a fast one but the building was long. It must have started in the front and was working toward the back. When we went to the rear of the building, I saw Mr. Zeller and Izzy carrying bolts of cloth and clothing out the back door. We moved over and stood by a pile of merchandise. Dad sniffed.

"What do you smell, Noah?" he said.

I sniffed. "Coal oil," I said. "Where is it coming from?"

Dad picked up a bolt of cloth and dropped it. "The cloth is soaked with it," he said. "Don't say anything about it, Noah."

"No, sir," I said, but I guess us keeping quiet didn't mean anything for by the next day it was all over town that Mr. Zeller had set fire to his store. People said he did it to get the insurance. Mr. Zeller said he didn't have any reason to do it. He was making plenty, he said. But somebody found out that he had had a fire before and this time the insurance company wouldn't pay him.

I never did believe Mr. Zeller set the fire.

CHAPTER 14

Vision of Miss Sally

A WEEK later the Zellers left town for good. I guess Izzy is being smart in some other town, now.

A couple of times after that Dad did mention the Zellers and the second time Mama jumped him.

"Anyway, Mr. Zeller worked every day. He'll get ahead and send Isadore to college. What will happen to our Noah, what chance will he have?"

Mr. Jesse rapped on the door and that saved Dad.

Hours later I heard that old one-cylinder engine putting away, coming up the river, and went down to meet them. They had caught some nice hardheads and fat white perch.

"What do you think we saw tied up at Quaker Neck Wharf, Noah?" Dad asked.

"Was it Grandpappy's ark?"

"No, it wasn't but some day we're going to have to tow him home. I saw him last week and Pap's got cataracts on both eyes."

"Was it the *B. S. Ford*?" I asked, wondering what Mama would do if Grandpappy went blind and had to live with us.

"It was the old *James Adams Floating Theatre*," he

said. "The showboat is coming up the river on the flood tide, early tomorrow morning."

Come to think of it I had noticed a man with a step-ladder and big brush pasting the showboat posters on the walls of Greenley's livery stable. Next Monday, they were going to open with *The Girl of the Golden West* and then they had a different show every night for a week, ending Saturday with *Peck's Bad Boy* for the afternoon matinee and *Ten Nights in the Barroom* at night.

"Can I go every night, Dad?"

"You don't want much, do you?" he said. "I'll give you the money to see *Peck's Bad Boy* on Saturday. Your mother wouldn't want you to see those other melodramas, anyway. You're too young."

"Aw, Dad," I said. "I've already seen *Peck's Bad Boy* three times." The showboat comes to our town once a year.

Me and Dad went up to the house to get something to eat.

"The showboat is tied up at Quaker Neck Wharf, Mother," he said.

"I hope you left them show people alone," she said. "The women they have with them ain't respectable, painting their faces and bobbing their hair. You didn't talk with them, did you?"

"Not for long," Dad said. "They're coming up the river on the flood tide, tomorrow morning."

"Can I go every night Mama?" I asked, thinking I'd try her too.

"Noah, I don't want to see you hanging around that old

barge. You might get some bad ideas from them show people. It ain't respectable living on a boat all the time."

"What's wrong with living on a boat, Mama?" I asked. "Maybe it would be fun to live on the boat."

Dad sort of laughed but Mama didn't. "You're almost eleven now and it's time you started talking sense. What's wrong with living on a boat!"

"Grandpappy lives on an ark," I said.

"You know how I feel about that," she said. "It's not respectable to live in a house that floats, a house needs to stand still."

I've always wanted to live in a place where I could throw a fishing line out of the window only I won't ever tell Mama that, it would make her worry more than ever.

After supper I saw Ric and told him the news.

"Let's go down to the river early tomorrow and watch the showboat come in," he said.

"If I can get away from Mama," I said.

Next morning, before I was up, I heard that showboat blow when she rounded the bend two miles below our town. She didn't sound like the *B. S. Ford,* but had an exciting note like a circus calliope. I jumped out of bed. It was Saturday and Mama usually lay late on Saturdays. Dad lay late every day, unless he was going down the river in the bateau.

"What are you doing up so early, Noah?" Mama said. "Mr. Leary won't have any deliveries before nine o'clock."

"Last Saturday you said it ain't good for me to lay so long," I said. She didn't say anything to that. I guess she didn't want to wake Dad.

I slipped downstairs and got a crust of the bread Mama had baked the day before and ran to the river. Ric was waiting for me. The showboat had passed the fertilizer factory's wharf and would soon reach the town landing. We ran so we could be there in time to help catch the mooring lines. She was a sidewheeler and threw up a lot of water. We got there in time to see the gangplank come ashore.

"There she is," Ric whispered, nudging me, and looking up, I saw a blonde, bobbed-hair girl sitting on the top deck with her feet propped on the rail.

"She's wearing tights," Ric said, keeping right on staring. I looked down to where a man with a white captain's cap was bossing a couple of deckhands.

"Hello, boys!" a screechy voice cried from the upper deck. "Hello, boys! Hello, boys! Sissies, sissies!" When I looked up, there wasn't anybody but the bobbed-hair lady and she was smiling.

"It's a poll parrot, Noah," Ric said. "See him by the lady?" I hadn't noticed the cage and parrot before, I guess those tights sort of held my eye.

"Sissies, ha! ha!" the parrot screeched.

"Who in the hell you calling sissies?" Ric yelled at the parrot, starting to get mad. Sissy is a fighting word with us river boys.

"Go to hell! Go to hell, sissies," the parrot screeched.

The showgirl was laughing all of the time, but I guess she didn't know what the parrot would say next, so she got up and took the cage inside. When she came out she had a bunch of letters in her hand.

"Boy," she said, "would you like to make a quarter?"

"You mean me?" Ric asked, moving over to the showboat.

"No," said the showgirl, "I'm speaking to the little boy." That was me.

"Yes, ma'am," I said, going over toward the boat sort of shy-like.

"Don't call me ma'am," she said. "It makes me feel old. Call me Miss Sally. Take these letters up to the post office and mail them. You can keep the quarter and if you come back tomorrow, I may have some more errands for you."

"Yes, Miss Sally." I took the letters and the quarter; I ran off for the post office. Ric didn't catch up with me until I reached the corner.

"Ain't you going to give me half of that, Noah?"

"I don't know why I should give you half."

"It was just lucky she picked you," he said. "If she had asked me I would have given you half."

"She didn't ask you because you cussed her parrot."

"He cussed us, didn't he?" Ric said. "How about giving me ten cents of it?"

"I'll tell you what, Ric, I'll give you a nickel, but I ain't going to give you more if she hires me again."

"All right," Ric said. "I guess that's better than nothing."

The next morning was Sunday, and when I went down to the town landing, the showboat was all closed up. I guess nobody was awake, and after hanging around awhile, I went home. Monday morning, I didn't have time before school and I knew if I was late Miss Bertie might keep me in until five o'clock. But right after school, I went down to the river.

The showboat people were getting ready for the first show that night. They were moving scenery around and I didn't see Miss Sally anywhere. The man with the white captain's cap came up to me with a big dust mop.

"Want to make a quarter, son?" he asked.

"Yes, sir." I thought these show people were really free with their money.

"You dust off all of the seats in the theater," he said, giving me the dust mop. I went inside and started dusting seats. There certainly was a lot of them, and I was getting tired when I heard a door open toward the stage. It was Miss Sally.

"Hello, boy," she said. "You look fagged out. Come on backstage and I'll give you a bottle of soda water."

I didn't know whether to go or not, but she took me by the arm and I couldn't help myself. We went through a little door into what must have been her dressing room. Anyway, there was a big mirror in it and all kinds of pictures and newspaper clippings stuck on the walls. One picture showed a group of pretty showgirls and it said "Follies, 1904" below. That was ten years ago. There were a lot of clippings that had "Variety" printed above them.

While I was looking, Miss Sally was opening a bottle of root beer.

"You must be just starting out in the show business," I said, for something to say.

"It's the other way," she said. "I'm finishing up."

"You don't look very old," I said, looking at the short dress she was wearing.

"How old do you think I am?"

I looked at her yellow bobbed hair and short dress and thought about her dressed up as Little Eva. "You can't be much more than twenty."

"Boy, how you flatter," Miss Sally said. "You're really going to be a lady's man when you grow up."

"I'm almost eleven years old, Miss Sally."

"You're a sweet kid," she said and reached over and patted me on the head. "How would you like to have a free pass so you can come to see all of our shows?"

"I'd like to, only Mama wouldn't let me go unless she went, too."

"Well, here are two free passes. One for you and one for your mother," she said and gave me two tickets, one printed on red cardboard and the other on green.

"Thank you, ma'am." I forgot to call her Miss Sally. "I guess I'd better finish dusting the seats." She went out with me and I dusted all of them, excepting the gallery where the colored people sat, before I gave the captain the dust mop. He gave me a quarter and I ran home with one hand in my pants pocket, holding the two tickets and the quarter.

Mama noticed right away that I was excited about something. "I've got two free tickets so we can see all the shows at the floating theater," I said. "We can go every night." I took the tickets out and gave them to Mama.

"Where'd you get them?" she said, reading what it said on each one. "Land sakes, I never know what you or your father will bring home next. These are reserved seats, too."

"I got them down at the showboat."

"Didn't I tell you to stay away from that showboat?" she said. "I've a great mind to put both these pasteboards in the stove. How did you get them?"

"I dusted the chairs in the theater." That was the truth.

"Well, that's honest work," she said. "What show are they going to have tonight?"

"The Girl of the Golden West, with real cowboys and shooting."

"I don't fancy that shooting," she said, "but I guess I could stand it one night, seeing your mind is so set on it."

After supper Mama put on her best dress, and I put on my Sunday suit and we went to the showboat. Of course, the heroine of the show turned out to be Miss Sally, and after the cattle rustlers kidnapped her and left her all tied up in a deserted shack, she was rescued by a handsome young cowboy who married her, only he didn't look very young from where we were sitting in the fourth row. Not as young as Miss Sally, anyway.

"Wasn't that cowboy girl with the yellow hair pretty, Mama?" I said as we were walking home.

"It's hard to tell with all that paint and powder she was wearing," she said. "You're awful young to be noticing women, Noah. You'd better get your mind on something else."

I tried to, but it seemed like my mind kept coming back to Miss Sally. Every night me and Mama saw her fall into the clutches of a villain. Tuesday night she just

missed the buzz saw, Wednesday night she was turned out
in a snow blizzard, and Friday night she flew up to heaven.
I wanted to cry when Little Eva died, but I couldn't. Every
afternoon I dusted off the seats and drank a bottle of root
beer with Miss Sally. Only I didn't tell Mama or nobody.

"What are you going to do when you grow up?" Miss
Sally asked one day.

"I don't know," I said. "My dad is a river man and so
was his pappy. I like the river but Mama wants me to go
to college and get an education."

"There's more to life than what's in books," Miss Sally
said. "You're a dreamer, boy, you've got imagination and
when a person is like that the most important thing is to
do what you want to do."

"Yes, Miss Sally."

Saturday came and I knew the showboat and Miss Sally
would soon be going down the river. She told me to come
and see her Sunday and I knew that would be the last
time. She opened up another bottle of root beer.

"You want to be good to your mother," she said, "and
help your father, too. You never know how long they'll be
here."

"Yes, Miss Sally." I thought how pretty she was in spite
of all that paint and powder she wore.

"Do you have any older brothers?"

"I have a half brother who works in Baltimore. He's
thirty years old."

"Does he look like you?"

"Folks don't say so. He's handsome."

"Boy," she laughed, "you're going to be handsome

when you grow up and you're very sweet now. Did I tell you that I have a little son just your age?"

"Ma'am," I said. "Ma'am, what did you say?"

Miss Sally laughed. "Didn't you know that I have several children of my own and that the youngest son is just your age?"

"No, ma'am, you didn't tell me that." I took a long gulp of root beer.

"Did you really think I was a young girl?"

"Yes, ma'am."

"I think I understand how you feel. Once when I was a little girl just your age, I fell in love with an actor who was old enough to be my father, only he seemed young. I think that you resemble him." She pulled out a drawer and showed me pictures of her children, all five of them. One of them was a senior in college.

I looked at Miss Sally and for the first time I saw the wrinkles on her forehead and the lines under her eyes. Somehow I had missed them before, or maybe it hadn't mattered.

"I guess I'd better be going," I said, "or Mama will worry about me."

"So long, boy," She patted me on the shoulder. "I'll be seeing you next year."

"Good-by," I said, somehow knowing that I would never see Miss Sally again, leastwise not as I had before, not even if I searched everywhere.

CHAPTER 15

Noah and Jonah

PRETTY soon it was summer again and I was out of school. The crabs were backing out of their shells again, too.

The hot weather must have dried up the swelling in Mr. Jesse's ear. Anyway Dad and he had been hauling seine for soft crabs all week. They would leave every morning, and before it was light I could hear that old one-cylinder engine pushing them up the river. Dad said that the water was warmer where the river was narrower. I guess crabs like it warm before they back out of their shells and change into softies.

"How about taking me soft crabbing with you tomorrow, Dad?" I asked one night. "Yesterday I caught a half a dozen softies with my dip net in Brewster's Cove."

"You might Jonah us," he said. "Me and Jesse's luck has been pretty good so far. I don't want to take no Jonah along."

"I ain't no Jonah, Dad," I said, "maybe I'd bring you good luck."

"Could you sit still in the bateau, going and coming?"

"Sure, Dad."

"Why don't you take him along, George?" Mama said.

"He's been underfoot here in the house ever since school was out."

"I can't figure you out, Mother," he said. "If I wanted to take the boy, you'd be dead against it. Women are contrary creatures."

"Can I take my dip net along, Dad?"

"All right," he said, "you can go if Jesse don't think you are a Jonah. He's peculiar about taking anybody along who might turn out to be a Jonah."

When Dad is crabbing he goes to bed with the chickens and gets up with them, so we all went upstairs early. Seemed I had just got to sleep when I heard Mama stirring in the next room. Soon I heard the fat sizzling in the frying pan downstairs.

"George, Noah," she called, "it's time to get up."

Mama had made up rising bread the night before and she took some of the dough and fried it for us. While we were eating, Mr. Jesse came in.

"Hurry up, George," he said. "It's graying towards the east. What's the boy doing up so early?"

"I thought I'd take him with us if it's all right with you," Dad said. "He can help us pick up the crabs and maybe catch a few strays with his dip net."

"The boy ain't no Jonah, is he?" Mr. Jesse asked.

"I ain't no Jonah, Mr. Jesse," I said.

"Well, he might as well come along, then," Mr. Jesse said. So I followed them down to the river.

"The tide ought to be right by the time we get as far as Buckingham's," Dad said.

The bateau was tied to a bush stake Dad had sunk in

the spring, so we rolled up our pants and waded out to it.
The water felt cold early in the morning. Mr. Jesse stuck
our lunches under the bow deck and Dad knelt before the
engine. He connected a wire to the battery and turned
the big wheel back and forward to warm her up. Mr. Jesse
untied the bateau from the stake and Dad primed the engine with a few squirts of gasoline. When everything was
ready Dad turned the wheel over and she went right off.
I guess these gasoline engines are all right if too many
people don't monkey with them. Dad sat down on the
stern seat with the tiller and I perched on the bow deck.
Mr. Jesse started to straighten up the stuff in the bottom
of the boat. The engine made so much noise there wasn't
any use of trying to talk; besides, Mr. Jesse is half deaf.
He leaned down and picked up one oar from the floor-
boards and looked around for the other one. But it wasn't
in the boat. He went back and yelled in Dad's ear and we
started back for the cove.

"Where do you suppose the other oar is?" Mr. Jesse said.
He looked at me. "I guess somebody is a Jonah." I jumped
ashore and looked in the marsh. There was the other oar.

"How'd it get up there?" Dad asked.

"Some Jonah must have put it up there," Mr. Jesse said,
looking at me.

When Dad tried to start the engine again he flooded
her, at least Mr. Jesse said so, and that meant turning the
wheel over and over until all of the gas was worked out.
It's like reviving a drowned man. He was tired by the
time the engine started again.

The sun was getting warm when we reached the cove

by Buckingham's. Dad and Mr. Jesse got the seine out of the boat and I took my dip net. Dad looped the painter of the bateau over his shoulder and, with Mr. Jesse, started hauling seine along the shore. I waded along by Dad, ready to dip anything that escaped the seine.

First time Mr. Jesse brought his end ashore, we caught three softies and a peeler. A peeler is a hard crab a few days before he sloughs his shell and becomes a softie. When you peel off his hard shell, the soft one is already there. A peeler is the best bait for fishing. There were small perch and sunfish in the seine but we let them flop back to the river. I put the soft crabs in wet moss and laid them in a shady part of the bateau. The peeler went into a live box, about the size of a chicken crate, which we towed to the stern of the bateau. We had a barrel for hard crabs.

"If we get three softies every time we come ashore, I'll say the boy brings us good luck, George," Mr. Jesse said.

Next time Dad and Mr. Jesse hauled the seine up on the beach, it was sparkling with little fish and crabs. We got three more softies and half a dozen hard crabs. You have to be quick to catch the hard ones or they'll crawl back to the river. A hard crab is a mean critter to handle.

'Long about noon the tide was getting too low so Dad rowed the bateau over to the old wharf with its grove of trees. All of the arks had gone down the river for the summer hard crabbing, they wouldn't come back until the fall. The pump worked. After priming it with river water, and pumping fifty strokes, we had a cold drink. I guess you only enjoy what you work for, at least that's what the preacher says. We took our lunches over in the shade of the trees, but the horse flies were pretty bad, buzzing around our heads all of the time.

"There ain't nothing like meat and potatoes to give you strength," Dad said. "Them and coffee."

"I'll take hog meat and hominy, any time I can get them," Mr. Jesse said. "Them and turnip greens."

We heard a little rumble down the river toward the bay and pricked up our ears.

"I guess that must have been a heavy wagon going across the bridge," Dad said.

"Sounded like thunder to me," Mr. Jesse said. "Ain't that a thunderhead coming up the river?" He pointed to a lot of white clouds piled on top of one another. As we looked a streak of lightning split them. "Yes, sir, it's a thundergust riding the flood tide. She'll hit us on the first of the flood."

"Ain't that something," Dad said. He looked at me. "Noah, somebody's putting the Jonah sign on us. It ain't you, is it?"

"Aw, I ain't no Jonah, Dad," I said. "Maybe it'll blow around and miss us."

"My pappy once told me that right before a thundergust is the best time to catch soft crabs," Dad said. "I guess the thunder hurries them out of their shells."

"Let's haul seine until it strikes us," Mr. Jesse said. "There ain't going to be much doing after that, anyway."

We left the grove of trees and started hauling seine. That thundergust was really riding the flood tide and the thunderhead had turned a dirty gray. Everything was quiet but the thunder, and it was awful hot. The marsh grass didn't stir and the water was like glass, only colored by the gray clouds. I guess Dad's pappy knew what he was talking about. We were catching plenty of soft crabs but all of the time we had our eyes on that thundergust coming up the river.

"When it's almost here, we can row over to the grove of trees," Dad said. "Maybe we won't get too wet." A streak of lightning slit the clouds down the river and we had a hard clap of thunder.

"We'd better be going," Mr. Jesse said. "That one wasn't much more than a mile away and it's coming fast." A puff of wind ruffled the glassy water and it began to blow.

"Dad," I said, "we read in one of our science books that it's dangerous to be in the woods during a thundergust. Lightning hits the tallest thing around." I looked at the grove. They were mostly tall pines.

"I ain't never heard of that," he said, looking down the river where we could see the whitecaps about one half mile away. "Did you ever hear of that, Jesse?" he said, resting on the oars.

"Sounds reasonable," Mr. Jesse said. "Lightning strikes church steeples and other high things. Them trees are the highest things around here. I guess they attract lightning just like rods."

"Where can we go?" Dad said. "I ain't aiming to get any wetter than I have to."

"Why couldn't we pull under the old wharf, Dad?" I said. "That would keep most of the rain off."

"It's a good idea, George," Mr. Jesse said. "The boy

has something in his head." Dad rowed back to the old wharf and we edged the bateau underneath it, tying up to a piling. About the time we got there it started to rain and the water poured through the cracks of the boards. It was as dark as night under the wharf except when the lightning flashed. Then the water was a bright green.

"I feel like I was in a trap, here," Mr. Jesse said.

"Anyway, we ain't drowned yet," Dad said.

"Suppose the lightning strikes the wharf," Mr. Jesse said. "The whole thing might fall on us." By that time the storm was on top of us. It was a bad one.

"Let's get out of here while we can, George," Mr. Jesse said. "I'd feel better in the open, even if we get wet."

He untied the line to the piling and was about to push the bateau out into the river when the lightning came right to us. Everything crinkled and my ears rang. There was a splitting sound and a terrible clap of thunder followed by a thud. It really poured but we stayed under the wharf.

"I guess if that one didn't kill us, we're going to live for a long while," Dad said. "You all right, Noah?"

"I'm all right, Dad," I said, but I was awful scared.

"Lightning don't strike the same place twice," Mr. Jesse said. "We'll be safe if we stay here." What Mr. Jesse said made me feel better and we stayed under the wharf until the rain began to slacken and it started to get light. Then we pulled out in the river.

"Good Lord, look," Dad said, pointing over to the grove. The tallest pine had been struck by that lightning bolt and cut off about halfway up its trunk. The top had fallen to the ground. Mr. Jesse looked at me.

"I take it all back, Noah, you ain't no Jonah," he said. "Only the good Lord knows where me and George would be now if you hadn't come along."

"I guess nothing ever happens to a riverman as long as he stays on the river where he belongs," Dad said.

CHAPTER 16

Catching the Devil

A LL of us boys had a hard time getting along with Miss
Lizzie. The main trouble was that her chicken yard
fence and the center field of our baseball diamond sort of
trespassed on one another. We had a ground rule like this:
"Anybody who knocks the ball over Miss Lizzie's fence is
out and has to go get it." It penalized the slugger. 'Course
Miss Lizzie didn't like us to climb her fence. She said that
weakened it, but usually we could slip over and come out
of her back gate, leaving it unhooked for the next player
who flied to deep center. It didn't always work out that
way, for if Miss Lizzie happened to be tending to her
chickens she would get the ball, and unless she was feeling
particularly good, that was the end of the game or maybe
we would ask Mama to make us a stocking ball. One time,
when I hit one over the fence, Ric was playing in the field
and ran to look through a knothole. He swore that Miss
Lizzie saw the ball coming and ran and caught it with one
hand. She didn't even wear a mitt!

One day we were playing ball and Mr. Jester came over
with posts and barbed wire. He started working on Miss
Lizzie's fence.

"Whatcha going to make, Mr. Jester?" Ric asked.

"I'm going to fix Miss Lizzie's fence so you young uns can't get over it without tearing your britches off. If you still try to climb it after I put the barbed wire up, Miss Lizzie is going to swear out a warrant for you. She says you're tearing her fence down."

When he was finished, Miss Lizzie's fence had three strings of barbed wire on top of the boards. "I guess you boys won't climb that!" he said, right satisfied-like, and went off home.

We were careful the rest of the afternoon but it ruins the game when you're scared to hit the ball as hard as you want to.

A couple of days later Crow Davis brought over a real horsehider and asked if he could play with us. That ball he had was a lot livelier than the old nickel rocket we'd been batting. The old rocket had been knocked lopsided and was about the shape of a small squash. Anyway, just about the first pitch, Ric knocked the new ball right over Miss Lizzie's fence. "You're out and you gotta go get it!" we all yelled, and sort of waited, hoping Miss Lizzie would throw it back to us. Once in a long while she did that. We looked through the knothole. It had landed right in the middle of Miss Lizzie's hen pen and all the old hens were grouped around clucking and looking it over.

"They think one of them laid it," Erny said.

While we were peeping through the knothole, Miss Lizzie came out of her back door and saw the ball. She picked it up and took it back in the house with her.

"Ain't that awful!" Crow said. "My pop just brought it home from the hardware store last night."

"The insides of this old nickel rocket are ready to come out. You got any tar tape, Noah?" Ric asked. I didn't have any tar tape.

We started to play with the nickel rocket but Crow was mad because we had lost his ball, so he really swung when it was his bat. He hit a hard one and the cover came right off, but the ball went over Miss Lizzie's fence.

"You're out and have to go get it," Ric yelled.

"That ain't the rule," Crow said. "I only knocked half of the ball over the fence. There's the cover down by second base!" He wouldn't even try to climb Miss Lizzie's fence.

"Go get that old stocking ball your mother made for us, Noah," Erny said. So we finished the game with an old spongy stocking ball.

The next Tuesday was my eleventh birthday and Dad came home with a new big-league baseball, black and red stitches. Boy! It was a beauty, almost too good to use in a game. I took it out and Ric happened to be around so we had a catch. We started throwing them harder and harder to see who would get enough first. Every ball I caught stung my hand right through the glove until it looked like a piece of raw meat, and Ric was getting stung too, only neither of us would say the word. I was backed up against Cullen's barn and Ric was standing down towards Miss Lizzie's. Ric threw one that nearly took my hand off and I knew that if I couldn't make him quit on my next pitch, I'd have to yell enough myself. I wound up and threw one with everything I had. I guess it was a trifle high. Ric raised his hand over his head to catch it but the ball hit his fingers just enough to send it higher and it went right over Miss Lizzie's fence. I felt like sitting down and crying. We crept over to the fence and looked through the knot-hole. Just as my luck would have it, Miss Lizzie was feeding her chickens. I peeped through in time to see her picking up my ball. She must have known it was a good one because she wiped it off and put it in her apron pocket.

"Why don't you go around to her kitchen door, Noah, and ask her for it?" Ric said. "I'll go with you."

We walked around to Miss Lizzie's back porch but the screen door was hooked on the inside. We rapped and waited. After a long while Miss Lizzie came out on the porch.

"What do you boys want?"

"I threw my new ball into your chicken yard, Miss Lizzie, on a wild pitch. Please, can I have it?" I looked down to where her apron pocket was bulging with it.

"Haven't I told you before that if you knock your base-balls into my yard, I'm going to keep them? They're liable to kill my best setting hens or send them into a two months' molt. They're scared to death of baseballs."

"Yes, ma'am, you told us," I said, "but I didn't knock the ball over. I threw it over."

"Don't make no difference, when that ball enters my yard, it's mine," she said, and went back in the kitchen. We stood around awhile and Ric got to talking sort of threatening-like. Miss Lizzie came out on the porch.

"You boys get off of my porch or I'll call Mr. Jester and have you arrested for trespassing!"

The rest of the day I couldn't get the loss of that big-league ball off my mind. Even when night came, and I finally went to bed, I dreamed about it. I had the sweetest dream. It seemed that I had caught a string of fish and took them over to Miss Lizzie for her chickens. She thanked me kindly and told me to wait a minute. Then she went inside her house. When she came back she had a whole peach basket full of baseballs — nickel rockets, dime hardies, twenty-five-cent horsehiders, fifty-cent rubber centers, and crowning them was my new big-leaguer with the red and black stitches.

"Help yourself, Noah," Miss Lizzie said.

I picked out a dozen of the best and hardest, squeezing them like Mama did when she bought peaches.

"If you need any more, Noah, just come over and rap on my kitchen door," Miss Lizzie said.

I woke up, but before I went to sleep again, I made up my mind to catch a string of fish the next day and try my luck with Miss Lizzie. Maybe I could get my new big-leaguer ball back, anyway.

After breakfast the next morning, I dug some worms and taking my bamboo fishing pole, went down on the old brick wall by the sewer pipe. That's where the fish bite the best. I took a couple of crab lines and my dip net along. First, I caught a few anchovies and tied them on the crab lines. Soon, I dipped a couple of hard crabs, and using the white knuckle meat for bait, I caught a nice string of white perch and yellow neds. Those were the kind Miss Lizzie liked for her laying hens. When the tide was right, I walked along the wall and was lucky enough to catch three big soft crabs, one of them just as it was backing out of its shell. That's when they taste the best. Miss Lizzie is powerful fond of fried soft crabs. I found an old piece of board and wrapping the soft crabs in wet moss, I put them on it. Softies have to be handled right easy. I got the string of fish and hid my fishing pole and net in the bushes. Then I walked over to Miss Lizzie's porch door and rapped.

She came to the door with a broom, and a rag tied over her head, so I guessed she was housecleaning.

"I've got a string of fish for your laying hens," I said, "and three nice soft crabs I just caught."

Miss Lizzie looked at the fish. "My Dominickers would fancy them," she said and reached her hand out to take the fish from me. "Are those crabs alive? They look mighty quiet to me."

"I just caught them."

"Wait a minute," Miss Lizzie said, and she took the fish into the kitchen. When she came out again, she had a butcher knife, and before I could stop her she cut through the shells of all three of my soft crabs. They squirmed around for a few seconds and lay still.

"They are alive," she said.

"Yes, ma'am, they were."

"I don't want any crabs today, Noah," Miss Lizzie said, "but here's something for the fish." She reached in her apron pocket, which was bulging with something round, and brought out an old lopsided nickel rocket. "If you can get a quart of sunflower seeds for my young pullets, I'll give you another ball. There ain't nothing like sunflower seeds to start young pullets laying." She went inside and left me standing with my three dead soft crabs and a lopsided nickel rocket that looked like it might have been laying in a muddy ditch for a year or two.

I didn't tell anybody about my dream and what really happened. I tried to forget all about it but the vision of a peach basket full of baseballs was hard to forget.

We all wondered what happened to our baseballs, which Miss Lizzie kept. Ric claimed she whitewashed them and used them to put in the laying nests. I thought maybe she sold them to the carnival men that came around every year. They always have a game where a man sticks his head through a hole in a piece of canvas and people throw baseballs to see if they can hit him in the head. You get three balls for a nickel and if you hit the man in the head you get a five-cent cigar. Usually it's a Negro because they're clever dodgers and their ivory is extra thick.

I never really knew what happened to our baseballs until one day when Mama was collecting things to send to the foreign missions in China. Miss Lizzie gave her a big bag for the heathen Chinese and in the bag were all of those baseballs of ours. Mama left them in the Sunday school room.

That next Sunday, during our lesson, the rector came in, and pointing to a big pile of bags in the corner of the room, asked all of us to look around at home and see if we could find some toys or clothes for the poor little Chinese boys and girls. All we had to do was put the things in a bag and leave them in the Sunday school room. The packages would be sent to the Chinese the next Saturday. The door was never locked.

Well, as the preacher says, I wrestled with Satan all the next week but he gradually wore me down. I didn't have the nerve to do it myself so I told Ric about it. We talked it over and Friday afternoon me and Ric took bags of old toys and left them in the Sunday school room.

Saturday morning, we went out in the pasture by the old barn and played catch. I tried to sting Ric and he tried to sting me with a real big-league ball that had red and black stitches.

"Say, Ric," I said, "if anybody finds out what we did, we'll *both* catch the devil when we get home."

CHAPTER 17

Mr. Lewy and the Age of Speed

I SOLD the soft crabs to Mr. Lewy. He gave me a shiny fifty-cent piece; he's not tight like Miss Lizzie. All of us boys liked Mr. Lewy. When he came back to town, Mr. Lewy opened a machine shop in Old Man Wood's barn, across the street from where we live. Folks said he was the wildest of the Hern boys, and old enough to settle down. He'd been in the Marines and fought in the Philippines against the Moros. When he first came home, he wore a faded khaki uniform but he soon put that away. Hanging in his shop were a couple of bolo knives, the kind the Moros use to cut your head off. A buddy of Mr. Lewy's got one of the knives when he stuck his head up to see what was coming. I liked to hang around his shop and watch him tinker, but Mama didn't want me to.

"That Lewy Hern was always a queer one," she said. "When he was a boy he rigged flying rings in the tallest trees of the old Hern place. He swung through the trees just like a monkey. It's a wonder he didn't kill himself, but old Mr. Hern couldn't manage any of his boys and Lewy was the wildest."

"Mr. Lewy is going to make a boomerang for me," I said.

"What's a boomerang?" she said.

"It's a stick," I said, "only when you throw it away it comes back to you."

"What kind of crazy talk is that?" she said. "That hot sun in the Philippines must have touched him, if he wasn't already that way. Don't you hang around him."

"There are boomerangs, Mama," I said. "There's a picture of one in the big dictionary."

"Boomerangs or rangatangs, you keep away from Lewy Hern," she said. "Next thing you know, he'll be telling you that you can fly through the air."

"He's already told me about that, Mama," I said. "Didn't you ever hear of the Wright brothers? They flew through the air in a big box kite with a propeller."

"The only Wright brothers I know are farmers down Quaker Neck. You're getting more like your father every day, Noah. You're never interested in the respectable people. It's always the strange ones — Isadore Zeller and now Lewy Hern — he doesn't have the sense he was born with."

"Yes'm," I said, thinking about what I had been reading in a book I had found in the school library. It said that a lot of good people were different from the rest — men like Thomas Edison and Henry Ford, not to mention Napoleon and Julius Caesar.

"If the Lord had wanted us to fly, he'd have given us wings," Dad said.

I thought he was asleep on the couch but I guess he'd been listening all of the time.

But even Dad liked to hang around Mr. Lewy's machine shop, especially when he needed a part for his boat engine. Mr. Lewy could make anything on his metal lathe and it took Dad weeks if he ordered an engine part from the factory. Not that Mr. Lewy was always in a good humor. Sometimes he was cranky. Take the day I decided to sharpen our old lawn mower and asked Mr. Lewy to lend me a file.

"What do you want a file for?" he said, looking contrary.

"To sharpen our lawn mower," I said, wishing I hadn't asked to borrow one. I guess most mechanics are stingy with their tools.

He looked around on his bench and handed me an old rusty rat tail file that wasn't good for anything.

"Thank you," I said and took it over to our back yard. That file couldn't cut hot butter but I did the best I could and took it back to him, right away.

"Thank you, Mr. Lewy," I said, handing him the file.

He took the file and squinted at it. He handed it back to me.

"You've ruined the file and you might as well keep it," he said. I never borrowed anything else from him.

But he made a boomerang and showed me how to throw it. The most fun was to take it down to the river and throw it toward the middle. It would sail like an oyster shell and if the wind and my twist was right, the boomerang

would curve around and come back to shore. Ric saw
mine and made one for himself out of peach basket staves.
Soon he was selling them for a quarter and it got so people
didn't like to walk along the river, the boomerangs were
that thick. 'Course Billy Unger had to throw one that
sailed back and broke his glasses.

One day, a bunch of men were pitching horseshoes in
front of Mr. Lewy's shop. Dad and Mr. Lewy were pitching against Mr. Jester and Old Man Wood. When you
pitch partners you don't have to do any walking. They
were arguing over a close one.

"Mine is closer," Old Man Wood said, "by the thick-
ness of this toothpick. That gives us the game."

"Not so fast," Mr. Lewy said, "I'll go over to the machine shop and get the calipers."

"If you leave the pitching box, you forfeit the game,"
Mr. Jester sang out from where he stood by the other peg.
"That's the rule."

"I guess there ain't no rule against dispatching a messenger," Dad said. "Noah, you go and get the calipers."

Mr. Lewy said, "They're hanging to the right inside the
door."

I wasn't sure what to look for but I used my imagination
and brought back the right thing.

Mr. Lewy bent over and measured the two distances.

"Ours is closer," he said, "scientifically, our shoe is three
millimeters closer to the peg."

"Drat scientifically," Old Man Wood said, "that's just a
new way to cheat. Let me measure the shoes with a piece
of string."

"Let's call it a tie," Dad said, and that's what they finally did.

"Are you going to enter your bateau in the regatta come August, George?" Mr. Lewy said, to change the subject.

"I might go in the handicap race," Dad said. "Speed don't mean anything, there, it's the steering that wins."

"Boats are getting speedier all of the time," Mr. Lewy said. "Soon they will be going a mile a minute."

"A mile a minute," Old Man Wood said. "Hear the man talk!" He tossed a ringer. "Top that, Speedy."

Mr. Lewy threw a twister that hit the stake and spun around, topping the ringer. He and Dad had special shoes with a raised hook that made them stay on the peg. Mr. Lewy had made them in the shop only nobody knew about them except Dad and him and me.

"There you are," he said. "You asked for it."

"That's the game," Dad said. "Pay up." They were pitching for a quarter a game.

The losers left their quarters and went up town.

"What say we make a speedboat and enter her in the races this summer, George?" Mr. Lewy said. "I can make the engine if you can furnish the hull."

"Boats are hard carpentering," Dad said. "Maybe I could find an old hull that would suit."

"I don't like to fool around with old boats," Mr. Lewy said. "My old man used to say never buy a new house or an old boat."

"That's about right but we might find something we could use."

"I already have the cylinders bored for an engine that will turn up a lot of horsepower," Mr. Lewy said. "If we could get the kind of hull that won't squat too much we might go a mile a minute."

"I guess a deadrise is hard to beat for speed," Dad said. "Just enough V-bottom to keep the hull from pounding."

"I'm not certain, George," Mr. Lewy said, "one man on the Great Lakes recently traveled fifty miles an hour in a flat-bottomed boat. She jumped right over the waves, like a rock chasing a school of minnows."

"Why didn't she squat?" Dad said.

"Her stern was tunneled," Mr. Lewy said. He took a block of wood and cut out a model hull so me and Dad could understand.

"How long a boat you want?" Dad said.

"A sixteen-footer ought to carry the engine, a mechanic, and the driver."

"That's the length of my bateau," Dad said. "You reckon she might do?"

"She might," Mr. Lewy said, "if we put a tunnel stern on her."

Dad grinned. "Think of my old girl passing everything on the river. I'll throw a wave that'll rock the *B. S. Ford.*"

"Where is your bateau?" Mr. Lewy said, ready to do something right away. That's how he is.

"She's drawn out on the cove," Dad said, and we walked down to see her. Mr. Lewy took a measuring rule along and used it to make a rough drawing on a piece of wood.

"She'll do if you don't mind changing the stern," he said.

"I'll try anything once," Dad said.

The next few weeks he and Mr. Lewy were busy. Boat work is slow and Dad always takes his time anyway. Mr. Lewy made a model and blueprint for them to follow. Every day I went to the cove after school. When they tore out the old transom, there was dry rot and worms.

"Do you suppose the worms are in the keelson, too?" Mr. Lewy said. "This hull has got to be strong to stand the power we're going to put in her."

"She's always taken me there and brought me back," Dad said.

"What is she fastened with?" Mr. Lewy said.

"Boat nails."

"That's not so good," Mr. Lewy said. "For our purpose she ought to have brass screws or copper rivets."

"That's an awful lot of trouble and expense for one race," Dad said.

"She may shake apart when we put the juice to her," Mr. Lewy said.

"I'm willing to take the chance if you are," Dad said. "We can both swim."

"All right," Mr. Lewy answered, and he never said anything more about it, at least I never heard him.

The engine Mr. Lewy made was a lot bigger than the one-cylinder Dad had used for years. They put it in the boat on a Saturday afternoon and all of the men in the neighborhood helped. It must have weighed a thousand pounds. The old bateau was tied to the brick wall and Mr. Lewy had painted the engine gray, trimmed in red. It was real pretty.

"It's going to go right on through the bottom of the boat," Old Man Wood said as they eased the engine down on the brick wall.

"It couldn't," Mr. Lewy said, "not with all of the river supporting the bottom."

He was right but the bateau went down about six inches when they placed the engine on the blocks. After Dad and Mr. Lewy got in, there wasn't much freeboard left.

"Don't shift your cud of tobacco, George," Old Man Wood said. "It won't take much to upset her, she's that low."

"She'll be all right when we can start the engine," Dad said. "She'll get up and go, then."

"She's just right," Mr. Lewy said. "You want to place any money on it, Mr. Wood?"

"She'll never make a mile a minute," Old Man Wood said.

"You wait until they have the races on the Fourth," Mr. Lewy said.

It took them the rest of Saturday and Sunday to get the engine lined up and the stuffing box in place. Most of the watermen stopped to look her over and they didn't mind saying what would happen when Dad and Mr. Lewy would take her out on a trial run.

"She'll go to the bottom before you ever get out of the cove," Captain Pete said. "As long as you've been around the water, George, you ought to know better, wasting your time and ruining the bateau, as well as making a damned fool of yourself."

"That big motor will shake the nails right out of her,"

Med, the one-armed seiner, said. "Then where will you be?"

"You'd better wear life preservers," Old Man Wood said. "You're going to need them."

By Tuesday they were all ready to make a trial run. I guess most of the people in town who weren't working came down to the river to see what would happen when Mr. Lewy started that big engine. Mama wouldn't leave the house. She was that excited but I guess she sat on the front porch and listened. Even Frank Muir, the undertaker, was there.

"You looking for a job, Frank?" Old Man Wood said.

"Business is slack," the undertaker said, "but I don't like drowning jobs. The bodies are too bloated."

Dad and Mr. Lewy must have heard them but they didn't say anything. Dad looked pale, though, under his tan.

The bateau was painted black and looked fast. The motor had a clutch so Mr. Lewy could start the engine while the boat was still tied. In the old bateau, when the engine started so did the boat, and they'd better be ready unless they wanted to take the dock with them.

Mr. Lewy primed the engine carefully and gave the wheel a spin. It started with a roar and everybody jumped. I guess they thought it had exploded. Mr. Lewy looked to see if the water pump was working and Dad took in the lines. They must have been excited but they didn't let on. Mr. Lewy put her in gear and the old bateau moved away like she had never moved before. She might be old but that new engine had put new life into her.

Professor Miles, who teaches Latin at the college, has a speedboat on the river. He is an old bachelor but he likes to take out the young girls and scare them. The boat even has a steering wheel and windshield. It looks fast. It just happened that he was out for a boat ride when Dad and Mr. Lewy took their trial spin. Seeing them coming, Professor Miles waved and headed down the river toward the black buoy. He was a quarter of a mile ahead of them but they went by him like he was stuck on a sand bar. I wondered if Mr. Lewy had opened her up. He was always talking about opening her up. They took the bateau around the black buoy and brought her back to the dock. She was down so her gunwale was almost touching the water.

"We forgot the bailing can," Dad said. "She almost sunk on us."

It was only ten days before the regatta and prizes for the winners were in the hardware store windows. The winners of the race that Dad and Mr. Lewy had entered would get a set of six life preservers. Old Man Wood said they would need them. Mr. Lewy spent most of his time working on the engine and Dad kept calking the seams, trying to find something that the engine wouldn't shake out. He tried everything, white lead and oakum, wicking and pitch, and even melted Mama's preserving paraffin and poured it into the seams. It was easy enough to get the bateau tight as long as they left her tied up. When the engine started, she never got very far, even when both of them bailed. The race was five miles long or twice around the black can buoy that marks the river bend.

"We ain't never been able to go the whole distance,

Lewy," Dad said the day before the race. "I've calked her with everything but my long underwear."

"Let's forget about calking her and I'll make a bilge pump," Mr. Lewy said. "We can pump the water out as fast as it comes in, maybe." He found an old bicycle pump in his shop and fixed it so that you could pump water instead of air. When he fastened it on the bottom of the boat with a piece of rubber hose over the gunwale, it worked fine. Dad and Mr. Lewy took the old bateau around the black buoy twice and came home, for the first time, and what was more, their pants were dry.

"That pump does it," Dad said.

Mr. Lewy was hot because he had been oiling the engine and pumping while Dad steered her.

"It'll be all right if I don't burn the cylinder or washer up, pumping her." he said. He put his finger against the pump and pulled it away in a hurry. "She's almost red hot."

"That's a chance we'll have to take," Dad said. "Maybe we'd better save the pump and not use it until the day of the race." And that was what they did.

Our town was all dressed up for the regatta, flags and bunting. Yachts came from all over the Chesapeake for the races. There were events for sailboats, speedboats, workboats, cruisers and even one for the old log canoes. There were six of the canoes left, hewed out of big logs, narrow, ballasted with men on springboards. They raced on a tenmile course where the river widens, with all kinds of sails, even one called a kite. But the speedboat race was the one I thought about because of Dad and Mr. Lewy.

"They'll never get over it if the old bateau wins," Dad said.

"Who's they?" I said.

"Eben Pauley and the rich men who own those other speedboats," he said.

"That old boat of yours don't look like much," Mama said. "Mr. Pauley's boat is pretty with all that shiny brass and mahogany."

"That gingerbread is all right for church rails," Dad said, "but it don't mean anything on water. Just show, that's all."

"We'll see," Mama said.

"Are you going to watch the race, Mama?" I said, knowing she never had before.

"If I get the housework finished in time, I might walk down to the river," she said, and I knew that meant she would be there.

The night before the regatta, I couldn't sleep a wink and, judging from the way the bed squeaked where Mama and Dad slept, I guess they didn't either. Dad was up earlier than when he goes soft crabbing with Mr. Jesse.

"How about some breakfast, Mother?" he said. "I want to go down to the cove and see how the bateau is."

"She's all right," Mama said, right jealous-like. "It might be better if you sleep in her at nights."

"Aw, Mother," Dad said, "won't you be glad if we win the race?"

"I'd be more than glad if you'd stop playing around and get a steady job," she said.

"I'll tell you what, Mother," Dad said, "if we win the race today, I'll get a job at the basket factory."

"I guess you know you're safe," she said, putting a plate of flapjacks on the table, "but I'm going to say a prayer for you."

Me and Dad bolted our food and hurried down to the river, but Mr. Lewy was there before us.

"Everything is all set," he said. "I strained the gasoline through a chamois, to make sure the fuel line wouldn't clog at the last minute, George."

"I'm going to scrub her out, anyway," Dad said. The bateau was cleaner than she had ever been, but Dad went over her inside and out with a scrub brush and a bucket of water. She didn't look like much compared to the yachts and speedboats anchored in the river and moored to the docks. I guess she looked all right to Dad and Mr. Lewy, the way they shined her up, or tried to.

The speedboat race was in the afternoon at three o'clock, so after working on the bateau and watching the sailboats race, we went home to dinner. Mama had fried squash and butterbeans, both of which Dad likes, but he didn't seem to be hungry.

"What's the matter with you, George?" Mama said. "Have you been eating crabs and drinking beer somewhere?"

"No, Mother," he said. "I guess it must be the excitement." He laid down on the couch. Usually Dad can go to sleep any time, but he turned and twisted. He got up and went out on the porch to smoke. Mama didn't like him to smoke in the house.

"Let's go down to the cove, Noah," he said, "and see how the bateau is."

"I guess we ought to guard it," I said. "In one of the Tom Slade books, a rascal tampered with Tom's boat just before the race."

"You're right, Noah," he said, "we mustn't let anybody tamper with the old bateau," and we went down to the river.

We beat Mr. Lewy this time, but he came a few minutes later.

"They're betting that Eben's boat is going to win our race, George," he said.

"Who's betting?"

"The fellows up town."

"What are the odds on our boat?"

"Doc Salmons offers to bet two to one that we won't even finish," Mr. Lewy said. "They all think we'll sink."

"Did you take Doc up?"

"I couldn't," Mr. Lewy said, "I'm awful short of cash."

"Me, too."

I sat on the bank while Dad and Mr. Lewy tinkered around, greasing this and oiling that. Every once in a while a race would be announced and the starter would count the seconds off before firing his gun. Then the judges' boat would cruise over to the finish line and wait. I never saw so many badges pinned on people before. They looked like pictures of Napoleon's generals in the history books.

"Unlimited speedboats, two laps, five miles," the announcer called. Mr. Lewy took in the one line that was holding the bateau and Dad sculled her out in the river.

The engine was running, but it wasn't in gear. There were six other boats in the race and the bateau looked like poor relations. All of the others were more varnish and brass than anything else. It hurt your eyes to look at them.

The starter counted off the last minute, a second at a time, and the boats ran slowly toward the starting line, then faster, as the seconds ticked away.

"Bang," went the starter's gun and I almost fell overboard even though I was expecting it. The engines roared as the boats sped down the river. The old bateau was last.

"Left at the post," Old Man Wood said. "They won't never finish."

"Your saying so doesn't make it so," said a voice that was familiar to me, and turning, I saw Mama all dressed up and carrying an open black umbrella to give her shade. Old Man Wood saw who it was and drifted away. He knew better than to get in an argument with Mama.

By that time the boats were halfway to the black buoy and I couldn't see who was leading. As they rounded the buoy one of them upset but it was too shiny for Dad. The boats came flying up the river and we could see that the bateau was still last, but not too far back. I could see Mr. Lewy pumping and there wasn't much water in her. I had heard Dad tell Mr. Lewy not to open her up until they rounded the black buoy on the second lap so I knew they still had a chance. But Mama didn't know.

"There your father is, last as usual," she said. "I'm going home." It wasn't no use to say anything to her.

The boats rounded the black buoy and started on the homestretch. I tried to see what was happening but they were too far away. Mr. Unger was standing beside me, looking through a pair of field glasses.

"There's a boat coming up from behind," he said, and I knew it must be Dad.

Soon we could see that the old black bateau had passed them all. Dad was out in front and pulling away from the others like they might have been rowboats. And I could see Mr. Lewy's arm going up and down, faster and faster, pumping the water out.

"I'll be damned," Old Man Wood said, and I knew he must have been betting against Dad.

Suddenly I saw Mr. Lewy's arm stop and he bent over like he was looking for something. The old bateau wasn't more than a hundred feet from the finish line, and everybody was laughing and shouting. But before you could spit on a bull frog, Dad's boat took a nose dive and disappeared under the water. Next thing we knew, two heads popped up and they swam across the finish line even before the other boats got there. The judges' boat took them aboard.

Old Man Wood was happy again. "Well, I bet they wouldn't finish and they didn't."

That sort of made me mad. "They crossed the finish line ahead of the rest," I said.

Old Man Wood looked at me like I didn't have a right to an opinion.

"The boat didn't cross the finish line," he said, putting me in my place. "That's what counts."

"How do you know the bateau didn't cross the line?" Mr. Unger said. "It probably did, under water."

While everybody was arguing about who won the race, the bateau came to the surface, bottom up, with a big hole where the engine had been. It was a good quarter mile past the finish line.

Even the judges seemed to be arguing. They were shaking their heads and pointing, first at the old bateau and then at Mr. Pauley's boat, which had been the first to cross the line on top of the water. The chief judge raised his megaphone. "The judges have decided that the black bateau, name unknown, was first in the race, Mr. Eben Pauley's *Shooting Star* was second, and Mr. John Carroll's *Speedy* was third. The time for the race was six minutes and ten seconds, which sets a new record for this division." The crowd cheered and I saw that Mama had come back and she wasn't hiding under the umbrella this time. Dad and Mr. Lewy came ashore looking like a couple of muskrats, they were that wet; Dad was carrying the life preservers they had won.

"You almost needed them life preservers, Mr. George," Rip Parr said.

"Well, Lew, you didn't do a mile a minute," Old Man Wood said.

"Not quite," Mr. Lewy said, "but next year we will."

Mama was waiting for Dad. "Don't forget what you promised if you won," she said.

Dad scratched his head. "What was that?"

"You said you'd get a steady job making baskets if you won."

Dad looked toward the river and what was left of his bateau.

"Maybe I should have gone down with my ship," he said.

But he fixed the bottom of his old bateau, put his old one-cylinder back in her — and went on being a waterman.

CHAPTER 18

Grandpappy's Foggy Day

THAT fall I was in the sixth grade, Grandpappy decided to bring his ark up the river. He didn't tell anybody, he just bought an extra pound of coffee, filled his water jugs and waited for a full moon tide.

The *B. S. Ford* passed him off Quaker Neck Wharf, floating with the tide, and tossed him a line. Only Grandpappy couldn't see the line. One of the deckhands came aboard the ark and made the line fast for Grandpappy. That must have been a funny sight, the *B. S. Ford* towing Grandpappy's little ark. I wonder if the smoke was coming out of the stovepipe. That was late in October.

Grandpappy hauled his ark out beside the other arks and shacks where the proggers live. The proggers don't do much of anything for long.

By that time he was so blind that he could only tell who people were by their voices. Dad took Mama to see him and when she understood how things were, she cried. Grandpappy came to live with us. That was in November.

But he wasn't happy. Our house was strange to him. I still remember that February day. . . .

"Where's my pipe?" asked Grandpappy, running his

fingers along the mantel. "Did you hide my pipe again, Evaline?"

Mama was washing dishes. "You're getting as blind as a
bat, Pap. Where do you think you are going with your
cap on?"

"I'm going down the river, that's where I'm going. I'll
tong us enough oysters for a pie."

Mama almost dropped a dish. "You're not going down
the river if I have anything to do with it."

Grandpappy tried a different tack. "What are you talking about, daughter?"

"You know what I'm talking about; you can't see your
hand in front of your face. If you don't see a doctor soon,
they will be coming after you."

I thought that Grandpappy was going to cry. "To think
that it would ever come to this — my favorite daughter-in-
law threatening to get rid of me. But I ain't fixing to be a
bother to nobody. Maybe I'd better go down and live alone
on my little ark."

Dad says that if he ever gets mad enough, he'll go, even
if he has to crawl. We're all like that.

Now Mama put her arm around Grandpappy's shoulders.
"You'll be seventy in May, Pap, and we don't want anything to happen to you."

He straightened up. "I feel as young as a boy, it's the
weather that's different. All the days are foggy now."

Dad was dozing on the couch. "What are you fussing
about?" he complained. "Why ain't Noah in school?"

"It's Washington's Birthday," Mama said, "and Pap is
talking about going down the river."

Grandpappy had that look he got when he was ready to argue. "If Washington could cross the Delaware in a rowboat, I guess I can go down the river in George's bateau."

Dad sat up. "You can't see where you're going, Pap, besides the river is still locked with ice. Old Chesapeake needs to snooze awhile."

"Don't you call me Pap," Grandpappy yelled, getting his dander up. "Here you are, a young man, stretched out in the middle of the day when you ought to be tonging the bar."

"You know I've got a weak back," Dad said.

"It's weak from lack of exercise. I never thought a son of mine would become a shiftless progger — all you want to do is to prog the marsh. You need a stint of exercise, handling a pair of thirty-two-foot oyster rakes."

Dad stretched on the couch.

Grandpappy found his pipe. "I'm clean out of tobacco, Evaline. Lend me a dollar so I can go up town and buy me a bag of tobacco."

"Noah can run and fetch it."

"No, sir, it's agin the law for a minor to buy tobacco."

Mama is stubborn but since Grandpappy is older, he can outdo her. She took a dollar bill from her purse. "You go along with your Grandpappy, Noah, and get a quarter-pound of chipped beef." She squeezed my arm and I knew that meant I was to keep a close eye on Grandpappy.

Mama never gave up. "Why don't you see Dr. Salmons about your eyes while you are up town, Pap? He used to go to school with you."

"Puss Salmons ain't getting a swipe at my eyes. When he was a lad, he couldn't whittle a willow whistle."

Outside it was a sunny day but not for Grandpappy. "Never saw such a foggy winter in all my days," he said. "My pap used to say that a cold fog was full of snow."

Grandpappy was proud. When we reached the smooth cement of the main street, he let go my arm and his eyes were good enough to see Meekins's Bar, or maybe he smelled it. "You wait outside for me, Noah," he said.

The hardware store is next door to the barroom and I looked at the penknives in the window. The trouble with owning a penknife is that you either cut yourself or lose it. Last Christmas, Mama gave me one on a chain so I lost it and the chain. I counted twelve muskrat traps in the window. Dad had twenty-two traps set now, only he didn't walk them early enough; he figured somebody else was taking his rats.

I was getting tired waiting for Grandpappy. A man came out of the bar but it wasn't him. When I looked through the window, I couldn't see anything but smoke.

Ric skated by on the ball-bearing skates he got for Christmas and made a slick turn. "What are you doing up town, Noah?"

"I'm waiting for Grandpappy."

"I just passed your Grandpappy; he was groping his way along Queen Street, heading for the river."

"He's in Meekins's Bar."

"I betcha he sneaked out the back door."

"You sure it was my Grandpappy?"

Ric crossed his heart and I knew it wasn't any use to

look in the barroom. Then we heard a one-cylinder motor start down on the river and I knew whose bateau that was. We listened. Grandpappy was going down the river.

When I reached home, Mama met me at the door. "Where's Pap?"

"He slipped out the back door at Meekins's Bar and went down the river. I heard the bateau."

Mama is like Grandpappy, she acts quickly. Now she roused Dad. "Get your boots on, George. Pap's run away to the river again, and you'll have to go after him."

Dad stirred. "We couldn't catch him if we both rowed. He'll come back when the tide floods. Can't anything much happen to him as long as he stays in the bateau."

"You go over and see if Jesse will lend you his bateau. Maybe he will go with you."

Dad saw the look in Mama's eyes and didn't argue. We slipped on our boots and Mama tied a wool scarf around my neck before going to the closet where she hid her bottle.

"Here's something I've been saving in case somebody got sick, George. You'd better take it along — for Pap."

Dad measured it.

Mr. Jesse was sitting beside the kitchen table watching his wife stir a pot of something that smelled awful good. "Get chairs and set up, George. You're in time for a bowl of snapper soup."

"Pap has run off to the river again, Jesse," Dad said. "He's so blind he can hardly see the sun. How about taking your bateau and helping us find him?"

Mr. Jesse went to the cupboard and found two more

bowls. "Your Pap doesn't need to see, George, he's been studying the river for more than fifty years. He can smell his way."

"Evaline says that I've got to go and fetch him and you know how set she can get."

"Just like your pap," said Mr. Jesse's wife, filling our bowls.

"All right, George, I'll help you, but let's fill up first. He can't roam far; the river's solid past Deep Point."

I walked between Dad and Mr. Jesse on the way to the river and I was hard put to keep up with them. After they got started, their boots carried them along while mine were getting heavier. Dad said you had to track the marsh for a long while before your boots learned to carry you.

"The river is wearing a pretty lace collar today," Dad said. He's always saying the strangest things.

The ice had locked the bateaus and he broke a channel with an oar while Mr. Jesse primed the engine. He worked the wheel back and forward a couple of times and she went right off. Watermen do things the easiest way.

Even though it was a sunny day, running against the wind took my breath until I got used to it. The crows were squatting in the marshy fringe and we flushed them. Maybe they thought we were shooting their way. Past the little gut, we saw an old man pawing with an eight-foot pair of nippers.

"He won't get more than enough oysters for a stew that way," Dad yelled, loud enough to be heard above the engine and by everybody for miles around, including the old progger.

He rested on his shafts and glared our way, muttering to himself. It was easy to read his lips.

We were well past the big gut when we saw Dad's bateau lying beside the ice off Skillet Point, but we didn't see Grandpappy.

Mr. Jesse shut off the motor and we coasted the rest of the way. Dad pointed to the ice and we could see the scratches of Grandpappy's heel plates leading to the shore.

"He likes to roam the woods," Dad said.

"Give him a hail," said Mr. Jesse.

"Where are you, Pap?" Dad yelled, and his call echoed. That would have been funny any other time.

Dad called a second and third time; we were getting worried when we heard a distant "Yeh!" and I knew that was Grandpappy.

"Where are you?" Dad yelled again.

Grandpappy didn't answer.

"Tell him you brung a bottle for him," suggested Mr. Jesse.

"Evaline gave me a bottle for you," Dad shouted.

I sort of expected to hear Grandpappy tearing through the woods; he did shout but we couldn't hear what he said.

"What's that?" Dad called.

This time I heard him. "I've got a coon treed."

"Did you hear what I heard, Jesse?" Dad asked. Mr. Jesse is a mite deaf and I reckon Dad wanted to be sure.

"Sounded like he said he'd treed a coon."

"What are we waiting for?" Dad said, and stepped out on the ice. We followed, slipping and sliding and hurrying where the ice cracked.

"We're coming," Dad yelled as he followed Grand-pappy's path through the marsh.

It was warm in the woods; the bare trees let in plenty of sunshine while keeping out most of the wind.

"Where are you?" Dad shouted after we had gone a good piece.

"Right here," Grandpappy answered, and there he was, standing beside a great oak tree. He was carrying a wooden tub and hatchet.

"Don't come too close," he said, "the critter might make a run for it before we are ready for him."

We looked aloft but there wasn't a sign of the coon.

"Did you see him?" Dad asked.

"I didn't see him but I smelled him." Grandpappy faced the oak tree and sniffed like a pointer. "I still smell him. Ain't there a hole in the trunk of the tree? I came ashore to get a few strips of red oak bark to brew liniment for my rheumatism and I figure this is the tree I've been using for nigh on twenty years. Ain't there a hole in the trunk?"

"You're right," Mr. Jesse said, "but it don't look like no coon hole to me." He reached inside the trunk and pulled his hand out fast, saying something evil. If I said that in school, Miss Barbara would wash my mouth out with soap. Mr. Jesse's hand was bleeding where the coon had grabbed him.

"You'll pay for this," he said. "I'll lay you amongst yams and turnip greens."

"We don't want to kill him yet, Jess," said Dad. "I've been wanting a coon for some time. Wouldn't it be nice to take him to the poolroom on a chain? They say that a coon is the only thing in these parts that can lick a tomcat."

"You be the one to snuff him out then, George," said Mr. Jesse, stepping back.

"Since I found the coon and have caught more varmints than the rest of you put together, I'm the one who says how to catch it," Grandpappy said.

We listened close.

"You boys can't match a pair of good coon hounds so we'll prog him with a red oak sapling. Then when Mr. Coon comes out, you catch him."

Mr. Jesse examined his bleeding hand. "I ain't grappling with that coon again."

"Me neither," said Dad.

Grandpappy sighed. "I wish I was young and had my sight. All you have to do is take off your coats and trap him in them. Sort of smother him."

Dad shrugged. "All right, you prog for him, Pap."

"Me, I can't see well enough to do much, you know that." But he did unbutton his coat like he might be getting ready to take it off.

Dad built a fire while Mr. Jesse was cutting the sapling; the stick was green and it took a long time to get it red hot. When Mr. Jesse gave it to me, it was glowing like a poker.

Dad and Mr. Jesse took off their coats and crouched down, ready to spring. The sapling had a hook and that made it just right for progging the coon.

Grandpappy's nose was fast. "Here he comes," he shouted.

The coon came out head first and fighting mad. Dad and Mr. Jesse didn't try too hard and they both missed. That should have ended the whole affair but for some reason the coon decided to jump Grandpappy; maybe he wanted to pay Grandpappy back for disturbing his long winter's nap. He climbed up his long legs like they were twin hickories. Grandpappy had his coat open and when the coon tangled with his vest, he closed it around the varmint and began to jump up and down. The coon was tickling Grandpappy. It was a cross between the Spartan boy who stole the fox and the hoochy-koochy girls at the county fair.

"Take him off me," Grandpappy shouted.

"He's your coon," Dad said.

Pretty soon the coon became winded and quieted down.

"Let him stick his nose out and get a breath of air," Mr. Jesse said. "He won't bite you."

"He's got teeth, ain't he?" Grandpappy said, but he did let the coon get a little air. The critter rode like a pig in a poke on the way back to the boats.

"Where's the bottle?" Grandpappy said. "All of this excitement has left me in need."

Dad found it. "You'd better give Mr. Coon a nip, too."

Grandpappy was making friends with the coon, it was easy to see that, and now the varmint had his whole face out; he must have been a young and trusting one. Only he didn't get to sample the bottle. Me and the coon were left out.

"You keep your friend warm and comfy and I'll run the boat," Dad said.

"You want me to go with you, Mr. Jesse?" I asked.

"You'd better ride with the coon."

When Dad started the engine, I thought that the coon

and Grandpappy would jump out of the boat. But the critter got used to it and dozed off. The old progger was still pawing and he almost fell overboard when he saw the coon with his head resting on Grandpappy's shoulder.

We tied up to the dock.

All the way home the coon rode easy, but his eyes were darting here and there.

Mama was waiting for us on the doorstep. She looked the coon in the eye.

"What won't you be bringing home next?" she said. But she was glad to see Grandpappy.

"He'll whip the shreds out of Mrs. Unger's yellow cat," Dad said and went on inside.

"Don't you bring that beast inside the house," Mama said. "I won't feed you if you do."

It may have been the way Mama looked at the coon, or maybe Grandpappy was getting too familiar with him. Anyway, the critter grabbed Grandpappy around the neck.

He yelled like an Indian, the coon jumped from his shoulder through the doorway. Mama reached for her broom and we heard a clatter in the parlor . . . then everything was quiet. It sounded like Dad had treed the coon.

Grandpappy was bleeding like a stuck pig. "The varmint scratched me," he said. "And after I treated him so nice."

The blood scared Mama. "Run and fetch Dr. Salmons, Noah, before your grandpa bleeds to death."

When I got back with the doctor, Mama had stopped the bleeding with a wet rag and Dad had cornered the coon in the springs of the couch.

Dr. Salmons examined Grandpappy, sort of measuring

him, like the undertakers do, and Grandpappy was as white as a snow bank. He must have thought that having a doctor meant he was dying. Every once in a while the coon would shake the springs. "I'm all trembly," Grandpappy said.

"That's the coon," said Mama, but in the excitement he had forgotten about the coon.

Dr. Salmons pressed the scratch on Grandpappy's neck and rolled his eyes back. "You'll be all right, Burt, just rest quietly for a day — if you can." He examined Grandpappy's eyes again.

"Do you remember when we were in the fifth grade together, Burt? Do you remember the day we played hooky and went down the creek?"

"I mind the time, Puss. That was a beauty of a day, the trees all breaking out their green, the sky and cove all blue. Mind you it was in May and my Mommy figured I'd played hooky when she saw all the sunburn. She whaled me but I still can remember that sunny day. The sun don't ever shine like that now — all of my days are foggy."

"The sun still shines that way but you don't see it, Burt, and that is because a thin skin has grown over your eyes. Have it removed and you could see things like you did when you were a boy."

"You mean the days would be sunny again?"

"That's right and the operation is much easier now. It's as easy as skinning a ripe peach."

Grandpappy heard the word "operation." "Nobody is going to tie me to a table and cut me open. I'm figuring on dying whole."

"I would go with you, Burt."

Grandpappy wavered. "And I could see with a young lad's eyes again?"

"That's right, Burt."

The rest of us were not saying a word for we knew how stubborn Grandpappy could be. You could see that he was about to get set again when Dad touched Dr. Salmons's arm.

"He'll be seventy come May, you know, Doc. Do you think he could stand it?"

Grandpappy sat up. "I never thought I'd raise a son to insult me," he yelled. "When do we go riding to that hospital, Puss?"

Dr. Salmons took Grandpappy to the hospital in Baltimore the very next day — before he had a chance to change his mind — and the big doctors said that the cataracts were ripe and ready to be removed. It was the first time Grandpappy had ever been in a hospital and it must have been awfully hard for him to keep still in bed. But he did for three weeks and came home wearing a pair of dark glasses. He sat around the house for a couple of weeks and it was plain that he was going to be all right. Grandpappy had his nose into everything, began to see everything and hear more. . . .

One day while I was in school and Dad was somewhere or other, Mama and Grandpappy had it out. He moved on board his ark on March the first. He was happier and so were we.

CHAPTER 19

Rip

A COUPLE of days after Grandpappy went back to his ark, while I was playing down by the river, Rip Parr came along sculling an old rowboat with a broken oar. I didn't pay any attention to him because Mama had told me more than once never to have anything to do with Rip. Everybody said he was the worst boy in town.

It was high tide and Rip brought the boat up on the beach as far as he could and dragged it into the marsh. He turned it over and stuck the broken oar under it. Then he sat down and began to pick the sand burrs from his feet. Even though it was early March, Rip was already barefoot.

"I guess she'll be safe," he said. Rip looked at me. "Ain't you Mr. George's boy Noah? You don't look as puny as you used to."

I didn't say anything but started to pick up the baseball players which I had spread on the bottom of Dad's bateau. I was scared Rip might take them away from me. I wondered if he knew I had one of Hans Wagner. You see I was the only boy in town who had a baseball player with Hans Wagner's picture on it. Usually we got the players' pictures by waiting in front of Mr. Billy Mac's store until somebody bought a pack of cigarettes. When they opened them we asked for the picture of the baseball player. But my half-brother Paul worked for a printing company in Baltimore and the last time he was home he brought me a big sheet of ball players just as they came off the press. And half of them were Hans Wagners.

I had all of my players picked up before Rip got the sand burrs off his feet.

"What are you doing with all them ball players, Noah?"

"Just looking at them."

"Want to match some?" he said, taking a big pack out of his pants pocket. You can match ball players, heads and tails, like pennies, but Mama made me promise not to do that because it's gambling.

"Mama won't let me," I said. "It's gambling."

"What's wrong with gambling?" Rip asked. "I saw your dad playing poker in one of them lawyers' offices last night." But he couldn't get me to match with him because I was afraid he would be too slick for me.

"Want to swap some?" Rip asked. When we get two of a kind you can trade for one you don't have.

"I got an extra Eddie Collins." I showed it to Rip on top of the others.

"Here's one of Nick Altrock I'll give you for that," Rip said, handing it over for me to look at.

"All right," I said, pulling Eddie Collins off the pack to give to Rip. He had mighty sharp eyes and, as luck would have it, Hans Wagner was next. He saw it and grabbed my hand.

"My God, Noah," he said, "where did you get that? Hans Wagner. I ain't never seen one like that." The way his voice sounded it might really have been the one he called on first. He let my hand go.

"My brother brought it to me from Baltimore," I said.

"Want to trade old Hans?" he asked.

"Naw, I don't want to," I said, sticking him deep in my pants pockets and putting my hand on top.

"I'll give you fifty players for him."

"Naw."

"I'll give you all the players I got," he said, and pulled out big packs from his pants pockets, scattering them on the bateau. "There's two Ty Cobbs in that bunch."

"Mama wouldn't want me to."

"I'll give you my barlow with a five-inch blade," Rip said, pulling out a long knife.

"I don't want to."

Rip stopped and thought things over. He unbuttoned his shirt pocket and brought out a little round tin contraption that had places to put pennies, nickels, dimes and quarters.

"This is my last offer, Noah," he said, and tossed the change holder on the boat with the ball players and the knife. I looked at the pile and felt the piece of cardboard in my pocket.

"All right, Rip," I said. "I'll trade," and handed over the picture of Hans Wagner. I gathered up the ball players, the barlow knife and the coin holder. Then I went home. When I got up to the top of the hill, I looked back and Rip was still sitting on the bottom of his rowboat looking at the picture of Hans Wagner. I didn't tell him I had half a sheet of Hans Wagners. I didn't tell anybody.

When I got home, I sat down on the porch steps and spread out all of the ball players. They were greasy, but I did find the two Ty Cobbs he said were there. I placed all of my players until I had full line-ups for most of the big-league teams. The floor of the porch was covered with them. I took out the coin holder and tried its springs. Mama came to the door with a broom and saw all of the ball players.

"Where'd you get all of the ball players, Noah?" she asked. "Didn't you promise me not to gamble?"

"I ain't been gambling, Mama," I said. "I traded for them."

"What did you trade to get all of them?" she asked, suspicious-like.

"I traded one of my Hans Wagners."

"What's that tin thing you have in your hand?"

"It's a change holder," I said. "I got that, too, for Hans Wagner." I didn't tell her about the knife because I knew she wouldn't let me carry one with a five-inch blade.

"Who didn't have any more sense than to give you all of that for one little piece of pasteboard?"

"Rip Parr."

"Rip Parr! Didn't I tell you never to have any dealings with Rip Parr? Helen was telling me only yesterday that Rip was taking to strong drink and him not more than sixteen. I guess he must have been drunk to give you all of that junk for one ball player."

"He weren't drunk," I said. "I'm the only boy in town that's got Hans Wagner. That's why it's worth so much."

"Sounds like gambling to me or maybe Rip's feeble-minded, too."

Dad must have been asleep and all our talking woke him up. He came out on the porch.

"What's all this fussing about?" he asked. "Seems like I can't ever get rested no more."

"Noah's been swapping ball players with Rip Parr."

"Did Rip cheat him?" Dad asked, looking at all the ball players spread on the porch floor.

"It don't look that way," Mama said, "but I've told Noah he shouldn't mix with the likes of Rip Parr."

"You're being too hard on Rip," Dad said. "His father drowned and his mother sick all the time. Rip's got to be tough to live. The other night he slept in the town jail."

"That settles it," Mama said. "Noah's going to take everything Rip traded him and give it back. He's probably stolen them somewhere and is trying to palm them off on you."

"Considering the time you spend in church, you're awful hard on Rip, Evaline," Dad said.

"What's that got to do with it?" asked Mama.

So I picked up the ball players and walked down to the river but it wasn't any use. Rip had gone.

Mama must have been watching because when I went home, she took the ball players and the coin holder. "I'll keep them until Rip comes back after that old rowboat," she said. "You keep your eyes peeled for him, Noah."

"Yes, ma'am," I said, figuring it would be late April be-ore I saw Rip again.

But March is a funny month on the Chesapeake. That March we had a quick hard freeze and a week of ice skating. Even Old Man Wood got his skates out and did all kinds of figures with his hands folded behind his back. He seemed young even though his beard did stick out with the breeze. Some of the little kids who couldn't really skate had double runners that looked like little sleds. Of course us boys sharpened our skates and had a big time. But it thawed after a week and the ice melted in the middle of the river where the current is strong. One night it got cold enough to harden the ice in Brewster's Cove and we could skate again, but the middle of the river was still open.

We were skating in the cove and playing hockey when Dad came down to the river. He took a look around and called me. "You, Noah, come off of that ice right away."

"What's the matter, Dad?" I asked, skimming over to the brick wall where he was standing.

"Can't you feel how the wind has sprung up from the north?" he said. "With the middle of the river open, the next thing you know it's going to blow this cove ice out in the river."

"Aw, Dad," I said, "ain't you too cautious?" But I sat down on the brick wall and took off my skates. Dad went home.

Richard Cullen heard what Dad said and so did his brother Willie, who was my age, and they took off their skates. But the rest went right on skating. I sat around awhile watching and then walked up the hill toward our house. I must have been halfway home when somebody screamed. When I turned, I saw that big hunk of ice moving out into the river just like it had an engine pushing it. Two or three of the skaters close to shore jumped off and swam, but the rest huddled and yelled for help.

That's when I saw Rip Parr again, for he was one of the skaters who swam ashore. He must have been cold but he ran toward the marsh where he had left his rowboat. Before anybody else could do anything, Rip had turned over his boat and dragged it into the water. With that broken oar, he was sculling his old leaky boat toward the ice. And the wind was blowing the ice toward the other shore.

Dad and Mama heard the commotion and came out of the house.

"Where's Noah?" I heard Mama say. She was wringing her hands.

"Here I am!" I called.

"Thank the good Lord," she said.

Dad was watching Rip and the skaters on the ice. "If he don't reach them before they hit the ice on the other shore, that floe is going to break up," he said. "Where will they be then? Come on, Noah, we'll get another boat."

Somehow Rip did reach the floe in time and they all got into the one leaky rowboat. Pretty soon a lot of boats were in the water and all were safe.

Rip was a real hero. One of the girls on the ice was Bessie Tilghman. Her father owned the basket factory. Mr. Tilghman was so thankful that he gave Rip a new suit of clothes and twenty-five dollars. But Rip took the money and went to Baltimore, where he landed in jail for fighting in a saloon. He didn't get back to the river till crabbing time. By that time, everyone — even Mama — had forgotten about the ball players and the coin holder and the barlow knife, that is, everybody but me.

CHAPTER 20

The Christian Thing to Do

SPRING starts the grass growing and I make most of my spending money cutting it. I cut Miss Lizzie's grass on Decoration Day. Every time I'd stop pushing the mower to rest, she would lift the curtain at the bay window and peep out. She had a scared look. She's that way. After finishing with the mower, I took the trowel and weeded the borders of the flower beds. Miss Lizzie is right particular about her flowers and she gave me strict orders not to touch them. When I thought I was finished, I rapped on the back door and she came out to inspect my work. I must have missed the plantain leaves close to the flowers. Anyway, it took me another half hour to satisfy her. She took a black purse out of her apron pocket and looked at the latch. It was hard to open but she finally managed it, and, looking inside it, she picked out a quarter for me.

"I was going to give you more, Noah," she said, "but I don't think you did a good job. You were in too big a hurry. If you want to do anything right, you must take your time. Now don't waste your money."

"No, ma'am," I said, putting the quarter in my pocket.

The twelve o'clock whistle on the basket factory blew while I was putting the mower in the woodshed.

When I make money, I like to spend it. During Lent, Mama made me put some of my earnings in a special little box the rector gave us in Sunday school. At Easter we all handed in our boxes, jingling them and carrying them to the altar like they were heavy. The money went to help the heathens in other lands. Dad said the church ought to help the heathens in our town, meaning himself, I guess. But Lent was over and the quarter I made cutting Miss Lizzie's grass was mine to spend. I'd been wanting a new fishing rig for some time, so after dinner I went up to the hardware store, it kept open on holidays. The clerk was greasing harness.

"Hello, Noah," he said. "Want to buy a new penknife and cut yourself?" He must have seen me looking at the knives in the window.

"No, sir," I said, "I want to buy a fishing rig."

"I guess you want to rig it yourself," he said, knowing my dad was a waterman.

"Yes, sir."

"Let's go upstairs and get a bamboo pole," he said. I like to be in a hardware store. They smell good.

"You want a short one?" he said. "See anything you like?"

I picked one out with a strong tip and we took it downstairs.

"What kind of hook you want, Noah?"

"A small one with catgut."

"That will cost you a nickel," he said, looking at me.

"I've got a quarter," I said.

I bought a line and a sinker.

"Don't you want a float?" he said.

"No, sir," I said, "I ain't used a float for a couple of years." Only little boys and sissies use floats, but it is fun when a big yellow ned pulls that bobbin out of sight. A real fisherman uses a sinker and tells by the feel.

"Let's see," the clerk said, wrapping up everything but the pole, "the hook was a nickel, sinker two cents, line five cents and the pole is a dime. That makes twenty-two cents." I handed him the quarter and he rang the bell on the cash register, giving me my three cents' change.

"You river boys are smart enough," he said. "The rig you have is better than the complete sets we sell for a dollar." He looked at the rack that held the shotguns and fishing rods. Those steel rods look good, but bamboo can't rust.

After I got home it only took me a few minutes to fix the rig and dig a can of worms.

"I'm going down to the old wharf, Mama," I said, "I'll bring you some fish home for supper."

"Don't you fall overboard," she said, "the *B. S. Ford* used to come in there." She meant it was real deep water.

"I can swim."

"That's what you say."

The old wharf is where the steamboats used to stop before they got rich enough to build a new one. There is a roof over most of it and you can sit in the shade and fish. If the tide is high you can stick your feet in the water. Even Dad likes to fish there on a hot day. But there wasn't nobody fishing when I got there so I picked out a fat worm and slapped it before I put it on that shiny new hook. As I let the line down beside one of the pilings, the old wharf creaked and I knew somebody was coming. I didn't even look because you often get a bite when you first put your line overboard.

"Move over, white boy," a voice said, and looking around I saw a strange black boy. I'd never seen him before and I knew he didn't belong in our town because he was wearing shoes and it was the last of May. But I didn't move over.

"Colored people don't fish here, black boy," I said. "You'd better go somewhere else."

"Move over, pale skin," the black boy said. "Can't you see that sign? It says 'Public Landing.' I'm just as much a citizen as you are."

I'd never heard that word "citizen" and I thought it was some kind of a nigger cuss word. "Don't you cuss me, nigger," I said. "I'll tell my father."

"Don't you call me a nigger," he said, "I'm an Afro-American. That's what my teacher told me."

"Do you go to school?" I asked.

"Where I live, white and black boys sit next to one another in school," the black boy said. "I live in Philly, where people are civilized. Move over, boy, or I'll push you in." He came closer.

He was bigger than me and I ain't used to smart talk from a nigger. I laid my pole down and started to get up. He was over me by this time and I don't know whether he pushed me or I tripped over the big cleat. Anyway, the next thing I knew I was overboard and going down fast, but I came up again. The boy had gone and when I looked at those old slippery pilings, I knew I couldn't climb them. I had been swimming doggy, a little, but this was the first time I had ever been over my head, and alone. The water was cold and I was getting tired, but my head was clear. I hadn't had time to get scared.

A rowboat was tied to one of the pilings and I just reached the gunwale in time. I hung on and rested. Maybe I'd better call for help, I thought, beginning to get scared. But there didn't seem to be anybody around, and besides, I didn't want anybody to know that I'd been pushed in by a nigger. After resting some more I kicked and climbed and pulled myself into the rowboat. Once in the boat, I stretched out on the seat and shivered but the sun warmed me up and I began to feel better and then I began to get mad. My lips began to tremble but I didn't cry. Mama says I never have cried, even when I was a baby.

I picked up my fishing pole and went home, dripping all the way, like the water sprinkler on a hot day. The screen door was hooked on the inside and I had to call Mama. She came out on the porch, her hands and arms covered with flour.

"I fell overboard," I said, "or maybe I was pushed."

"Are you all right?" she said, seeing my lip trembling.

"Yes, ma'am."

I heard the couch spring creak in the front room and knew Dad must be getting up. He came out and looked me over.

"You been fishing on the brick wall?" he asked.

"I was at the old wharf, Dad, and a nigger pushed me overboard."

"A nigger!" he said. "What's a nigger doing down there?"

"He was a city nigger and wore yellow shoes. I told him he didn't belong there and he pushed me in."

"Didn't I tell you never to argue with a nigger?" he said.

"You ought to know better than to argue with a nigger," Mama said. She always calls them colored people so I guess she was mad, too.

"Anyway, we know you can swim, now," Dad said. "You're all right, ain't you?"

"What will Ric and the others say when they know I let a nigger push me overboard?"

"It is shameful," Mama said.

"Why didn't you push him in, after you got out?" Dad said.

"He was gone," I said. "Besides, he was bigger than me."

"There's only one thing to do," Mama said. "You go back and push that nigger off the wharf."

"He's a lot bigger than me, Mama."

"You take your baseball bat along," she said. "When you get on some dry clothes and eat something, you'll feel better."

Mama made some chipped beef and gravy, which is a favorite of mine, and I did feel better, but I still didn't want to tackle that big city nigger. Dad must have known what I was thinking.

"I'll go with you, Noah," he said. "If you have any trouble, I'll be there to help you."

I took my baseball bat and we walked down Water Street. "What'll I say, Dad?" I asked.

"You don't say nothing," he said. "You just walk up behind him and push him in. After the nigger gets wet he'll lose all his flip. If he tries to fight conk him one with your bat."

When we neared the wharf, Dad stopped behind a hedge and I went on alone. "Maybe he didn't come back," I thought, but something told me he was there. I was barefoot and he didn't hear me until I was right behind him. The black boy was sitting down with the yellow shoes beside him, his feet dangling in the water. I guess those shoes had really blistered him. As he started to turn I gave him a good shove and he hit the water before he knew it, going down like a hunk of lead. But he came up again and started to thresh around and yell.

"My Gawd," he cried, "I'm drowning." I could see the big whites of his eyes turn red, he was that scared. "Help me, white boy," he said. He couldn't swim either. I reached my hand toward him but it was too far. I remembered the bat and picked it up.

"Oh, my Gawd, don't hit me," the black boy cried. "Help me, please!"

I stuck the bat toward him and he grabbed it and I towed him over to the rowboat. He hung on for a while and pulled himself out. Stretched on the seat, he shivered, just like I had, and the same sun began to warm him.

"I didn't push you in, white boy," the black boy said. "You slipped. I was just talking."

"You did push me in," I said.

Dad came along and heard us. "Didn't I tell you never to argue with a nigger?" he said. But I sort of felt he was proud of me, the way he put his hand on my shoulder as we walked home.

When we got home Mama was waiting on the porch.

"What happened?" she said. "Was the colored boy there?"

"Yes," Dad said, "Noah pushed him in and then pulled him out."

"Why did he pull him out?" she said.

"That was the Christian thing to do, Mother," Dad said.

"Don't get sacrilegious, George," she said. Mama always has the last word.

CHAPTER 21

Mr. Lewy Had Wings

DAD and Mr. Lewy were pitching horseshoes against Old Man Wood and Mr. Jester. Us boys were watching and listening to their talk.

"Where were you born, George?" Mr. Jester asked. "You've been paddling around ever since I can remember."

"Me," Dad said, "I'm a native. I was born over on Water Street. They say old Doc Bascombe stepped down to the river and washed me there."

"I was born in Caroline County," Mr. Jester said.

"That's nothing to brag about," Mr. Lewy said. "The way I heard it, that makes you a red belly, creeping and crawling over that red clay they have down there."

"I'm no foreigner, anyway," Mr. Jester said. "You were born in Baltimore, Lewy, in a hospital. I remember that."

"Being born on the Western Shore is worse than being born across the sea," Old Man Wood said.

"And where were you born?" Dad asked Mr. Wood.

"I was born," he said.

"We'll take that for granted," Mr. Lewy said, "but where?"

"If you must know, I was born in Delaware," Old Man Wood said.

"Ain't that awful," Dad said. "You'll never be able to live that down."

"You can spit across Delaware on a windy day," Mr. Jester said, even though he was Old Man Wood's partner.

"Three counties at low tide and two counties come high tide," Dad said.

"I guess you can't help where you were born," Mr. Jester said. "What I can't stand is these foreigners moving in from Pennsylvania and New York and trying to tell us how to live. We had a case with one of them before the magistrate the other day — this Mr. Goldblatt, he's the chap who built the big house on the river. He claimed Ferky Crouse poisoned his pedigreed dog. Well, they were both standing before the magistrate after Mr. Goldblatt had made the charge.

" 'What do you have to say to that, Mr. Crouse?' the magistrate asked.

" 'This man is a foreigner, Your Honor,' Ferky Crouse said. 'Everything was all right until these foreigners started coming in.'

" 'What do you say to that, Mr. Goldblatt?' the magistrate asked.

" 'Your Honor, I am an American citizen, and since it is said that I am in a foreign land, I demand to be tried by an American consul,' this Mr. Goldblatt said."

"What happened then?" asked Mr. Lewy.

"The case was dismissed because of insufficient evidence."

"I heard that the fellow who jumps in a parachute at the fair is a Russian," Old Man Wood said.

"Only a damn fool or a foreigner would do a thing like that," Mr. Jester said.

"He gets fifty dollars every time he jumps," Mr. Lewy said, "besides being a pioneer in aviation. I hear he's using the money to build an airplane."

"Damn foolishness and tempting the good Lord, I call it," Old Man Wood said.

"If the good Lord had wanted us to fly, He'd have given us wings," said Dad.

"You boys are all wrong," Mr. Lewy said. "Didn't you ever hear of the Wright brothers or Langley? They've been flying machines heavier than air."

"How could anything heavier than air stay aloft?" Old Man Wood said. "It sounds crazy."

"Birds are heavier than air," Mr. Lewy said, "and ain't we all flown kites? An airplane is a big box kite with a propeller on it."

"You know so much, why don't you build one and fly?" asked Mr. Jester.

"I might at that if there was something in it," Mr. Lewy said.

"I'll bet you a hundred dollars you can't fly," Old Man Wood said. He is always willing to bet on a sure thing.

"You would?" asked Mr. Lewy.

"I would."

"How long do I have to stay in the air?" Mr. Lewy asked.

Old Man Wood thought awhile. "Ten minutes."

"It's a bet," Mr. Lewy said. "George and Mr. Jester can be a witness as to the terms."

"I hope you won't have to sell your tools to settle it when the time comes," Old Man Wood said, sarcastic-like.

"You needn't worry about that," Mr. Lewy said. "I hope it won't kill you when you part with your hundred dollars."

"Speaking of large sums, I wonder if George and you will pay up for the two games you've lost," Mr. Jester said.

Dad and Mr. Lewy fumbled in their pockets and somehow got fifty cents together. The game broke up and the men went up town.

But I guess everybody heard about Mr. Lewy betting Mr. Wood he could fly. Even the women were talking about it.

"I never heard such crazy talk in my life," Mama said, "flying through the air like a bird. It's sacrilegious."

"Religion don't have nothing to do with it," Dad said. "It all depends on whether Lewy can get that box kite off the ground."

"I don't want you fooling around that machine shop, Noah," Mama said. "It would be just like that Lewy to put you in the contraption and hoist you, or try to."

Most everybody had a bet on the proposition. The church people sided with Old Man Wood because it was sounder and more proper but the watermen and farmers were betting on Mr. Lewy.

He was spending his time building box kites of different sizes and shapes. This took time and the odds soon were two to one that Mr. Lewy wouldn't fly. Us boys watched him work. One day, while he was working on a box kite the size of a chicken coop, he ran out of tissue paper.

"I'm going to stop until I get more paper," he said. "I guess I'll have to send to Baltimore."

I remembered Mama's dress patterns. They were tissue paper and some of them were big. "I could get you one of Mama's old dress patterns," I said. "She's gone over to sister Helen's."

Mr. Lewy looked up and down the oyster shell road. "All right," he said, "but be sure it's an old one. I don't want to get your mother after me."

Ric kept watch and I went home. In the bottom drawer of Mama's sewing machine, I found a pattern called Mother Hubbard and it had Miss Louisa's name on it. She is a nice lady but she's plenty plump and I figured it would be just the thing for Mr. Lewy. Ric gave a long whistle and I knew that Mama was on her way home, so I got a crust of bread and stuck the pattern in my blouse. I met her at the gate.

"Can't you wait for dinner?" she asked.

"No, ma'am," I said. I headed for the river but when I was out of Mama's sight, I cut around and went in the back door of the machine shop.

"That was a close shave," Mr. Lewy said. "Did you get the tissue paper?"

I gave it to him and there was enough to finish the box kite. "How would you boys like to help me fly it?" asked Mr. Lewy.

"I don't aim to be a guinea pig," Ric said, winking at me.

"I wouldn't want a human to go up, yet," Mr. Lewy said.

"Why don't you try a cat in it?" I asked. "They've all got nine lives and always land on their feet."

"How about getting Old Tom, Miss Lizzie's cat?" Ric said. "She's been keeping a lot of our baseballs lately."

"Old Tom has sharp claws," I said. "He's mean if you try to pick him up."

"We'll get a fish head and lure him," Ric said.

That's what we did, and pretty soon all the cats in the neighborhood smelled the fish and collected around us, purring and rubbing against our legs, trying to make out they were hungry and acting pitiful. But we gave the fish head to Old Tom and when he stuck his nose inside the gills, Ric threw the sack over him. He didn't seem to mind too much and I could hear him crunching away on the fish head.

"You boys help me put the box kite on this wheelbarrow," Mr. Lewy said. "We'll take it over to the yellow cliff by the dump. That ought to be a good place with the wind where it is."

"We'll take the cat the back way," Ric said.

A screen door slammed and I saw Miss Lizzie standing on her side porch.

"Tom, Tom, Tom, Tom," she called.

Old Tom heard her, even if he was in the bag, and started to squirm and mew. He must have stuck his claws in Ric's back.

"Damn you," Ric said. "Do that once more and I'll drop you in the river." Old Tom must have understood.

When we got there, Mr. Lewy was standing on the cliff. "This seine twine ought to be strong enough to hold her," he said. "You boys go down on the dump and I will toss you the line. When I give you the word you can run and tow it."

"What about Old Tom?" asked Ric.

"I'll let him out of the bag just before you pull," Mr. Lewy said. "The sunlight will blind him and then it will be too late for him to jump." We helped Mr. Lewy prop his kite on the edge of the cliff and slid down to the level ground below.

Mr. Lewy stood on the cliff and waited for a strong puff of wind. "Get ready," he shouted as the wind bent the willows along the creek. "Pull away," and he gave the kite a shove. We ran and it was hard pulling, like towing a sled uphill in thawing snow, and we didn't dare stop to look back.

Suddenly something eased and I knew that the wind must be taking hold of the kite.

We stopped running. "Let out string fast," Ric said, panting, and we let the seine twine slip through our fingers. It burned us but the kite was climbing. Huddled inside was Old Tom, too scared to meow. But the wind died and the kite started to drift downward.

"Run, boys, run," we heard Mr. Lewy yell, so we started off again. It seemed harder pulling than before, but lucky for us a puff of wind came along and held the kite. It was about two hundred feet above the creek.

Toward home, I could hear Miss Lizzie calling, "Tom, Tom, Tom."

And bedoggone if Old Tom didn't hear her, too. He stood up and faced toward home.

"He's going to jump like the parachute man at the fair," Ric said.

"Only he ain't got a parachute," I said.

"It's suicide," Ric said as Tom got ready to spring. He couldn't seem to make up his mind but the wind caught the box kite and turned it over. Old Tom hung on for a minute, clawing and yelling, then somersaulted down to land in the creek. He was out in a minute, shaking himself, and ran off toward home.

"It's funny how cats don't like water," Ric said.

"Look out," Mr. Lewy yelled, and we looked up and saw the kite coming down on our heads. We got out from under it in time.

After that the odds went up to three to one that Mr. Lewy wouldn't fly. Every time anybody saw him on the street they would say, "When are you going to take off, Lewy?" or, "What undertaker is going to take care of you, Lewy?"

The new kite he was making was bigger than a barn door and stronger than the others. In place of tissue paper, he was using old newspapers.

"It's going to take more than two to pull this one," Mr. Lewy said, "especially when I'm aboard."

"We'll get the three Cullen boys to help us," Ric said.

"If I win the hundred dollars, I'm going to give you boys ten dollars to divide among yourselves," said Mr. Lewy. "Of course, if I lose, you don't get anything." I guess he figured that would be a good way to make us pull.

The Cullen boys said they would help but Richard, the oldest one, thought we ought to get Mr. Lewy to sign a paper first. "Suppose we pull him and he gets killed," he said. "His folks might sue us."

"What for?" asked Ric.

"Accessories or something like that," Richard said. He was thinking about studying law.

That sounded bad but Mr. Lewy promised he would sign a paper.

"We're going to try on a day when there's a strong nor'wester," he said. "That'll blow me out over the river and if I should crash, the water is softer."

"Dad might follow you in his bateau," I said.

"You ask him for me," said Mr. Lewy.

We had an easterly spell of bad weather with two days of rain and one day of clearing, but on the fourth day the wind hauled around to the nor'west and it really blowed. Saturday, Mr. Lewy said he was going to take off at three o'clock in the afternoon. The word spread and by two o'clock half the people in town were milling around on the cliff where Mr. Lewy planned to leave the ground. This time the kite was too large for a wheelbarrow and it took a horse and wagon. Us boys guarded it. Old Man Wood was all dressed up and walking around important-like. He licked his lips every once in a while — he seemed sure of getting that one hundred dollars. Just before three o'clock the odds were four to one against Mr. Lewy. I stood around reading about Happy Hooligan in the funny papers on the kite. It looked like Mr. Lewy was going to get a kick worse than that mule ever gave Happy Hooligan.

"You boys are going to feel mighty bad about this," Old Man Wood said to us. "Suppose Lewy breaks his legs or his neck?"

"That's all taken care of, Mr. Wood," Richard Cullen said. "The proper papers have been signed."

"Don't forget your consciences, boys," Mr. Caldwell said. He's the Methodist minister. "Legal connivances can never cleanse a guilty conscience. You will regret it as long as you live if Mr. Lewy is seriously hurt."

When the town clock struck three, it seemed like the wind blew harder to help Mr. Lewy. The new box kite had the seat from an old cultivator fastened to the frame, and Mr. Lewy took his place. We had a big ball of the twine Dad uses for trotlines to tie on the kite. It's stronger than the seine twine. Us five boys slid down the cliff and got set. I wondered if Dad had his bateau on the river. I couldn't hear it.

The kite was sitting on four rollers and chocked but now the chocks were pulled out and it started to roll. We trotted away like five horses drawing a stage-coach. The crowd yelled as we ran, and we knew that Mr. Lewy must be flying, at least something awful heavy was on the other end of that trotline. Ric dared to look over his shoulder.

"She's up," he yelled. "Let's stop and let out some line."

As we turned the big kite shook and for a second I thought she might turn over like the other one had, but she didn't. The kite was about two hundred feet above the ground and rising. We were having a hard time holding it until Ric made a turn around a tree.

"How far do you think Mr. Lewy wants to go?" Richard Cullen asked as the trotline came to its end.

"He didn't say," Ric said. "Gee whizz, how're we going to get him down?"

"Why can't we pull the kite in?" asked Willie Cullen.

"This line has got about all the strain it will stand," Ric said. "If the line breaks, where will that leave Mr. Lewy?"

The kite was over the river. Mr. Lewy threw his hat at a fish hawk that happened to soar by, and the bird dropped the eel he was carrying. The hawk must have figured Mr. Lewy had wings.

"How are we going to get him down?" Ric asked.

"Do you reckon he's been up ten minutes?" John Cullen asked.

Mr. Jester was the official timekeeper and we saw that he was eying his watch. He came running over to us.

"The ten minutes are up," he said. "Lewy's won."

Everybody was watching Mr. Lewy and the trotline. The line stretched and we waited for it to break.

Mr. Wood's eyes were glued to the line. "I guess Lewy won't ever collect that one hundred dollars," he said.

"Why don't you boys pull him down?" asked Mr. Jester.

"We're scared to," Ric said. "The line might break."

"You can't leave him up there," Mr. Jester said. "It's mighty confining."

Several of the men took a grip on the line and we all pulled. It snapped and the kite drifted up the river toward Buckingham but losing height fast. We all ran toward the river and I hoped Dad wasn't asleep on the parlor couch.

When we reached Brewster's Cove, it was all over. Dad was coming down the river in the old bateau and he had a passenger. We could see that it was Mr. Lewy and that he was swinging his arms to get warm. Dad ran the bateau along the brick wall and Mr. Lewy stepped ashore.

"Where's Mr. Wood?" he said. "I want my hundred dollars."

I guess Old Man Wood had sneaked off somewhere; he hates to part with money. Mr. Lewy found him and he paid up. But Mama wouldn't let me and Ric build a box kite and, for once, Dad agreed with her.

CHAPTER 22

The Prodigal Son

I RAN down Water Street past the big houses. Most of the rich people in our town live in brick houses which have lawns sloping down to the river. All of Water Street ain't like that, though, and the part just before you get to the basket factory is just the opposite. That's where the proggers pull their little arks out and live during most of the year. Grandpappy lives there, now.

I like the part of Water Street where the proggers live. If I was an artist, that would be the place I would paint, not the big brick houses.

I was taking some of Mama's vegetable soup to Grandpappy. She don't want him around our house but she wouldn't want him to starve to death. Sometimes his pickings are mighty slim. His teeth are bad and he drinks a lot of coffee, besides taking a drink of whisky when he can get it. He's still real smart, though, and one of the young college professors who teaches mathematics says Grandpappy can do things with arithmetic that most people can't do even with college figuring.

I rapped on the ark door, thinking he might be asleep. But I heard him shuffle over and unbolt the door.

"Good morning, Grandpappy," I said. "Mama sent you over this vegetable soup."

"Thank you, Noah," he said. "Come on inside."

The coffee pot was boiling on the stove and Grandpappy had on his spectacles, which meant he was reading. Now that his eyes were good, one thing he got every day was the *Sun* and he had time to read it from cover to cover.

"Sit down, boy," he said, "and tell me how you are getting along. You don't look well with that pale skin. When I was your age I was as brown as a marsh hen by May. How many times have you played hooky to go swimming this spring?" His hair was white but his blue eyes had a young look when he talked about swimming.

I just sort of sat there and grinned.

"I won't tell your teacher on you," he said, "nor your mama."

"Mama won't let me go before school is out," I said, "and she says I can't go unless Dad is with me."

Grandpappy snorted. "Ain't that awful?" he said. "They're ruining you before you're half grown. Who's going to take care of you when you grow up if they don't let you learn to fend for yourself when you are young? Why don't you run off and go swimming, anyway? But don't tell your mama I told you to. Nothing can happen to you."

"I couldn't disobey Mama."

"There's times to obey and times to disobey," Grandpappy said. "A young boy has got to rebel sometime if he's ever going to amount to anything. 'Specially in the spring when he ought to be out on the river, swimming and fishing. How many times have you been fishing?"

"I ain't really been fishing yet," I said. "School keeps me busy and I've been delivering groceries for Mr. Leary on Saturdays besides cutting grass. Mama don't want me to go fishing on Sundays."

Grandpappy grunted. "Next Saturday, my skiff will be ready to put in the river and I'm going fishing on Sunday under the big bridge. I want you to go with me. Besides, I need somebody to help me launch her, Saturday. I'll be looking for you to help me."

"All right, Grandpappy." He opened the door for me to go. "Saturday is three days off," I thought as I ran toward home.

Those three days I was busy studying for the final exams. I didn't have much time to think about helping Grandpappy launch his skiff and going fishing under the bridge. Us boys don't often get a chance to go fishing there. We mostly fish from the brick wall or the old wharf, and sometimes we go out on the bridge and fish over the rail.

All of a sudden school was over for the week and I had to make up my mind what to do. One thing was sure, I'd better not tell Mama because she didn't like me hanging around Grandpappy. I guess she was scared I might get some of his notions.

I had been working Saturdays right steady since before last Christmas. I delivered the groceries in my express wagon and Mr. Leary paid me fifty cents for the day. He doesn't have the biggest grocery in town but he doesn't work me too hard. Besides, every now and then he lets me take a piece of candy from the glass case. Once he gave me a whole handful of chocolate nigger babies. I had a good many deliveries on Water Street, and it would be easy to take time out and slip down to Grandpappy's ark. That is what I did.

My express wagon was loaded full when I pulled up beside the ark. Grandpappy was fooling around the river.

"I've come to help you launch your skiff, Grandpappy," I said.

"It's about time," he said. "If you had been much later we would have had to wait for the next tide." He was mighty proud of his skiff and gave her a fresh coat of paint every spring. She was about fifteen feet long and built mostly of white cedar, which is the best we have for boats. He painted her white with a green gunwale and seats. She never leaked a drop and Grandpappy used to say he could clean her out with a dustpan and brush. She was setting up on two rollers now, ready to push into the river. I guess he really didn't need any help for she moved into the water like she was on ball bearings. A few trickles were coming in between the bottom planks.

"She'll be all swelled up by tomorrow," Grandpappy said. "You be here by one o'clock, Noah, so we can catch the tide right. It ain't no use to go if we don't fish on the right tide."

"Yes, sir," I said, wondering how I ever could go fishing and to Sunday school at the same time.

Sunday is the hardest day of the week for me. The only good thing about it is when I go to bed on Sunday night I feel that I've done the right thing. Dad never goes to church but Mama makes me go with her in the morning at eleven o'clock. I have to wear a stiff white collar and sit still for a long while. In the afternoon, we have Sunday school at one-thirty, and, as if that wasn't enough, I sing in the children's choir during the evening services. I like to sing the *Magnificat*, whatever it means.

After getting my bath on Saturday night I lay awake wondering what to do. I couldn't go back on Grandpappy and miss the chance to go fishing under the bridge. There was only one thing to do and I knew it all along. I would have to trick Mama and play hooky from Sunday school. Somehow, that seemed worse than playing hooky from school. There wasn't any truant officer to track you but it seemed evil. If I asked Mama to let me go fishing with Grandpappy I knew what her answer would be. Before going to sleep, I knew I was going to have to sin if I wanted to hook any white perch.

Sunday morning I went up town and got the paper for Dad. When I got home it was time to get dressed for church. I couldn't even read the Katzenjammer Kids in the funny paper. Mama always wears a dress that rustles and I had a suit and shoes that were as stiff as the collar. We left Dad sitting on the porch, barefooted, reading the paper. He looked comfortable.

"You should be ashamed of yourself, George," Mama said as we went out the gate.

"Sunday is the day of rest," Dad said, turning to the sports page.

Church was harder to stand than usual because I knew that if I went fishing with Grandpappy I would be a hypocrite as well as a sinner. Just by chance the preacher's text had to be the one about the prodigal son. Mama always asks me to repeat the text at the dinner table. When she was a little girl, she didn't get the dessert if she didn't know the text. We don't often have a dessert so she can't use that on me. The text was, "And bring hither the fatted calf, and kill it; and let us eat, and be merry." I kept repeating it to myself during the rest of the sermon, wondering if Mama would kill the fatted calf for me if she found out I went fishing with Grandpappy.

Getting out of church feels even better than Friday afternoon when the bell rings for school dismissal. It was easy to smile at everybody just like we all had been enjoying ourselves as we went out of the church door and walked home. I felt free and fine.

"Mama," I said as we walked along, "how would you feel if I ran away and consorted with harlots?"

"Noah," she almost shouted, "if you use that word again, I will wash your mouth out with soap."

"The preacher used it. What would you do if I was the prodigal son?"

"You could never be a prodigal son," she said. "Let's talk about something else. Have you been fishing this year?"

"No, ma'am." I didn't speak again on the way home.

Dad was resting on the couch in the front room. Mama peeked at him sharp-like and went out in the kitchen to get dinner.

When she asked me for the text at the dinner table I rattled it off without a hitch.

"What do all them words mean?" Dad asked.

"It means the father should forgive his prodigal son," Mama said.

"If Noah was prodigal I would be the first to forgive him," Dad said. "What does it say about prodigal husbands?"

Mama didn't answer and we filled our plates. We had roast chicken, one of Miss Lizzie's hens that had molted, along with fresh peas and lettuce and onions from our garden, not to mention potatoes. Then there was a jar of Mama's watermelon rind preserves.

After dinner I went out to the woodshed and slipped a couple of fishing lines into my coat pocket. I tried to read the funny papers but I kept looking at the clock. Mama came in from washing the dishes and looked at the clock. "You'd better get started for Sunday school," she said, "or you'll be late."

"Yes, ma'am." I picked up my cap and went out the door.

I walked up Queen Street toward the church but after I passed Mr. Leary's, I cut through the alley to Water Street and hurried along the river front. I met Ric on his way to Sunday school.

"Ain't you going to Sunday school?" he asked, looking at my clothes and stiff collar. I guess he saw the fishing lines bulging from my coat pocket, too.

"Not today, Ric, but don't tell anybody you saw me. I'm going fishing with my Grandpappy."

"I won't tell nobody," Ric said, "but ain't you afraid you'll go to hell when you die?"

"That's a long way off. Maybe they'll forgive me like they did the prodigal son."

"Are you prodigal?" Ric asked.

"I'm going to try mighty hard," I said.

When I reached the ark, Grandpappy had his new spectacles on and was reading a book. He put it on the table and took the spectacles off when I came in.

"I've been reading a book one of the young college professors brought me," he said. "It's by a fellow named Thoreau who lived by himself in the woods for two years. Did you ever hear about him in school?"

"No, sir," I said. "We've been studying Longfellow's poems lately."

"Ain't that coincidental?" Grandpappy said. "The young professor who lent me this book is Longfellow's grandson, name of Dana, son of Edith, the one with the golden hair in the poem. He ain't like his grandpap, though. Sort of wild, he'll get into trouble sooner or later."

"Yes, sir."

"This Thoreau got into trouble, even spent the night in jail, but he could write! He said what he thought and, my, how he could think! Before you're my age you'll know about him. Ideas like he had have a way of getting around, only it takes time."

Grandpappy put his spectacles in a cigar box and got up. "We'll catch some peelers for bait on the bridge pilings," he said. Outside the ark he got a long-handled dip net and a pair of oars from under the old monkeynut tree. "You can carry the dip net," he said.

I would have rather had the oars because Grandpappy had a pretty pair. They were so light, made of ash, with copper tips and leathers that rested in the rowlocks so that you could row easy and quiet. By the river the skiff bobbed up and down to the little dock where it was tied.

"Where's your fishing line?" he asked. I patted the lump in my coat pocket.

"You can't get in my boat with that stiff collar on," he said. "Take it off and we'll both feel better. You certainly are dressed up to go fishing. Must be because it's Sunday."

I took my Sunday coat off and tucked it under the bow deck but I had a terrible time with the stiff collar because Mama always helps me with it. I finally got it off but the gold collar button went overboard and sank out of sight.

"Let me row, Grandpappy."

"It's just a little piece to the bridge," he said. "You can try your hand at catching the peelers."

Crabs like to hang to the old bridge pilings and while not many of them are peelers, some are bound to be. They're hard to see and usually all you have to go by is the red on their big claws. But it was a nice, sunny day and that made it easier to see them. Grandpappy sat on the stern seat and rowed by pushing. Most of the old watermen row like that so that they can see where they are going without bothering to turn. He rowed over by the draw pilings and pretty soon I had three peelers.

"That's enough," he said, and let the skiff drift under the draw. He looked the pilings over until he found a certain one. "There's a deep hole here where the biggest perch go to get cooled off," he said. He tied his stern line to the piling and I tied the bow line to one close to me. We both used two half hitches.

The water had that clear green look it always has under the bridge on a sunny day. It's easy on the eyes, like the green shades bookkeepers wear. The sun came through the cracks of the bridge and one ray placed a halo on Grandpappy's head like the disciples wear on the painted windows of our church. I thought of my sin and wondered if I was wearing a halo, too.

We baited our hooks and let the lines slip over the gunwale until the sinkers struck bottom. Then we pulled up a little to get out of the mud. Grandpappy was right about it being deep. I guess it must have been all of twenty feet. But we didn't have any bites.

Grandpappy watched the tide slipping by the piling. "It's running too strong for the perch to bite," he said. "We'll have to wait until the high water slack."

About that time I felt something sucking around my hook and when I gave the line a yank I hooked an eel. He gave me a great battle but eels are awfully slimy and I had to cut the hook out because he had swallowed it.

"Throw it overboard," Grandpappy said. "I don't want no slimy eel in my clean boat." He looked at me sharp-like. "What are you worrying about, Noah?"

"Nothing much, only I played hooky from Sunday school so as to go fishing and now all I catch is an eel. Looks like the good Lord has already taken a hand."

"It ain't Him, it's the tide."

"I can't help from worrying, Grandpappy. Don't you ever worry?"

"Not since I reached fifty and got some sense," he said. "I must be one of the luckiest people in town, I guess."

I'd never thought of Grandpappy as being lucky, he seemed so poor and alone.

"I've got a place to live in, enough clothes to keep me warm and I don't go hungry," he said. "Besides I've got time to read and fish or set in the sun. The richest men in town don't have as much as I got."

"Wouldn't you rather be president of the bank, like Mr. Eben Pauley, and wear a stiff collar every day, Grandpappy?"

"Lord, no," he said. "Eben has got a chain attached to that stiff collar. We grew up together and he was a nice boy, free and easy. Now he can't look around without wondering what people will think or say. Spends most of his spare time showing folks how honest he is by leading the church choir and things like that. I'll bet he'd like to go fishing on a Sunday, only he's afraid of what people might say. I can go fishing any time I want."

"Wouldn't you like to live in a big house and have servants to feed and wait on you, Grandpappy?"

"I don't need nobody to wait on me," he said. "I can take care of myself. What does that fancy food get you? A pot gut and a visit to the hospital. Look at me, I'm as slim as when I was a boy." And he was.

"What do you want to be when you grow up, Noah?" he said.

"I kind of thought I'd like to be a writer, Grandpappy."

"Well, there's been one great one in our family, an Englishman, though we don't claim no relation. That's all right, write about the river. But don't leave the river. It's a fine life and a free life. People like Eben have given up their freedom for something else and if they live long enough they'll be sorry. They're all caught just like shad in a pound net. They follow the school in and they can't get out."

Grandpappy gave a quick yank and brought a pretty white perch over the side of the skiff. "They've started to bite," he said. "Let's stop thinking and have some fun."

It was fun, the way those perch bit just like they hadn't eaten anything for a week. I even forgot it was Sunday, pulling the perch out of the green water. Grandpappy caught one that must have weighed a pound and a half.

"Look at this big one," he said, laughing. "He looks like a bank president."

The perch stopped biting as suddenly as they had started and after waiting a few minutes without a bite, Grandpappy pulled his line in. "We might as well go home," he said. "They've had enough."

We untied our lines and Grandpappy let me row the skiff back to his ark. There he made me take half of the fish and put them on a string.

"I guess you're ashamed to carry a string of fish down Water Street on Sunday, ain't you?" he said.

"I ain't ashamed but I'm scared of what Mama may do. She ain't licked me since she used the hair brush."

"Always do what you're scared to do," he said. "You take those fish right home and tell her where you've been. She may talk a lot, that's the way of most women, but she won't do anything."

"Maybe she'll kill the fatted calf," I said.

"What's that you said?" he asked, thinking he hadn't heard me right.

"Maybe she'll treat me like the father treated the prodigal son in the Bible," I said. "Our preacher talked about that this morning."

Grandpappy laughed. "Why don't you walk right in and give her the fish and say, 'Mama, your prodigal son has returned,' and see what she says."

"You don't know Mama, but I'll try it," I said, and started home with my string of fish. I couldn't put the stiff collar on because I'd lost the collar button, my coat was rumpled, and I had sticky river mud on my shoes. But the white perch were real pretty.

Water Street was deserted. I guess everybody was sleeping off their big Sunday dinners. Mama was sitting on the front porch when I got home.

"Where'd you get those fish?" she asked.

"I caught them, Mama," I said. "I've been fishing under the bridge with Grandpappy."

She looked at my clothes. "Oh, my," she said, "fishing on Sunday and missing Sunday school. We'll never live this down. I should think you would be ashamed. Ain't you ashamed?"

"I'm like the prodigal son, Mama," I said, looking at her with a little smile.

"The prodigal son," she snorted. "What's that got to do with it? You take your clothes off and go to bed." She looked at the string of white perch. "You'd better clean the fish first."

CHAPTER 23

Cupid and the Little City Girl

EVEN though my Grandpappy lives in an ark, I am allowed to play with some of the best children in town.

Every summer Billy Unger's city cousin visits him for a couple of weeks. She always seemed to be a scraggly little thing. The summer I was twelve, when she came over, something had happened to her. She was as pretty as a picture. Not that I'm much judge of girls or women. Mama says if I ever get married, the woman will have to come and get me, I'm that shy. When I was in the third grade I used to sit next to Ginny Bruce and sometimes we'd walk home together. But one day Micky and Erny saw us and called me a sissy. I had to fight both of them and since then I ain't had much to do with womenfolk, except Mama. But when Billy's little city cousin came over to visit him, I got interested again.

I was fishing on the brick wall next to Billy's house, and had just caught a fair-sized eel, when she came up in back of me.

"Aren't you afraid of that wriggly thing?" Betty said.

Her name was Elizabeth, but everybody called her Betty.
"Why, it's Noah, isn't it? I didn't hardly know you, you've
grown so big." And she smiled and showed all of her teeth.

"Afraid of what?" I cut the hook out of the eel's mouth
with my penknife. "Sometimes I catch them as big as a
rubber hose. You want to touch it?" I held the eel over toward her and she sort of screeched like she was scared. I
cut it up for crab bait. Pretty soon I caught a big hard
crab. It swaggered around on the grass throwing up its big
claws like it wanted to fight.

"My, it certainly takes a lot of nerve to catch big hard
crabs," Betty said. "Can you pick it up?"

"Sure," I said, but when I reached for its back fin, it
swung around and grabbed hold of my finger, bringing
blood.

"Oh," Betty said, "you're hurt and it's all my fault. Let
me tie your finger up for you."

Before I could stop her, she took out a little flimsy handkerchief and tied it around my finger. The blood came
through the linen.

"It's going to ruin your handkerchief," I said.

"That's all right," she said. "It was my fault, and you
are so brave." She smiled again and showed all of her
teeth.

We sat there all morning with our legs dangling over the
wall, catching fish and crabs. I showed Betty how to kill a
crab and use it for bait and pretty soon she wasn't afraid of
them. My finger stopped bleeding and I offered to give her
the handkerchief but she said she wanted me to keep it.
When the twelve o'clock whistle blew, Billy's mother

called her home for dinner but before she went she asked me down to play with her and Billy that afternoon.

When I went home, Mama noticed my finger right away.

"I told you that penknife was too sharp. Now you've gone and cut yourself. How did you do it?" she asked.

"A hard crab bit me."

"A hard crab, don't you know they bite? Come here and put it in this basin of hot water so it won't get sore." She noticed Betty's handkerchief. "A lady's handkerchief, and linen, too. What won't you bring home next! Where'd this come from?"

"Billy's little cousin from the city tied it up for me."

"She did," Mama said, sort of jealous-like. "These city females know how to go after the men, even when they're only knee high to a grasshopper! I suppose she invited you to come down to Billy's house and play with her this afternoon."

"Yes, she did," I said, wondering how Mama guessed that.

"You'll have to wash up and put on clean clothes," she said. "You smell like an old crab that's been laying in the sun too long."

I went upstairs and washed and put on a clean shirt and a pair of breeches. I wet my hair and slicked it back.

"Do I look all right now, Mama?" I asked when I came downstairs. She took a good look at me and washed behind my ears with a soapy rag. She could be awful rough around your ears.

"You're just as good as Billy Unger any day," she said.

"Always remember that, even if your father won't work steady."

"Yes, ma'am," I said, and walked down the hill to Billy's house. His father is a lawyer and they live in a big house. Billy was always nice to me, but sometimes it looked like Mrs. Unger didn't like him to play with me too much. Dad said she was trying hard to belong to the four hundred, that means society folks.

There wasn't anybody on Billy's front porch, but when I went around in the back yard, there was Betty sitting on the porch steps, only she wasn't alone, for besides Billy there was Erny and Micky. I couldn't figure why they had come; they belonged up town.

"Hello, Noah," she said, smiling that way of hers and the boys sort of grunted. I sat down on the steps.

"I was telling these fellows about what the city boys do when they come to see a girl," Betty said. "They always bring her flowers or a box of candy. Micky and Erny didn't bring me a present, did you?"

For some reason I felt right spunky. "How'd you like to have a four-leaf clover to bring you good luck?" I said, trying to remember where I saw one the other day in Billy's yard.

Betty thought about it a minute. "That would be fine, maybe all of you boys could find me a four-leaf clover, and I will forgive you." She smiled that smile.

Part of Billy's yard had gone to clover so us four boys went on pasture and started looking for a four-leaf clover.

"Ow!" Micky yelled, coming up from his hands and knees right quick.

"Did you get one?" we all said.

"I got one," Micky said. "I knelt on a honey bee and he stung me."

He pulled out the stinger and went and sat on the brick wall where he could stick his leg in the water.

All the time we were groveling and creeping around with our noses almost in the clover, like animals, Betty was sitting back on the porch steps, like a queen.

"Here's a five-leaf one," Erny said, standing up.

"That ain't no good, that's bad luck," I said, so Erny pitched it in the river as quick as he could.

I began thinking of sticking an extra leaf on a three-leaf one and faking it, when I came across the real thing. It was a puny one, and a bug had eaten part of one leaf, but anybody could see it was a four-leaf clover.

"I found one," I called and carried it to Betty. She looked it over and so did the rest.

"It's not a pretty one," she said, "but I guess it will do. For finding it I'm going to give you a special favor, Noah. You can take me to the movies Friday night when they have *The Iron Claw*. Aren't you a lucky boy?" She smiled.

I didn't answer that question but I didn't feel lucky and then I did, sort of half scared and half lucky. I never had taken a girl to the movies but I guess you have to start sometime. Anyway, Friday was three days off, lots of things might happen before then.

"Well, you don't seem very happy that you're going to be able to take me to the movies," Betty said. "Maybe I'd better ask Micky or Erny." They didn't say anything either so she sort of shifted the subject.

"Let's play hide and seek," she said. "Noah, you can be it." That wasn't our way of doing it but I went it just to be polite. I didn't have any trouble finding Billy and Erny but I couldn't find the other two anywhere until I looked down in Mr. Unger's cellar. Micky and Betty were hiding in the corn cob bin and it was so dark I wouldn't have seen them only they moved and the corn cobs started to stir.

"One, two, three for Betty and Micky," I called.

Erny was it and the rest of us hid. Betty took me by the hand and we hid in the corn cob bin. It was awfully dark in there but not as dark as it gets in the movies. Betty made out she was scared and held my hand all the time.

While we were hiding I heard somebody walking around on the back porch. It sounded like grown-up footsteps. "Where's Betty?" we heard Mrs. Unger call. Betty sort of nestled up close to me and giggled.

"We can't find her and Noah anywhere," Billy said.

"You'd better stop the game," Mrs. Unger said. "It's time for Betty to have her afternoon nap."

"All in! All in!" Billy shouted, so we crept out of the cellar and ran toward the back steps. Mrs. Unger looked at me sort of funny-like and said, "Oh, this is Noah, isn't it?"

"Yes, ma'am," I said, right shy-like.

"Noah found me a four-leaf clover, Aunt," Betty said, "and he's going to take me to the movies Friday night."

"Is he?" Mrs. Unger said. "Well, you'd better come in and take your nap now and the rest of the boys can run along. I have some work for Billy to do." We went down to the river and skipped oyster shells.

"These city girls are right nice, ain't they?" Micky said.

"You ought to have some fun in the movies Friday night, Noah."

"That old corn cob bin ain't a bad place to spoon," Erny said. "It's not pretty, but it's comfortable."

"Do you reckon you'll really take her to the movies Friday night, Noah?" Micky said.

"Noah ain't got nerve enough to take her," Erny said. "Let alone hold her hand when the Iron Claw sneaks out on the screen."

"Sure I'm going to take her, and what's more we'll stop at the Candy Kitchen and have a sherbet after the movie is over!" That kind of stopped them and they couldn't think of anything else to say. We all went home.

Mama was sitting on the porch when I got there. "Did you have a good time, Noah?" she asked. "Did Mrs. Unger treat you all right? What sort of dress did Betty wear? Who else was there?"

"Yes, ma'am," I said. "I didn't notice."

"You're as tight-mouthed as an oyster," she said. "I never can find out anything from you. All I do is ask questions but what sort of answers do I get?"

"I don't know, Mama."

"You're the hardest child I ever had to talk with," she said.

"Yes, ma'am." I went over to give my piggy-bank a shake.

"What are you thinking of spending money for now?" she asked. "Remember you promised not to take anything out of that before next Christmas."

I figured I would need fifty cents for Friday night. The

movies would cost me ten cents apiece and the sherbets ten cents more. But I didn't even have a red cent except the money in the piggy-bank. I didn't want to be a bank robber, not after I had promised Mama. By Wednesday, I was getting worried because I couldn't get a job to earn that half dollar. Besides, I was spending a good bit of time playing hide and seek with Betty and Billy. Only by this time, half the boys in town were playing there, bringing her presents, and someone had taken her to the movies every night. Wednesday afternoon, I took my wagon and collected those old bones I'd seen over in Bosy Robertson's field. The junkman only gave me twelve cents for them. By Thursday, I was thinking of shaking down the piggy-bank, anyway, and then my luck came back.

I was doing a little work in the garden when Miss Louisa called me.

"Noah, I've got a letter that ought to catch the ten o'clock mail," she said. "Will you mail it for me right away?"

"Yes, ma'am." I was glad to get out of doing the hoeing. Mama's father was a farmer and I was named after him but that don't make me a farmer.

I took the letter and ran off without even giving her time to pay me. "It's worth doing for nothing to get out of the hoeing," I thought, after rounding the corner. "Miss Louisa has always been nice to me." When I got to the post office, the ten o'clock mail had left for the train. I could just drop it in the chute, Miss Louisa wouldn't ever know but she'd always been so nice to me. I sprinted for the railway station and made it in time. I was ready to walk home and began to feel tired when I picked up that hoe again. I heard the screen door slam down at the Ungers' and it was Miss Louisa again.

"Did you get there in time?"

"Yes, ma'am, but I had to go to the station and put it on the train."

"That's wonderful," she said. "It was to a gentleman friend and I was anxious that he get it. Thank you, Noah, and here is something for you." She reached over and put a fifty-cent piece in my hand. It was so big that it felt heavy laying there on my palm.

"Thank you, ma'am," I said. "Thank you so much." And all my worry left me as I put it in my pocket.

Miss Louisa went home and I started hoeing again. That hoe felt as light as a feather. Mama came out in the garden to see how I was getting along.

"I guess you ain't never going to be a farmer," she said. "You're as slow as molasses in the winter time."

"I ran an errand for Miss Louisa."

"That's all right, then. Did she give you anything?"

"Fifty cents."

"Good Lord, that's way too much, she don't know the value of money like her father does. You go and give it back to her right away. She's been too good for you to be taking her money like that."

"I can't do that, Mama."

"Why not?"

"I need that fifty cents."

"Fiddlesticks, I ain't going to argue with you, you either take it over right away or I'll shake fifty cents out of your piggy-bank and give it to her." She had me.

"Yes, ma'am," I said, and went to the Ungers' house and rapped on the side door. A maid came to the door.

"Can I see Miss Louisa?" I asked. She looked at me a minute and let me into a room as pretty as I'd ever seen. After hoeing in the garden I didn't like to sit on that furniture.

Miss Louisa came in. "Miss Louisa, Mama says I can't keep the fifty cents you gave me. She says you've been nice enough to us without me taking money for running a little errand."

"Your mother is too proud," she said. "After all, you might need it to take your girl to the movies." She laughed. "I'm sorry but it was my giving and I won't take it back."

I went on back to the garden, where Mama was hoeing and waiting.

"She wouldn't take it back," I said, feeling that coin heavy in my pants pocket.

"Louisa is as stubborn as her father, even if she don't have his money sense," she said. "Well, you might as well put it in your piggy-bank."

"I can't do that," I said.

"Why not?"

"I'm going to take Betty to the movies tomorrow night."

"Well, why didn't you say so?" she said. "It takes a crowbar to pry anything out of you. If you had told me you needed fifty cents for that, I would have given it to you."

Thursday afternoon, when I went down to play at

Billy's house, besides Betty and the town boys, there was a new boy I'd never seen before. He wore horn-rimmed spectacles and Billy introduced him as Francis Cummings from Philadelphia. He didn't talk like the rest of us but it looked like he was getting along with Betty. She was from Baltimore, so I guess they had something in common. Every time we would go off and hide, Betty would go with that city boy and they always hid in the corn cob bin.

"Ain't you going to hide with me just once, Betty?" I asked, after waiting a long while for her to come with me.

"Noah, don't you know you mustn't say 'ain't'?" she said. "Such words are not used by gentlemen." She smiled at the city boy in the horn-rimmed glasses. He looked like a sissy to me but she must have liked him. I didn't say any more to her after that and the first chance I got, I went off to the cove and skipped oyster shells.

Well, that was Thursday. Friday was about the same. When I went down to Billy's, old four-eyes was squiring Betty around like he had the day before and I couldn't get a word in edgewise. But before I went home I sidled up to Betty and said, "I'll be over to get you about seven o'clock."

"What's that strange boy talking about?" the city boy said to her.

"Oh, something that happened before you came," she said, smiling and showing all of her teeth. I didn't know anything else to say, so I went home.

After supper I started getting slicked up. I sneaked into Mama's room and got a little of her headache cologne and looked in her big mirror. I looked pretty good, even if I do say so myself. Then I got a bouquet of nasturtiums from Mama's flowers and walked down the hill to Billy's house. I could hear my heart beating and stopped by the honeysuckle to suck a little honey and calm myself. When I got to Billy's, I didn't see Betty, but Mrs. Unger was sitting on the front porch.

"I'm going to take Betty to the movies," I said.

She looked at me and laughed. "You must have made some mistake," she said. "Betty left awhile ago with Francis, that fine boy from Philadelphia. You must have got things mixed up, Noah." She laughed again.

"No, ma'am," I said. "I didn't get things mixed up but it don't make no difference. Here is a bouquet of flowers for you, Mrs. Unger."

I walked over to the cove. I sort of felt like crying until I felt that fifty cents in my pocket, besides the dime and two pennies I made selling the bones. Doggone if I wouldn't go down to the movies anyway and sit in the balcony where Mr. Jester couldn't catch you if you yelled when the Iron Claw grabbed the heroine. And I'd have a double banana royal at the Candy Kitchen afterwards, with four dippers of ice cream and three flavors of syrup.

CHAPTER 24

Long Pants or a Mustache

THE next day I was sick and Mama had to send for Dr. Salmons. I spent three days in bed and had time to think about Betty, Mrs. Unger, and the fifty-cent piece that Miss Louisa gave me. Money must be important, and I began figuring on how I could make some during summer vacation, not by just cutting grass and delivering groceries on Saturdays but getting a real job.

After I was over that stomach attack, I heard that Mr. Chris, the Greek who runs the Candy Kitchen, was already hiring boys to sell ice cream hokey-pokies at the County Fair in August.

"Mama," I said, "can I get a job selling ice cream hokey-pokies at the County Fair for Mr. Chris? He's going to pay fifty cents a day and you get into the Fair free."

"You're too young," she said. "There's too many evil things going on at the Fair for you to see. Gambling wheels, horse racing, and dancing girls without a stitch of clothes on their backs."

"You mean the hootchy-kootchy girls?" I asked, thinking of how we used to beat on our school desks and say, "da, da, da, da, da" when the teacher was out of the room.

"Don't you speak that word, Noah," she said. "You're too young to even think about it."

Dad came in the back door for his dinner. "What's Noah too young to even think about?"

"Working at the Fair and watching those Oriental dancing girls," Mama said.

"It might do him good to do a few licks of work, seeing it's only for a week," Dad said. "Sooner or later he'll have to see the dancing girls anyway."

"Ric and Erny and Micky have already got jobs with Mr. Chris," I said. "I'd like to earn enough money to buy a new saw."

"So you can cut your finger off," Mama said.

"Why don't you go ahead and let the boy earn some honest dollars?" Dad said. "You're always nagging me because I don't have a steady job. Now when Noah wants to work, you don't want to let him."

That sort of made her think. "Well, I guess if the other boys are going to work it won't hurt you none. But remember you are to keep away from the Oriental dancing girls."

"Yes, Mama," I said, thinking that those dancing girls really must be good with even Mama talking so much about them.

After dinner I went up to see Mr. Chris about the job at the Fair. He was in back of the fountain in the Candy Kitchen, stirring around and looking in the mirrors. There were so many mirrors you never knew when Mr. Chris or his partner was watching you.

"Mr. Chris," I said, "I heard you are hiring boys to sell hokey-pokies at the Fair next month. Do you need any more boys?"

"How old are you, boy?" he said. He looked at me real close.

"I'm twelve."

"You know how to make the change?" he said. "Suppose the man bought three hokey-pokies and gave you the dollar bill, how much change you give him? Quick, how much?"

"Eighty-five cents," I said.

"That's right," Mr. Chris said, and walking over to the candy case, he slid back the glass and picked out a big chocolate cream drop.

"You can work for me," he said, giving me the candy. "Come in here Saturday before the Fair and I'll give you the free pass."

"How much are you going to pay me, Mr. Chris?"

"Fifty cents a day," he said. "If you treat me right, you get hokey-pokies and maybe some candy."

"Yes, sir," I said. "I'll treat you right." I ran all the way home to tell Mama and Dad that I had a job.

I saw Ric down by the river the next day and told him I was going to work for Mr. Chris.

"What sort of clothes are you going to wear to the Fair?" Ric asked, throwing an oyster shell that skipped four times.

"I ain't thought nothing about that," I said, "I guess I'll wear my khaki breeches and a shirt."

"I'm going to wear long pants," Ric said. He was only a

month older than me. "Long pants make it look like you're almost a man and that helps at the Fair."

"How does that help?"

"You'll see," said Ric, "just wait and you'll see," and he snickered right smart-like.

"Aw, why can't you tell me, Ric?"

"You ain't old enough," he said, "but when the Fair comes, you'll see why you wished you were wearing long pants."

The Fair that year was the week of August 5-12, and July passed so slowly, I could hardly wait. I even got tired of fishing and crabbing. The week before the Fair I went to Mr. Chris's and he gave me my free pass. It was a button with a blue ribbon on it and mighty pretty. Then it was Sunday, and that night I couldn't sleep, I was so excited. When it started to get light, I got up, put my clothes on, khaki breeches, white shirt, and a pair of sneakers. I pinned the free pass button on the front of my shirt.

"Is that you, Noah, stirring around?" Mama called from the next room. "What's wrong?"

"I don't want to be late getting to my job."

I heard the springs squeak as Dad turned over. "Why don't you let me sleep?" he said. "About the time it gets cool enough to sleep, somebody wakes me up."

"I'll get up and get your breakfast, Noah," Mama said, "but if you eat so early you'll be hungry before dinner time."

"If I get hungry, I'll eat a hokey-pokey."

"You'd better not unless Mr. Chris says so," she said.

After breakfast I started out for the Fair Grounds running like those trotters in the afternoon sulky races and by the time I got to the gates of the Fair Grounds I was panting. But the man who tended the gate wasn't there yet and everything was locked. Pretty soon Erny and Micky came along and we talked while we were waiting.

"Here comes Ric," Erny said. "Gee, he's got on a pair of long pants."

"Hello, fellows," Ric said, and when he sat down on the box beside us, he pulled up his pants so as not to ruin the crease in the knees.

"I guess you think you're hot stuff, don't you?" Micky said to Ric. "Wearing long pants."

"I been wearing these long pants so long they're almost worn out," Ric said. "You just never noticed them before."

And they were worn around the cuffs and pockets.

The gate opened and we found the hokey-pokey booth.

"You boys early birds, eh?" Mr. Chris said. "All right, you crack the ice." So the four of us cracked the ice until we were all hot. Mr. Chris gave us hokey-pokies to eat. That cooled us off.

"Get your coats on, boys, and take the hokey-pokies down by the gate where the farmers can buy them as they come in," Mr. Chris said. We put on the white coats and went down toward the gate, each of us carrying a metal box that had ice and twenty-five hokey-pokies.

"There's no use of all us sticking together," Ric said to me. "Let Erny and Micky go ahead, the people have got to walk a ways before they get hot enough to buy a hokey-pokey." We stopped by a big tent where a group of men were raising a canvas sign.

"What do they have in here, Ric?"

"My Lord, Noah, you're dumb," he said. "This is where they dance the hootchy-kootchy."

The canvas sign straightened out and on it were pictures of pretty girls, dressed in something as thin as cheesecloth. They had all kinds of jewels on their hands and legs. The printing on the sign read, "Oriental Dancers — from the Harem of the Sultan of Turkey — Admission 25¢ — Men Only."

"Here comes Mr. Chris," Ric whispered.

"Hokey-pokies, five cents," I shouted, and we walked on toward the crowd that was coming through the gates. By the time we got to the gate all our hokey-pokies were sold and we went back to the booth to get more.

"Every time you boys sell twenty-five, you can eat one," Mr. Chris said, so we ate one.

By twelve o'clock, Ric and I had each sold out seven times and each of us had eaten seven hokey-pokies, not counting the two bottles of pop we bought. I was getting awfully hot and the dust was blowing in my eyes. Ric didn't feel too good either.

"Let's go up into the top of the grandstand and rest awhile, Ric," I said.

"Yeh, I feel like the time I smoked my first cigar," he said.

And we both got awful sick before we began to feel better.

"I ain't going to eat any more hokey-pokies, today," I said.

"Me neither," Ric said. "Maybe we can sell the ones Mr. Chris gives us and keep the money." So that's what we did from then on.

By the middle of the week I was making more money by selling the free hokey-pokies Mr. Chris gave me than the fifty-cent piece I was paid each evening. And I hadn't spent any money for bottles of pop since that first day either. But there were two things I really wanted to do. I certainly would have liked to win one of those big cowboy pistols and holsters that they chanced off at the gambling wheel booths. They were real pistols and shot big .38-caliber bullets like the Texas Rangers used. The other thing I wanted to do was to go inside that tent where those girls danced the hootchy-kootchy.

Right before every performance the ticket seller would bring the girls out on a little platform and give his talk. A little fellow would beat on a big bass drum and the girls would screech and wiggle before they went inside. Then they would sell tickets. That ticket man had a pleasing voice.

"Come on over here, men," he'd yell. "Hurry, hurry, hurry. Gather closely and I'll tell you the story of these Oriental dancing girls, favorites in the harem of the Turkish sultan and brought to America at great expense for your entertainment. These girls dance with every muscle of their beautiful bodies, and inside the big tent you will see those muscles shake like a bowl of jelly on a frosty morn." He stopped to get his breath and introduce the girls and have them shake a little. He always ended up the same. "But the little lady on the end is the chief attraction. Come right up, men, it's only twenty-five cents. Nobody admitted unless they have long pants or a moustache."

That last part was what stopped me. One afternoon, I saw Ric coming out of the hootchy-kootchy tent. He looked sort of pale.

"Gee, Ric," I said. "Have you been to the hootchy-kootchy?"

"Yes," Ric said, spitting. "I guess that makes me a man. What I saw in that tent!"

"What did you see, Ric?"

"It wouldn't be good for you, Noah. You're too young."

"I'm only a month younger than you," I said.

"A month makes a lot of difference sometimes," Ric said. "I'll tell you what, Noah."

"What?"

"I'm going to see the hootchy-kootchy again the last day of the Fair and if you get yourself a pair of long pants you can go with me."

"I don't know where I can get a pair of long pants."

"Ain't you got a pair of overalls?" he asked. "That's what some of the farmers wear. They'd be all right with your white coat on top."

"Maybe I could keep the overalls under the counter in Mr. Chris's booth," I said. "I could put them on before I go to the hootchy-kootchy Saturday afternoon."

"Yeh, that would be the way to do it," said Ric.

Every time I went by the hootchy-kootchy tent, I took a

look at the sign and twice I watched the girls parade on the platform. That ticket man had a real cunning voice. He sort of lured the men over to buy tickets. Once I saw Dad in the crowd but he didn't see me.

I couldn't get my mind off them hootchy-kootchy dancers. Friday I was selling hokey-pokies in the grandstand, thinking of what I might see the next day and I yelled, "Here you are, gents, buy a cooling hootchy-kootchy for five cents." The crowd howled and I ran.

I took several chances on one of those big cowboy revolvers with the holster but I didn't have any luck. Seems like nobody ever won but one man who I saw win three of those revolvers at different times. Ric said he was in cahoots with the fellow who ran the gambling wheel and that proved the wheel was crooked. This one man was allowed to win so that suckers like me would buy paddles.

Saturday morning I wrapped my blue denim overalls up in a piece of newspaper and took them to the Fair with me. I hid them under the counter in Mr. Chris's booth. I saw Ric at dinnertime.

"What time are we going this afternoon, Ric?"

"The last show is the one to see," Ric said. "Boy! They say the last show is really hot. If they had the last show first the sheriff would have to close them down, but being's it's the last one, they can get away with it."

We went to the last show. That old ticket seller really let himself out and said a lot of extra things about the girls.

"Well, gents, since this is the last time you'll be able to see the Oriental beauties shake their jelly roll, we're going to have a special show after the regular routine. Be sure to take a dollar bill inside the tent with you and for that extra buck the girls will do their final dance in the nude." He ended up with his sentence about the long pants or the moustache and we lined up to get our tickets, Ric in front.

When it came Ric's turn to get a ticket he plunked down a quarter and the man gave him one off a big roll. The ticket man looked at me.

"How old are you?" he asked.

I couldn't say a thing, I just froze, but Ric came to the rescue.

"That's my brother, he's tongue-tied but he's over sixteen," Ric said.

The ticket seller took another look, picked up my quarter, and handed me a ticket. We were inside.

Besides the little man with the big bass drum, there was a cornet player and they started to play "Da, da, da, da, da," together. There weren't any chairs, we stood up. The girls came out and started wiggling and shaking all of the bracelets they had on their arms and legs. They wore themselves out in short order but the men seemed to like it, judging by the way they hollered.

"Come on up close where you can enjoy it, gents," the bass drummer said, and before we knew it the men in back of us had pushed me and Ric close enough so we could have reached over and touched those hootchy-kootchy girls.

I heard one of them say, "Look at that little boy in overalls, they grow up quick in the sticks, don't they?"

One of them reached over and grabbed Ric's hat off his head before he could stop her and shook all over it. The rest of the men laughed but Ric didn't like it. The music stopped and the ticket man came over.

"Now, gents, this is the last show of the week, and we're going to give you something real choice but you're going to have to pay for it. One of these beauties will dance in the nude for all those who put up an extra dollar."

"What's nude mean, Ric?" I said, feeling for my dollar bill.

"Ain't you ignorant about some things," he said. "That means naked."

We all put up the extra dollar bill and two of the girls left, leaving the one they called Madame Fatima. Even the musicians and the ticket taker were gone. Madame Fatima wiggled for a while.

"Come on and take it off!" a big farmer yelled. "We want our money's worth!"

The madame looked real coy and backed toward the rear exit of the tent.

"All right, boys, here goes," she said in a high screechy voice and pulled off all of her clothes.

I looked, and Ric shouted, "She's a man, dammit, it's a he!"

It didn't take the big farmer long to realize that we had been cheated and he was the first to make a dive for Madame Fatima. But she, I mean he, had gone out the rear exit like a flash and we couldn't find him. Later we heard that he had hid in the bearded lady's wagon, but that was too late.

And me and Ric couldn't brag to the other fellows about seeing the hootchy-kootchy.

CHAPTER 25

Wig

I BOUGHT a new baseball glove with the money I earned at the Fair. Me and Ric were breaking it in when a colored girl came by carrying Mrs. Unger's wash in a wicker basket. She brought the clean clothes every Tuesday. She'd been using something to take the kink out of her hair and it sailed out from her head.

"Hello, Wig," Ric said to her, grinning and looking ornery.

The colored girl didn't say anything but she cut her eyes the other way.

"Wig," Ric said again, "Wig," and I said, "Wig, Wig," and we both heehawed.

The girl set the basket of clean clothes on the ground and turned to face us.

"You'd better stop calling me Wig," she said, "or I'll tell your mothers on you."

"You don't even know our names, nigger," Ric said.

"Don't you call me nigger, you pale faces," she said, getting so mad she started to tremble.

"Wig," Ric said, "aah, Wig."

"Wig," I said, "Wig."

The girl stooped over and picked up a couple of oyster shells. "You call me Wig again and I'll slit you open with an oyster shell."

It was getting better all of the time. "Nigger Wig," Ric said, sticking out his tongue. "Wig nigger."

The girl threw a shell at Ric but he ducked behind the big oak tree. He stuck his head out. "Wig," he said.

The three Cullen boys must have heard us bantering the girl and they stuck their heads over the garden fence.

"Yeh, Wig," one of them said, thumbing his nose, "Wig, Wig, Wig."

By that time the girl was so mad she didn't know what she was doing. She picked up oyster shells and started throwing at the Cullen boys. They ducked and came up with clods of dirt and started to chunk her. One clod hit her and one landed right in the middle of the basket of clean clothes. That was enough for Wig. She grabbed the basket and ran toward Mrs. Unger's. I hadn't thrown at her when the others did, but for some reason I picked up a shell and sailed it toward her. We were all throwing shells. Anyway, none of them hit her, but one sailed over her head and through Mrs. Unger's front window. It might have been the one I threw but I'm not saying it was.

"Come on, Noah," Ric said, "let's go down to the river and we'd better run."

All that afternoon, at different times, Mama would come out of the house and call for me. I knew better than to answer but I hated to have her worrying because she might think I was drowned. But I knew that Wig's mother,

Mrs. Unger and maybe Mr. Jester were with her. I didn't go home until it was almost dark and I was hungry. It wasn't any use. Mama was sitting on the front porch, Wig and her mother were standing in the yard.

"There he is," Wig said. "That's one of the boys who deviled me. He threw the shell that broke Mrs. Unger's window."

"Noah," Mama said, "where have you been all afternoon? I called and called. Did you break Mrs. Unger's window?"

"Down by the river, Mama," I said.

"Answer me," she said, "did you break Mrs. Unger's window?"

"I don't know," I said, "there was a whole flock of shells going that way."

"Ain't you ashamed of yourself," she said, "calling this poor little colored girl Wig and making her cry?"

"She threw oyster shells at us," I said, "and she almost cussed us."

"What do you mean, almost cussed you?"

"She didn't say it, she just looked it."

"What do you have to say to that, Mrs. Wig?" Mama said to the colored woman, forgetting herself. The woman must have been using the same stuff on her hair that her daughter used. Anyway, it sailed out all directions like a wig. She was a little spindly thing but when Mama called her "Wig" by mistake, that set her off.

"I'll have you know, Mrs. Marlin, that my name is not Wig. It is Mrs. Marshall and I try to be an honest colored woman and get along with you white folks."

"It's just that your hair does look like a wig," Mama said. "It fooled me, too."

"Mrs. Unger won't pay me for the wash until her window is paid for," the little woman said, "and your boy was one of the ones who threw shells at my poor little girl." She sniffled and I thought she was going to cry.

"How much did the new windowpane cost?" Mama said.

"A dollar and a half."

"Noah, go inside and shake a quarter out of your piggy-bank."

"Can't I take it out of the church box?"

"I said your piggy-bank."

"Yes, ma'am," I said, and got the money.

"Here you are," Mama said, giving the woman the quarter, "and be sure you give it to Mrs. Unger. You can get the rest of the money from the other boys' parents. They've got more money to give."

"I'll see them right away," Mrs. Wig said and she took little Wig by the hand and went off toward the house where the Cullen boys lived.

You might think that ended the Wig affair but it didn't. Mrs. Wig got fifty cents that Ric was saving for a new air rifle and the Cullen boys paid the rest for a new windowpane. Ric minded it most of all because he felt that Wig had got the best of him.

"Look here, Noah," he said, "we've got to make little Wig pay for this."

"Aw, let's forget it, Ric," I said. "Like as not we'd break another windowpane."

"Well," Ric said, "you know that was your shell."

"You can't be sure of that," I said.

"Let's go and talk it over with the Cullen boys," he said. "I'll betcha they want to do something about it."

Mrs. Cullen always keeps her boys busy and they were in the back yard working. Willie and John were cleaning out the hen house and Richard was beating biscuits.

"You fellows satisfied to let them two Wig niggers get the best of us?" Ric said.

"I'm not aiming to pay for any more windows," the oldest Cullen boy said.

"We ought to be able to figure out something," John Cullen said. "It's not right to let a girl get the best of you, particularly a nigger girl."

"We might build a pitfall," Ric said, "like they catch wild animals in. That girl lives in coontown and goes by the dump on her way with the clothes."

"She comes to get the dirty clothes every Saturday," I said, "only old Wig came with little Wig last time."

"Has she got a father?" Willie asked.

"Sure," Ric said. "Old Pokey's her father. He and old Wig go fishing down the river in the spring."

"I guess I saw that little woman carrying the oars," Richard said.

"She does the rowing, too," Willie said.

"Old Pokey carries the jug and a can of worms," I said.

"He won't give us no trouble," Ric said, "even if he owns to being the father of little Wig."

"They're probably not married, legally," Richard said.

"Why can't we hide and devil the girl?" Ric said. "She

could only guess who it was and our word is better than hers."

"We could hide here in our back yard," Willie said.

"That wouldn't do," Richard said, "that would make our father responsible before the law."

"You mean if we deviled her from your yard, the owner would be responsible?" Ric said.

"That's right," Richard said.

"Let's hide in Miss Lizzie's chicken yard and devil her," I said. "She's kept three of our baseballs in the last two weeks." We laughed at the idea.

"She goes to the store Saturday morning, about the time little Wig comes for the dirty clothes," Willie said.

"Maybe they'll put Miss Lizzie in jail," Ric said.

That made us laugh again. "That would be killing two birds with one stone," Richard said, getting legal again.

"Do you think we ought to stone her?" Willie said.

"I didn't mean that," Richard said.

"I wish we had some big nickel firecrackers to set off on her tail," John said.

"That's a lot of money to spend on a nigger," Ric said.

"It would be worth it to see her run," Willie said.

"Let's get Froggy Duncan to help us, he's got a dozen five-centers he's saving for Christmas," Richard said.

"Miss Lizzie's got a long garden hose she uses to water her chickens," I said. "We might use that."

"To put out the fire," Ric said.

"This thing has got to be planned just right," Richard said.

Mrs. Cullen came out of the summer kitchen and saw

us. "What are you boys planning to get into now?" she said. "Noah, you and Rickard better go on home. My boys have a lot of work to do before dinner."

Me and Ric left but we saw the Cullen boys the next day and made our plans to devil little Wig.

"Here's the way I see it," Ric said. "When little Wig comes along, somebody at the far end of the fence will say 'Wig.' She'll stop and look, that's the time to pitch the firecracker. That'll start her legs moving, only we'll have a wire stretched across the road to trip her. Then we play the fire hose on her or toss another firecracker or spit devil for good measure."

"What'll she do, you think?" Willie said.

"She won't stop short of the river," Johnny said.

"Maybe she'll jump in and drown," I said.

"Girls are afraid of the water," Ric said. "She won't jump in."

The next Saturday, Miss Lizzie left for the store with her big basket tucked under her arm and the fellows boosted me over her back fence. I slipped through her chicken yard and unlatched the side gate so the rest could come in. There were six of us, counting Froggy, and he had two of his five-centers. 'Course he was the one who would light and throw them. Ric found a knothole big enough to squirt the hose through and the rest of us found knotholes along the fence. It was six feet high and had three strings of barbed wire on the top, like the trenches in the war.

"Here she comes," Richard said. "I see her coming along the oyster shell road by the big willow."

"She's alone," Ric said.

I saw little Wig, her hair sailing out behind, walking toward us. Once she stopped to talk to an old hound dog that was stretched out beside the ditch. When she reached the street that led past Miss Lizzie's, she stopped and looked toward Mrs. Unger's, at the other end. She turned and looked behind her and then looked toward Mrs. Unger's again. It seemed like she was sniffing the air and I guess she was wondering why the street was so quiet on a Saturday morning. Usually some of us were playing two-batter-two or deviling around. Little Wig picked up a couple of oyster shells and a big stick from the ditch. She straightened up and came on. When she was abreast of Miss Lizzie's fence we started.

"Wig," a voice said from somewhere. I knew it was Ric, only he had disguised his voice and sounded like something out of the graveyard. "Wig, we've got you," the voice said. Little Wig turned and started to go back but it was too late.

"Wig," a different voice said. It was high-pitched, Willie Cullen's. "Wig, we've got you." The girl whirled and looked toward Mrs. Unger's. That was when Froggy pitched the lighted firecracker. His aim was good and it exploded right in back of her. Wham!

It didn't hurt her but little Wig jumped high and yelled. She started running and tripped over the wire Ric had rigged.

"Fire!" Johnny Cullen yelled and squirted the hose on her through the fence.

Poor little Wig had stood all she could and I was sick to

my stomach. But Froggy pitched the second firecracker. The sound it made aroused her and she got up and ran toward home. She reached the oyster shell road just as Mr. Brewster was driving home in his horse and carriage. He has the fastest rig in town and touched his mare up when he saw little Wig running. But that didn't mean anything to her. She left Mr. Brewster's horse behind and the last we saw of her was a dust cloud leading past the dump.

Ric laughed, but the rest of us, even Froggy, didn't feel so good. I heard a noise and turned. There was Miss Lizzie standing on her back porch, a basket of groceries beside her.

"I saw it all," she said. "I saw it all, and if your parents don't lick every one of you good, I'm going to turn you over to the town constable for trespassing."

Mama used the hair brush on me — she's an easy whipper — but Mr. Lawrence used a strap on Ric. The Cullen boys got it, too, only Richard is too old for whipping and he had to clean out their privy, for punishment.

It's funny, but while Mama was whipping me, all of a sudden I thought of Rose Mack. It was the first time I had thought of Rose Mack for a long while.

CHAPTER 26

The Passing of the River Rats

ONE day in September, while I was walking home from school, I saw a stranger in town, and he was wearing a uniform. His hat had the widest brim, something like what the National Guard wears, and he had on breeches with leather leggings. Leaving out the policeman, we don't see many uniforms. I had a penny and stopped in Mr. Billy Mac's to get a sour pickle.

"How'd do, Noah," Mr. Billy said. He wrapped the pickle in a piece of old newspaper for me to hold on to. "Are you going to join the Boy Scouts?"

"I ain't heard about it, Mr. Billy," I said, "but I just finished reading about Daniel Boone in a book." We saw the stranger in uniform come out of the National Bank.

"There he goes," Mr. Billy said, "that man in the big hat with a belt for a hatband; he wants to organize a troop of Boy Scouts here. He's been interviewing the bigwigs and hunting around for a scoutmaster."

Ric came along. "Hey, Noah, give me a bite of your pickle." He can take an awful big bite if he wants to, so I moved the newspaper up.

"You heard about the Boy Scouts, Ric?" I asked.

"Sure, I don't want to join no scouts. Do you think old Davy Crockett or Kit Carson would have joined the Boy Scouts? Naw, I'd rather be a lone scout and prowl the woods by myself or maybe with some other guy. Pop says it's a scheme to get us boys into the army."

The next day when we went to school, Miss Gussie, our seventh-grade teacher, gave each of us boys a little folder telling all about the Boy Scouts. And on the cover was a picture of a scout all dressed in his uniform and carrying a knapsack on his back. We all wanted one of those uniforms for Christmas. But it said in the folder that only Boy Scouts could wear the uniforms. Ric said if he wanted to he would wear one, Boy Scout or no Boy Scout, but that folder said it was protected by an act of Congress. I didn't want to break no laws, that means trouble. That afternoon, who should come into our classroom but the stranger in uniform. He didn't have much size to him but he was right dapper. Miss Gussie asked us boys to stay after school to meet him. That was the first time I was ever glad to stay after school.

"Boys, this is Mr. Claude R. Woodstrum, and he wants to talk to you about organizing a troop of Boy Scouts in our town. He comes from the National Headquarters of the Boy Scouts of America," Miss Gussie said.

Mr. Woodstrum was some talker. He told us all about how the Boy Scouts were first organized by an Englishman after the Boer War and how the idea was brought to America. He showed us a tenderfoot badge and explained what it meant and he gave us copies of the scout oath and law.

Then he passed out copies of the *Boy Scout Handbook*. They were new with a nice smell and inside the waterproof cover it told you everything a scout would want to know. How to build a leanto, how to cook a bear steak, how to take care of snake bite.

"Are there any questions you'd like to ask, boys?" Mr. Woodstrum asked.

"How old do you have to be to join the Boy Scouts?" Billy asked.

"Twelve years old, that's why I talked to you fellows. Most of you are twelve."

"What do you have to do to join the scouts?" Erny asked.

"Well, you have to pass certain examinations," Mr. Woodstrum said.

That sort of sobered all of us. Examinations were next to the woodshed and we all dreaded them.

"Just a few tests," the organizer continued, "like tying ropes and learning the scout oath and law. After that, you become a member of the Boy Scouts and receive one of these membership certificates."

He showed us a small celluloid-covered certificate with a picture of two Boy Scouts signaling on it. It was real official-looking and pretty and I knew I wouldn't rest until I got one of those certificates and a uniform.

Mr. Woodstrum tied a few knots, only he wasn't so good on some of them. Us river boys can't tie many knots but the ones we use, like the bowline, we can tie blindfolded or behind our backs.

"Did you ever see the masthead knot, Mr. Woodstrum?" Ric asked. That's a knot the schooner men use in case they

lose a mast in a storm. It takes both hands and your teeth
to tie it. Mr. Woodstrum was right surprised but he showed
us timber knots we had never seen before.

"What kind of a gun do Boy Scouts carry?" asked Ralph
Meekins.

The Meekins boys carry their cat rifles with them most
of the time. They shoot cats.

"The Boy Scouts do not carry guns, they are strictly
nonmilitary," the organizer said. "But they do carry a six-
foot staff," and he showed us a picture.

"How do you get to wear that uniform? That's what I
want to know," Erny asked, right plain-like.

"After you have passed your tenderfoot examinations,
your name is recorded at National Headquarters and you
can buy the uniform, knapsack, canteen and other equip-
ment from the headquarters store. How many of you boys
want to join the scouts?"

All our hands shot up except Ric and the Meekins boy.
Ric was just plain contrary and I knew that Meekins boy
would not give up his rifle even to join the Boy Scouts.

"I'll be back in a week to give you the tenderfoot ex-
amination," Mr. Woodstrum said. "In the meantime I'll
leave these handbooks with your teacher. You fellows study
hard." He gave us the three-fingered salute of the scouts
before he marched out of the room.

The next week Miss Gussie kept most of us boys in every
afternoon because we didn't have our schoolwork done,
but we were learning something else instead. Every night
I got my schoolbooks out on the kitchen table under our
big nickel lamp. But it was that *Boy Scout Handbook* I

really studied. It had everything in it from rabbit tracks to barbecuing a hog. I don't know why they don't write school-books like that with interesting pictures and telling you something worthwhile. Only one thing I had trouble with, that was the test on the significance of the badge. Those French words, "fleur de lis," sort of stuck me — that and the double carrick bend used to join tugboat lines. It didn't seem practical for Dad's rowboat.

The test was going to be given Monday night in the Masonic Hall and we would have the chance to meet our scoutmaster if we passed. That young lawyer, Joe Parker, was going to be our scoutmaster. Judge Parker, everybody called him in fun, had always been interested in the woods and Mr. Billy Mac told me one time when he was a boy, Judge had run off to the woods and lived for several days until his parents found him and brought him home. Any-way, being a young lawyer, he would have plenty of time to work with the Boy Scouts, that's what our parents said.

The night of the tests, I went with Billy and Hicky New-man, who had just moved to our town, because none of us liked the idea of going to the Masonic Hall by ourselves. We didn't want to ride one of those live goats the Masons had. The tests weren't as hard as I thought and I breezed right through everything but those French words about the badge. At the last moment I forgot them, but Mr. Wood-strum said since I passed everything else, it was all right. Some of the up-town boys had trouble with the bowline knot but they finally tied it by laying the rope on the floor. I don't know what will ever happen if they need to tie it in a hurry, but they passed the tests. All of us passed and we said the scout oath together. I felt just like I did when the Bishop confirmed me, only happier. The organizer divided us up into two patrols of eight tenderfeet each. He didn't know that the two patrols were the same as our two gangs. My patrol was made up of the River Rats and the other patrol of the up-town boys were all Town Bums. Only Ric, the chief Rat of our River Rats, hadn't joined the scouts so the other Rats elected me patrol leader. We picked our patrol name, too, Muskrats, which wasn't much of a change. The up-town patrol called themselves the Lions. When we left the Masonic Hall, I saw Ric lurking in the shadows and waved to him but he didn't say anything. He must have been looking in the window.

The next day in school I found a note on my desk. It read, "There will be an important meeting of all River Rats in the old boathouse by the river after school today." It was signed by Ric, the chief Rat. When I tried to talk to him at recess, all he would say was for me to be sure to be at the old boathouse. I had to stop at the store for Mama on the way home and when I got to the boathouse, all the rest were there.

"Don't you know a Boy Scout is dependable, Noah?" Ric said. "Why ain't you here on time?"

"Aw, Ric, don't get mad," I said.

"Now all us River Rats are here," he said, "I want to know which is it going to be, are you River Rats or Muskrats? What about the promises we signed in blood when we formed the River Rats, are you going to go back on them for your sissy Boy Scouts?"

"Why can't we be both, Ric?" I said. "I know some men in town who are Elks and Masons, both, and there's Mr. Eben Pauley, he joins everything, even the Owls."

"You can't do that," Ric said. "Look here what Article Three says: 'We River Rats pledge ourselves to war continually against the Town Bums.' They're your pals now, the Lions. Do you think you puny Muskrats can ever get along with the Lions? They'll eat you up." Ric kind of laughed but he was plenty mad.

"Aw, Ric," I said, "don't get mad with us. If you'll join the Boy Scouts, you can be patrol leader of the Muskrats. I'll resign."

"I don't want to join no Boy Scouts," Ric said. "They're making sissies of you and you ain't got sense enough to know. You won't be able to carry your air rifles or shoot even tit sparrows no more. You can't never play hooky no more. You can't never throw an oyster shell through the windowpane of an old house, or cuss if you hit your finger with a hammer no more. You're giving up all your rights just so you can wear that uniform."

"Aw, Ric," said Billy, "why don't you join the Boy Scouts and you can wear a uniform, too?"

"I don't want to wear no uniform," Ric said. "If I wanted to wear one, I'd join the army and get a real uniform."

"We'll all help you study for the tenderfoot tests if you'll join the scouts, Ric," I said.

"You fellows are all traitors to the River Rats, every single one of you," Ric said. "Here we made our promises and signed them in blood and you're going back on all of them for a uniform. You're just a bunch of sissies."

"Sissy" is a fighting word for us River Rats, I mean Musk-rats. And that made us mad.

"Ric, you're so contrary we can't do nothing but vote to do away with the River Rats," Billy said. He was the Rat in charge of records and he got out the old can with the stones we used to vote on new member Rats. He gave each of us a pebble. "All in favor of ending the River Rat gang drop a stone in the can."

The sound of the stones dropping in the tin can told what was happening. Everybody but Ric dropped their stones in but when it came his turn, he turned and threw the stone through the only windowpane left in the old boathouse. The breaking glass made a loud noise and we all thought we'd better go home, that is, all but Ric. He still sat on a chunk of wood. "Good-by, Ric," we said as we went out of the door, sort of sad-like.

"Good-by, Marsh Rabbits," Ric answered. "Don't get your nice new uniforms dirty."

CHAPTER 27

Batty: Wilderness Scout

I'M going on a scout hike tomorrow, Mama," I said. It was Friday afternoon, after school.

"Is that so?" she said. "Where are you going?"

"Baker's Woods, by the mill pond."

"Oh, my," she said. "I don't know whether or not I should let you go there. Leaving out the mill pond, there's a swamp on the Baker farm and quicksand. Paul got stuck there once, before you were even thought of."

"Yes, ma'am," I said, "that's why we are going. A scout has got to be brave and know how to face danger without cringing."

"Why didn't you tell me before that you were going?"

"It wasn't no use to let you worry too long," I said. Mama has got to worry over me. Sometimes I think she likes it and I guess she's never thought how hard it is on me.

"You're not going," she said. "For once I'm going to put my foot down." Mama is always putting her foot down and sometimes it's hard to get her to pick it up.

"I've got to go. I'm the patrol leader of the Muskrats. All the fellows would say I was scared if I backed down."

"You'll look like a muskrat if you fall in that swamp. But you can't go."

"You wouldn't want all the fellows saying I was a scared-cat, would you?" I said, trying a different tack.

"I want everything good for you, Noah," she said, "and I don't want you lost in that quicksand."

Dad came up from the river with a peach basket full of oysters. "Where's my shucking knife, Mother?" he said. "I've got some oysters for supper. There's nothing like a mess of fried oysters to fill you up."

"Where'd you leave it the last time you used it?" she said. "That's where you'll find it."

I remembered seeing it stuck in the cherry tree and got it. Dad sat down on the back step and started shucking the oysters, dropping them into a saucepan, sticking about every second one into his mouth.

"Want a couple of raw ones, Noah?"

"I'll wait till suppertime," I said. I can eat them raw but I'm more partial to them fried.

"George, Noah was planning to go on a scout hike to the swamp by the mill pond," Mama said. "I told him he couldn't go."

"Now, Mother," Dad said, "you don't have to worry so about the boy. Like as not that quicksand is all dried up since Paul got mired."

"Do you think so?" she said.

"Sure," he said. "I ain't heard of any cow being stuck there for years." Dad knows how to soothe her.

"Can't I go, Mama?" I said. "I've got to know right away so as to plan my provisions."

"That's another thing," she said. "The food you eat on them hikes is bad enough if you had a good stomach. But you were such a poor little thing when you were a baby, and about died. Now you want to ruin your stomach, just when you're beginning to outgrow it."

"There ain't nothing wrong with the boy's stomach," Dad said.

"Can I go, Mama?" I said.

"All right, you can go," she said, "but with one provision."

"What's that?" I said, careful-like.

"As soon as you get home I'm going to give you a dose of castor oil, and you've got to take it without balking."

I didn't say anything for a minute because if there was one thing my stomach didn't like, it was castor oil. But I had to go on the hike, being the patrol leader of the Muskrats. "All right," I said, "I'll take it and you won't have to hold my nose."

Thinking about that dose waiting for me when I got home didn't make the fried oysters taste any better.

After supper, I got out my scout knapsack and started thinking about provisions. "You got any smoked sausage, Mama?" I said. "Scouts like to cook them on a stick, it's easy."

"I don't have much to eat in the house," she said. "You'll have to get some baloney in the morning."

"Baloney is already cooked," I said. "I want something to cook."

"Why don't you make yourself a hunter's stew?" Dad said. "That's real food to eat in the woods."

"Listen to the man talk," Mama said. "I ain't never seen you fry an egg, George."

"I used to cook in my younger days, when I was sailing," he said.

"How do you make a hunter's stew, Dad?" I said, thinking it had a good name.

"It all depends on what you got," he said. "It's sliced potatoes and an onion mostly. If you have that, you can add a tomato, carrots and whatever scraps of meat you can find. The old hunters would shoot a squirrel and skin it."

"I can't shoot a squirrel," I said. "A scout is kind."

"Maybe the squirrel has been stealing the farmer's corn," Dad said. "Can't you even shoot that kind of a squirrel?"

"I don't know," I said. "The scout manual ain't clear in places." Dad is always getting me mixed up when it comes to what is right and wrong. I started looking for the things to make a hunter's stew with.

"Can I have this hunk of bacon, Mama?" I said.

She took a look. "Cut it in half," she said, "and you can help yourself to the potatoes." It didn't take me long only I found out later that I forgot to take salt and pepper.

The next morning I got up earlier than usual and put on my scout suit. It was October and warm enough to make the leggings feel sticky.

"You'd better eat a good breakfast, Noah," Mama said. "Like as not you won't get much else until you get home." She hadn't never been on a scout hike. That's about all we did, eat. "And don't you go near anything that looks like quicksand or jump in to see if it is."

"No, ma'am," I said, hoping she wouldn't get started on that again. After breakfast I filled the water bucket and the woodbox.

"Good-by, Mama," I said.

"Come here and kiss me," she said. "I'll be worrying about you until you come back."

I let her kiss me and, picking up my scout staff and knapsack, started for our meeting place, traveling scouts' pace, ten steps walking and ten steps running. We were to meet in front of our scoutmaster's law office at nine o'clock but I was early. Even so, when I got there five of the boys were sitting on the steps, their knapsacks and scout staffs on the sidewalk.

"Hi, Muskrat," Micky said. He was a Lion. "Are you going to lead the way through the swamp?"

"I don't know the way," I said, "I ain't never been through the swamp. Mama would never let me play around the mill pond."

"I guess some of us up-town Lions will have to show you river boys the way," Erny said.

"Ric knows the way," I said, "but he ain't in the scouts."

Batty Benson came walking down the street. He's about my age, but he's not a scout, either. Batty don't even go to school any more, but most everybody's glad about that. Anyway, his teachers are because Batty never could learn. He spent three years in the third grade and Mr. Manning decided to let him quit. Not that Batty's dumb, but he couldn't learn to read. I don't know who gave him his nickname but that never helped him much. Besides his people are awful poor and there's a lot of them.

"Hello, Batty," Micky said, but the rest of us didn't say anything. Mama has told me more than once not to mix with Batty.

"Hello," Batty said and stopped. He leaned his back against the building and spat clean to the road. "Where you fellows going?"

"We're going to take a hike through the swamp near the mill pond," Micky said.

"I ain't never taken a hike," Batty said. "Is it anything like walking?"

"Sure," Erny said, "only you go in a bunch and cook a meal in the woods."

"You fellows are liable to get lost in that swamp," Batty said. "And if you don't get lost you're liable to have trouble with the hobos that stop off there."

"Hobos?" Micky said, and the rest of us picked up our ears.

"Sure, tramps," Batty said. "They stop off there on their way south. I saw a couple of them heading that way this morning." He took a chew off a piece of plug tobacco and offered it to us.

"You boys chew on a hike?" he said.

"It's against the scout law," Micky said.

"The scout law, I ain't heard about that law," Batty said. "Does it say you can't chew tobacco?"

"It says 'A scout is clean,' and that includes smoking and chewing," Micky said.

"I guess that includes a lot," Batty said. His clothes were dirty and so was Batty but he didn't seem to know it. "Do you reckon Judge might let me go hiking with you?"

"You don't belong to the scouts," Billy Unger said. "And you don't have a uniform."

"That's right," Batty said. "I don't belong."

"Judge might let him go if we asked him," Micky said. "Batty knows the swamp."

"I guess old George Rogers Clark wouldn't have turned Batty down if he knew the swamp, just because he didn't have a uniform," Erny said. He knew his history.

"Let's ask Judge when he gets here," Micky said. You could see that Billy Unger didn't like it but there were more of us poor than the other way. The Judge came along in a couple of minutes, wearing leather puttees, like a real scoutmaster.

"Hello, scouts," he said, looking us over. "Is everybody here?" Us patrol leaders reported.

"Can we take Batty Benson along, Judge?" Micky asked. "He doesn't belong to the scouts but he knows the swamp trail."

Judge looked at Batty. "Why not," he said, and Batty almost swallowed his cud. "Batty, you can carry the new first aid kit." It was bigger than our knapsacks and had a Red Cross painted on the khaki, official-like. The Judge got the kit from his office and gave it to Batty. He slipped it over his shoulder and straightened up. We started out, going in twos, by patrols, and Batty walked beside our scout-master. I hoped none of our womenfolks would see him with us, it might hurt the scouts. We marched up High Street, past the school and cemetery, swinging our scout staffs, almost like soldiers. The people came out on their porches to watch us go by.

Past the cemetery we hit the railroad track and turned to follow it. There wasn't any need to worry about being run down. The morning train had left and it wouldn't be back until late afternoon. Judge and Batty led the way, followed by the Lions and us Muskrats. The leaders stopped before a strange-looking tree. It had a fruit, something like an apple.

"Do any of you scouts know what kind of a fruit this is?" Judge asked, picking one of them from the tree. None of us knew.

"I know what that is," Batty said. "That's a persimmon. Only it won't be ripe until we have a good frost. Ain't none of you boys ever bit into a green persimmon?" I bet Ric had but he wasn't with us.

"I'll try anything once," Billy Unger said, and took a bite. I never saw anybody make such a wry face. "I'm poisoned," he said, spitting most of it out, but his lips were still puckered.

"They won't hurt you," Judge said. "Anybody else want to try?" We looked at Billy Unger and decided not.

After following the railroad for about half a mile, we came to the mill pond and the swamp. Pond water is different from river water but we flushed a shitepoke along the shore and he flew off complaining like those that live on Brewster's Cove.

"You boys are going to get your feet wet and those uniforms dirty pretty soon," Batty said, and we came to a piece of marshy land bordered by a creek.

"How do we get across?" the Judge said.

"Follow me," Batty said and led the way along the creek.

We came to the crossing, an oak plank about a foot wide, and rotten-looking. We hesitated.

"It'll hold you," Batty said, and walked across. We all followed, one at a time, but I felt shaky, wondering how deep the creek was and whether it had a quicksand bottom. I was the last to cross, being the rear guard, and the rest were looking at something on the ground.

"They're fresh," Judge said, and I saw they were looking at footprints.

"That's them two hobos I saw coming this way right early," Batty said. "They look tough but they can't hurt us if we stick together."

"Can't we follow them?" Judge said.

"Sure," Batty said. "Like as not they're on the way to their camp."

"Do they have a camp?" Judge said.

"They call it that," Batty said, "only it's not much, cans to cook with and a place to get out of the rain." We followed the footprints down a narrow path which was wet and slippery.

"Don't you fellows get off the path," Batty said. "There ain't no bottom to this swamp, once you break through." We walked single file and held on to the scout staff of the one ahead. Only I was last and scared to look behind, and nobody held on to my staff.

We came to another creek, only this wasn't as wide as the first one, but there wasn't any bridge, not even a board.

"How do you get across?" Judge asked Batty.

"I jump," he said, "but sometimes I get wet."

"Let's make a bridge out of our staffs," Judge said, "like

it does in the handbook." But we didn't have any rope to lash the staffs together.

Batty took a short run and leaped the creek, clearing its bank by a foot or more, but most of us didn't fare that good. We all got across but we weren't any cleaner when we reached the other side. That marsh mud is like paint. Along the creek there were bushes bearing the prettiest red berries, the color and size of holly berries, only there weren't any leaves, just red berries. They were so pretty, there in the bare marsh. Batty said his pappy called them coonberries.

"When the foraging gets poor in dead winter, the old raccoons come out and eat the coonberries," he said. "Pappy sees them when he's tending his muskrat traps."

The going got wetter and slipperier before it got better and we came out in a grove of big chestnut trees. A few burrs had already fallen from the trees and we tried to open them with a stick.

"Come a good frost and they'll open themselves," Batty said. I stuck a spike from a burr in my finger and was given first aid. Only somehow even the pain from the spike felt good, it was so nice in the chestnut grove, after the swamp.

"I guess the hobos must have left," Batty said, "but their fire is still burning." We went over to the fire and there was a meal cooking in a couple of tin cans hung on a stick. I heard a rustling in the leaves and two men came out of the woods.

"We saw them uniforms and thought you were soldiers," one man said. It was Johnny the umbrella man. He came to town spring and fall, mending umbrellas, and slept in the town jail. You could hear him half a mile away shouting, "Umbrellas to mend, umbrellas to mend." Us boys answered him, "Umbrellas to mend," like an echo.

"Hello, Batty," Johnny said. "Why ain't you got on a scout uniform, too?"

"I'm just guiding them through the swamp," Batty said. "I don't belong. What are you cooking?"

"That's mulligan in one can and coffee in the other," Johnny said. The other tramp didn't say anything. He never did.

"What's mulligan?" Judge asked, sniffing. "That smells mighty good."

"It's hobo stew," Johnny said. "Most anything you can pick up boiled in water and thickened with a little flour. It goes down easy." It sounded like hunter's stew to me.

"You boys might as well make camp here," Judge said. "A fire for each patrol ought to be enough." When we first started taking hikes each scout had his own fire but it got too dangerous, not to count all of the wood we burned. Soon we were busy with our cooking. Batty hadn't brought any food but we shared with him.

"Wish there was a chicken yard near," he said. "I'd show you scouts how to mud roast a hen."

"Speaking of roasting, did you boys ever roast a loon?" Johnny the umbrella man said. None of us had and he told us how.

"First, you have to shoot the loon and that's hard enough," he said, "but if you shoot often enough you'll catch him once coming up. Take him home and don't bother to clean him but put him in your baking pan. Go outside and get a red brick from your pavement and put the brick in the pan with the loon. You cook the loon all day. Then you cook him all night. Next day, at dinnertime, take out your baking pan carefully, remove the loon and throw it away. Eat the brick, you'll find it's deliciously flavored."

We almost died laughing at that. Johnny the umbrella man was a slick talker. He saw the muskrat on our patrol flag. "Seeing that muskrat reminds me of the time I went muskratting," he said. "I used to shoot them with a cat rifle. Well, I hunted all day and didn't see a muskrat, it was that cold. 'Long about suppertime, I built myself a fire in a field close to the marsh and set down to rest. I was sitting there half asleep when I heard a little rustling and there was a muskrat coming up to the fire to get warm. He sat on his haunches and warmed his footsies like a person. Pretty soon another one came up and before I knew it there was a couple of dozen of muskrats, sitting around the fire warming up. But they had one eye on my rifle and I knew they weren't any use to try and shoot them. Well, the fire burned high and the heat started to soften the dirt around the fire, and the muskrats began to settle in it. Then the fire went out and the ground hardened, catching all them muskrats hard and fast."

"You must have shot them then," Judge said.

"Shoot them," Johnny said. "It wasn't necessary. I just slit each one down the back and cut myself a bramble switch. I gave each one of them muskrats a crack across his back and they all jumped right out of their skins and ran off to the marsh. I got two dozen prime hides out of it."

"Muskrats are good eating," Batty said.

"I wouldn't want to eat anything called a rat," Billy Unger said, turning up his nose.

"You're missing plenty," Batty said. "Muskrat gravy is better than squirrel."

My hunter's stew was all right but it took so long and looked more like soup, being's I didn't have any flour to thicken it. But it filled me up and I felt like sleeping, listening to Johnny, the umbrella man, tell his stories. But I had to wash my mess kit. That's the only trouble about cooking, there's always dishes to wash.

When everybody had finished and everything was cleaned up we were ready to play games. The best game we play is where one bunch goes off and the other tries to find them. It was time for us Muskrats to hide. That's more fun than hunting.

"Remember you fellows can't separate until we sight you," Micky said. He's the Lion patrol leader.

"Don't you Muskrats hide in the swamp," Judge said That sounded funny, muskrats not being allowed to go in a swamp.

"You fellows wait until I blow my scout whistle," I said. "I'll blow one long and one short blast."

"Remember, three long blasts means everybody come back to camp," Judge said.

We started off, traveling scout's pace, and as soon as we were out of sight we doubled and sneaked in back of the camp to see if any of the Lions were cheating on us. But they were all sitting around with the Judge listening to Batty and Johnny the umbrella man. We started to travel.

The woods covered the high ground bordering the swamp. We walked careful so as not to break any twigs or leave footprints on the soft ground. There were pretty little red berries growing around the roots of the trees. They called them partridge berries because the birds like to eat them. After walking a few minutes we came to a big oak tree that had been uprooted. It looked like a good place to hide.

"How about this place, fellows?" I said.

They liked it and the hole in back of the tree was big enough for all of us to hide in. I took my scout whistle and blew a long and short blast, not too loud, so they would think we were a long ways off. We listened but there wasn't any answer.

"You'll have to blow it louder," Billy Unger said. I blew again, this time much louder, and the Lions answered, meaning they had heard us and were coming. We lay low and listened. Pretty soon we heard them coming, making plenty of noise. The idea of the game was for us to beat them back to camp without being tagged.

If they tagged us we were caught but if we could get back to camp and touch the biggest of the chestnut trees, that counted for us. But we had to wait until they saw us before making a dash for it. Besides, they probably had left a couple of Lions in camp to guard the base.

"Maybe they'll walk right by and not see us," Hicky said. "That'll give all of us a chance to beat them to the base."

We saw Micky skulking along, trying to keep behind the tree trunks. After that, four more Lions, spread out, came trailing, searching the grounds for signs of us. Micky stopped and we could see that he was looking in our direction. He called the other fellows over and they talked awhile. They spread out again and came toward us. If we hid much longer, it would be too late, so I stuck our patrol flag up and waved. All eight of us gave the Muskrat call and jumped out of the hole, running away in different directions to make it hard for the hunters. The Lions roared and came after us.

Me and Hicky ran together, away from the swamp and fast. After about five minutes we stopped and listened. Everything was quiet and we turned toward the camp base, walking easy on our toes like the Indians used to. Neither one of us had ever been in this woods before and it seemed like we might be lost. But soon the woods thinned out and we heard a hound dog crying like he was chasing a rabbit. Somewhere, the crows were making an awful racket, cawing and talking among themselves. We walked in that direction and came to a cornfield. The crows were in the trees planning how they would get the corn from the two scarecrows. Listening to them, you could tell that some of the crows thought the scarecrows were fakes, but most of them didn't want to take any chances. On the other side of the cornfield we could see a farmhouse. That made us realize we weren't too far from civilization.

"Let's walk along the edge of the cornfield until we hear the fellows at the base," I said. "Then we can make a dash for it."

Hicky got an ear of corn from one of the shocks and started crunching the kernels between his teeth.

"Is that good?" I said.

"It was good enough for the old Indian fighters," he said. "Ain't you ever read about Kit Carson? It gives you strength."

I tried some, but it didn't taste good to me. Maybe Mama is right about me having a weak stomach.

"Listen," Hicky said, and I stopped, pricking up my ears. It was Batty talking to Johnny the umbrella man.

"What's the heaviest load you ever saw go over the Chester River, Johnny?" Batty said.

"As I remember," Johnny said, "it was a wagon of pig bladders, all blown up and traveling toward Wilmington." We heard a lot of laughs after that and knew the base was close. We dropped to our knees and crawled toward the voices. I nudged Hicky. Through the trees we saw six of the Lions and their five Muskrat prisoners. They were close to the tree base but all of them were sitting, tired-like. Batty and the Judge were standing up and so were the two tramps. Their backs were to us and we had a good chance of tagging the tree first if we kept low enough. It was hard on our uniforms but we crawled along on our stomachs, like two snakes. We got up and ran for the base, and got there first. That won the game for the Muskrats.

"I'll call the other fellows in," Judge said, and put his whistle to his mouth. The scoutmaster's whistle makes a louder noise than ours, but that's the way it ought to be. He blew three long blasts. We listened and from far away there was an answer.

"I guess that's Micky and Erny," Judge said. "Maybe they've caught Billy Unger."

"Billy was the last one in a couple of weeks ago," Hicky said. "He sort of likes to worry us."

"He'll really get lost sometime," Batty said.

We sat down and waited. In about five minutes, Micky and Erny came in, and they were tired enough to drop.

"Did you see Billy Unger?" Judge asked.

"We trailed somebody along the edge of the swamp for a couple of miles but we never caught them," Micky said.

"He'll be in pretty soon, Judge," Hicky said. "Billy is just trying to worry us."

Judge blew three long blasts but he didn't get an answer. He tried again but it wasn't any use.

"If he's not here in ten minutes we'll have to hunt for him," Judge said. "Something might have happened to him."

None of us said anything but I knew we were all beginning to think about the swamp with its quicksand. And we all knew how Billy was, he usually did what the teacher told him not to do.

Judge kept looking at his watch and I never knew ten minutes could be so long. He blew three long blasts again. There wasn't any answer.

"We'll spread out and search the woods," he said. "If anybody finds him, blow four blasts. Don't any of you scouts go into the swamp."

"He might be stuck in the swamp, Judge," Batty said. "I'm going to look along the edge."

"All right, Batty, but be careful," Judge said.

It wasn't too far from the swamp to the cornfield — the woods were long but not very broad — and I could see the scouts on each side of me as we searched for Billy Unger. I walked a long ways, far past the fallen oak tree where we had hidden, but nobody blew those four blasts. It was getting dark and when the sun went down it started to get cold. Just when I thought nobody would ever find Billy, somebody yelled and I recognized Billy's voice, only he seemed a long ways off. He shouted again and I started running toward the sound. I tripped over a fallen tree and tore the knee out of my scout breeches, but I got up and ran on toward where Billy was shouting for help. Somebody started blowing four big blasts on a scout whistle and I speeded up. When I reached the edge of the swamp it was too late to help but everything was all right or almost so. Billy Unger and Batty were stretched out on the ground, only it was hard to tell who they were. Both of them were covered with black marsh mud from head to foot and looked like two black boys.

Billy was too tired to talk but Batty told us about it.

"Billy was down to his shoulders in the mud when I found him," he said. "I sort of crawled and swam on top of the marsh, and that big sapling helped. I bent it over like a rabbit snare and pulled Billy out."

It was dark by this time and I knew Mama must be almost worried to death.

"Let's carry Billy and Batty on emergency stretchers," Judge said. We made two stretchers using scout staffs and shirts, only it was cold when you took your shirt off. We nearly froze going back to town.

When we got there, the people heard us marching by and came out on the porches to see what had happened. Billy was too tired out to pay much attention to anything, but Batty rode his stretcher like a general who had won a battle.

CHAPTER 28

The Lord's Oysters

ONE Saturday in early October Dad took me with him in the old bateau, down the river. Towards noon, it got awful hot and we ran into Quaker Neck Wharf to find some shade. A schooner was laying beside the pilings and Dad tied to her. A black boy was fingering a fishing line stretching over her rail.

"Anybody aboard?" Dad called, but the boy didn't say anything, he just grinned. I heard bare feet slapping the deck, in a hurry, like they were hot, and a man with more wrinkles than I've ever seen on a turtle's neck stuck his head over the rail. His face and neck were lined all criss-cross, but his eyes were blue and young.

"Hello, George," the man said. "Come aboard and get a bit of shade, it's free."

"Hello, Captain Pete," Dad said. "We're coming." He boosted me over the rail first. I couldn't wait to get in the shade of the half-hoisted mainsail, the decks were that hot.

"That your boy, George, ain't it?" Captain Pete said, sort of panting. He winked at me and I knew he remembered.

"This is my Noah," Dad said, and to me, "This is Captain

Pete, son, he is the owner of this schooner, the *Kessie Price*. How is your old girl, Captain?"

"She's been doing better since I had her hauled out at Solomons in April. Davis put a whole new stern in her and part of the keel where the worms had been working. I just brought a load of lumber from the Carolinas to Baltimore and came in the Chester to rest awhile. It's too hot and I ain't stirring again till oyster season opens."

"I guess she's an old boat," Dad said, watching the pitch ooze out of a deck seam.

"She's not too old," Captain Pete said. "She was built in 1888, the same year as the great blizzard. A fellow by the name of Rome Price built her over on Rock Creek. He called her the *Kessie C. Price*, and now most everybody's forgotten about that middle 'C.' "

Captain Pete picked up a black chunk of pitch, rolled it awhile and stuck the ball into his mouth. "It's better than chewing tobacco in hot weather," he said, firing one over the rail. "George, I'm looking for a mate to sail her when we go drudging. You used to be right smart with the canvas, ten years or more ago. How about sailing her for me?"

"I ain't done any sailing since the year Noah was born," Dad said. " 'Twas when I helped you take the *Kessie Price* down to Solomons and we were frozen tight in the Patuxent for most of the winter. The missus almost died alone, and this boy only a few months old."

"I'll make it worth your while," Captain Pete said. "I'll give you a tenth of all the oysters we drudge."

"That don't sound like much to me," Dad said, "only one in ten." I could see he was bargaining.

"If you will bring your boy along to help out, I'll make it an eighth," Captain Pete said.

"He's been in school since September," Dad said, "and the missus wouldn't let him stop. She's even talking of sending him to the college on the hill when he gets old enough."

"Damned foolishness, I call it," Captain Pete said. "When I was his age I was as good a culler as any man on the Bay." He looked at me. "Don't you let her do it, boy. You got too much of the river in you to be happy in a stiff collar."

"He's going to finish public school, anyway," Dad said. "I want him to have a better chance than I had."

"Good Lord, George, you don't know when you're well off," Captain Pete said. "Here we have a scorcher and where are you? Working in a bank adding figures or clerking store? No, sir, you take a little trip down the river and go fishing with your boy, or set in the shade and chew pitch. How about a drink?" He pulled a half-pint bottle out of his pocket and handed it to Dad. Dad wiped the sweat off his mouth with his shirt sleeve and took a long swallow.

"I'll sail for you if you give me an eighth without the boy," Dad said, handing the bottle back to Captain Pete. The Captain took a swig and set the bottle on the deck. He thought awhile. "It's a deal, George, if the boy will work for us on Saturdays. There ain't no school then."

Dad picked up the bottle and took another one. "What about it, Noah?" he said. "I'll buy you a bicycle."

"It's all right with me, Dad," I said, thinking of the blue

bicycle in the window of the hardware store, "but you know Mama."

"We'll talk her into it," he said. "She'll come to terms when she sees the money involved." Dad always starts to using big words when he's had a couple of drinks. He took another swig and so did Captain Pete.

"I'm coming up the Chester, middle of October, to get my drudging machinery, George," the Captain said. "I aim to lay at Queenstown near the mouth, while I'm oystering. I'll pick you up at Chestertown."

"Where will you get me Saturdays, Captain Pete?" I asked.

"I hadn't thought of that," he said. "Well, I guess that part of the deal is off." He took another drink. "I'll give you an eighth anyway, George. You're worth it, if you'll keep sober except Sundays. Will you give me your word on that?"

"Unqualifiedly," Dad said, or a big word like that, and they finished the bottle to bind the bargain. Then they both went to sleep and I walked aft to see what the black boy was catching. He had a couple of hardheads and had just pulled in an old toad fish. His line was tangled.

"I'se going to have to cut the hook out," he said, more to himself than to me, and pulled out a big barlow that opened when he pushed a button on the handle.

"Do you work for Captain Pete?" I asked.

"Yessir," he said. "I'se his man."

"What do you do?" I asked.

"I'se a handy man most of the time," he said, "and during the oystering, I'se the cook."

"My Dad is going to be the mate when you go drudging," I said.

"Yessir," he said, grinning. "I heard the Captain and him bargaining."

Dad and the Captain didn't wake up until the sun was low enough to shine under the canvas and hit their eyes, or maybe they smelled the hardheads and fried potatoes the Captain's boy was frying in the cook shack. They both stirred about the same time.

"I guess we snoozed awhile, George," the Captain said, when he sniffed the cooking. "How about you and the boy eating with me?"

"We better be getting home before dark," Dad said. "My running lights ain't working and I dropped my whistle overboard yesterday. If them inspectors ever stop the old bateau, it will be too bad. I don't know why they had to pass that new law down at Washington."

"They're taking our freedom away, little by little," Captain Pete said. "You'll live to see the day when people will be punching time clocks on the Chesapeake."

"I'm scared of them federal inspectors," Dad said. "They're worse than the state officials from Annapolis. Come on, Noah, we want to get home before dark."

We got into the bateau, Dad primed her, being careful not to flood her, and she started the first time he spun the wheel. We coasted up the river, the flood tide and the southwest wind both helping the engine. But it was hot running before the wind, and the flies were pesky.

"You reckon your mother will wait supper for us?" Dad

said. "Those fish frying made me awful hungry. I'm so hungry I'm weak," and he lay back on the stern seat, steering with his big toe.

"She'll make out she's all cleaned up, but there'll be something in the oven," I said. "Look out for the fish stakes, Dad!" I yelled, and he stuck his head up in time to steer between two of them. If you run a fish stake down, it's liable to stave a hole clean through one of the garboards. Once that happened to Dad and he took off his pants, dived under the bateau, and stuck them in the hole from the outside. He got home without his pants.

It was almost dark when we ran under the old wooden bridge and slid across Brewster's Cove to the stake where Dad tied his boat. Mama was sitting on the front porch, rocking the way she does when she is excited or scared.

"Supper ready, Mother?" Dad asked.

"Supper ready," Mama said. "I waited two hours for you and then I ate. But I couldn't enjoy my food, wondering if you and Noah were drowned. Where's all the fish you were going to catch?"

"I caught something more important than fish, Mother," Dad said. "I've got a job."

"A job?" she snorted. "How could you get a job going fishing?"

"Dad does have a job," I said. "He's going to be Captain Pete's mate when he goes oyster drudging."

"A-sailing," she said. "Well, the last time you sailed a schooner, I didn't see you for six months, and Noah a baby at the same time."

"It won't be that way this time, Mother," Dad said.

"We're going to lay at Queenstown and Sundays I'll be home to see you and the boy."

"How much will you be paid a week, George?" she asked, getting practical.

"I get an eighth of all the oysters we drudge," Dad said.

Mama snorted again. "I thought there was a catch in it somewhere," she said. "Always a gambler, and always short of cash." She looked at the old coffee pot where she kept the food money and I knew it must be close to empty.

"Sometimes a schooner drudges enough oysters to make two hundred dollars a day, if the market is right," Dad said. "I'd get twenty-five dollars for our share."

"It'll be your luck to drudge a dollar a day," she said.

"Even if that happens, you won't have to feed me," Dad said, sort of disgusted. Mama always takes the bad side of things. Usually she's right.

Captain Pete brought the *Kessie Price* up the river and Dad went drudging. It was mighty hard, sitting in those desks and thinking about Dad sailing the *Kessie Price* with a drudge dragging behind her. I wondered how they were making out. Dad came home on Sunday about the last of October. Mama had been right. They weren't drudging enough oysters to pay their food bill.

"The state legislature passed another food bill last spring and now we can only work a few of the bars," Dad said. "There's more schooners than there are beds to drudge, not counting the skipjacks and bugeyes. Someday, that fool legislature will give the bay to the big boys and it will be all over."

"Who are the big boys, Dad?" I asked.

"Big companies and the like."

"Why don't you be a big boy, Dad?"

"I'd rather sleep at night."

"He don't want any responsibility," Mama said. "He's smart enough to be rich if he wanted to. Then we could eat less chipped beef and gravy."

"We've talked this all over before, Mother," Dad said.

"I like chipped beef and gravy, Mama," I said.

"It's a good thing you do," she said. "That's what we are going to have for our Sunday dinner."

I didn't see Dad again for two weeks. It was a Thursday, after school, when Billy Unger came running.

"The *Kessie Price* is coming up the river, Noah," he said. "I saw her from my back yard. Let's go down and watch your father sail her in."

We ran to the old wharf, where she used to lay, and sure enough, she was beating up the river, close hauled, for the wind was from the northwest. About a quarter of a mile down the river they dropped the staysail and came on under the fore and mainsail. With the wind where it was the rest was easy, and Dad gradually brought her head into the wind, allowing enough headway to coast alongside the wharf. One of the schooner's men tossed me a line and I slipped the loop over a piling.

"It's a good thing you boys were here to get the lines," Dad said, "or I would have had to really come in close. How's your mother?"

"All right, Dad," I said. "Why ain't you drudging to-day?"

"We broke one of the drudge's gears and have to take it to the blacksmith's shop," he said.

"You might as well go home and see the missus, George," Captain Pete said. "We won't be sailing before tomorrow afternoon, anyway."

"I'll be here, Captain," Dad said, and we walked home together. When Mama saw us coming she came to the gate to meet us.

"I thought it was about time you were coming home," she said. "Have you had enough sailing for this time?"

"We're here to have the blacksmith fix one of the drudging gears, Mother," he said. "Like as not, I'll be going down the river tomorrow."

"Got any money?" she asked.

Dad shook his pockets but nothing jingled. "Captain Pete is getting desperate," he said. "We can't even feed ourselves. The only boys who are making any money are the tongers and they are raking it in. One of the Queenstown boys made forty dollars yesterday and he only worked six hours."

"If one man with hand tongs can make that much, I would think five men with a drudge could make a lot more," Mama said.

"The state has saved the bars at the mouth of the Chester River for the tongers and we drudgers can't touch them," Dad said. "They've got all the cream and the way things are going, it'll soon be lapped up for them, too."

"Dad," I said, getting an idea, "if you sail tomorrow afternoon, can I go with you? It's Friday."

"Of course you can't," Mama said. "You might get

drowned, besides you'd miss Sunday school and church."

"That wouldn't hurt him, Mother," Dad said. "It would do Noah good to have a sail with me. He's been looking pale since school began."

"Aw, Mama," I said. "Please, I'll go to church Sunday night, after I get home."

"How are you going to get home?" she said.

"He can catch the *B. S. Ford* at Queenstown Sunday morning," Dad said. "He'll be home before sundown."

"If he can get home before sundown I guess it will be all right," she said, "but I hate to spend them two nights by myself. Something might happen."

"Why don't you stay at sister Helen's?" I said.

"I could do that," she said, so it was all settled. I was going drudging with Dad.

The blacksmith had to make a new cogwheel for the drudging gear and it took him most of Friday to do it, but the *Kessie Price* was ready to catch the first of the ebb tide late in the afternoon. I thought I would help Dad sail her, but Captain Pete sent me to the cook shack to help the cook peel potatoes for supper. By the time I finished the potatoes, we had passed Quaker Neck Wharf and the river was widening. It was getting dark.

The cook lighted the oil lamp in the cabin and put supper on the table. Dad steered her while the rest ate so I stayed with him.

"Go up in the bow, Noah, and see if you can spy a black can buoy," Dad said. "If you see it, yell which side it's on, port or starboard. The way we are breezing along, I'd hate to hit that big can."

"Yes, sir," I said. It was almost dark. I looked and looked and then I saw the black can buoy well off to the starboard, where it belonged. I yelled to Dad but he didn't raise his hand and I knew he hadn't heard me. By that time, the can was about one hundred feet off our beam and I knew Dad couldn't run it down if he wanted to. I went aft and joined him.

"Did you see it, Dad?" I asked.

"I saw it," he said. "Why didn't you yell?"

"I did, Dad, but you didn't hear me."

"There's the Queenstown Light," he said. "It's going to be tight sailing taking her in now it's dark. Noah, go down and tell Captain Pete we'll need to down the staysail in ten minutes. I don't want no headsails on her when I hit the harbor."

I told Captain Pete. The men had finished eating and were sitting around picking their teeth and smoking.

"Boys, that George really knows the Chester River," Captain Pete said. "He can see better at night than an old hoot owl."

"He gets it from his pappy," one of the schoonermen said. "His old man can see through ink. How are your eyes, boy?" he said, looking at me. I was blinking in the lamplight.

"I just spied the black can buoy for Dad," I said.

"He knew where it was all the time," Captain Pete said. "Well, boys, let's go on deck and help George take her in." He turned the oil lamp down and we all went to help Dad.

"Get the boys to trim the fore and main, Captain," Dad said. "We need to sail closer to it."

"All right, let's trim her," Captain Pete said, going forward.

"It's time to take the staysail off of her, Captain," Dad said a minute later. "I'll lay on the wind and make it easy."

Charley, the smallest and quickest of the schoonermen, climbed out on the bowsprit, Captain Pete unloosed the staysail halyard, and the other fellow and I manned the downhaul.

"Here I come," Dad yelled, bringing the schooner into the wind. The sails flapped, we pulled the jib down in a jiffy. The moment Dad saw we had it, he let the schooner fall off before she had lost her headway.

Dad had the range lights lined up and we were boiling along. It seemed to me that we were going to run high and dry on the beach.

"The deepest water is closest to the point," he said. "That northeaster we had the second week of September moved the channel over ten feet but the government ain't moved the ranges."

The tide was out and I could see the sandy beach, we were that close.

"You want to step ashore, Noah?" Dad said, and in a twinkling we were through the narrow slough and into the harbor. The men had the anchor unlashed and ready to drop. The rest of us, even the cook, were with the sails, all set to pull sheets in and drop them. The lights from the homes gave Dad something to steer by and I saw two anchored schooners, after we had passed them. I guess Dad must have seen them or maybe he was just lucky.

"I'm coming about!" he yelled and spun the wheel. The

Kessie Price came up into the wind, the anchor hit the water with a splash and you could hear the cable rattling against the windlass drum. We pulled in the two sails and dropped them before the schooner would have a chance to fill again.

"Let's put the stops on while we are about it, boys," Captain Pete said after he put the brake on the windlass. "I guess the right bower will hold her tonight, so long as it blows northwest."

We all helped to snug down the sails and get things shipshape. It was quiet and warm after anchoring the *Kessie Price,* and it was good to be with men after all week inside with a bunch of women. I didn't say anything, I kept quiet and listened.

"That old nor'wester sure brought us down the river," Captain Pete said, cutting enough tobacco from his plug to fill a corncob pipe. "Beats any engine they'll ever make, the free wind."

"It'll be blowing nor'west again tomorrow," Dad said. "Three days of nor'west wind after a three-day easterly, that's what my pappy always says."

"Did you con the sky come sundown today?" the schoonerman named Charley said. "It looked like a weather breeder to me."

"A nor'wester really kicks up the bay when the tide is flooding," Captain Pete said. "It's going to be rough sailing in the bay tomorrow."

"In the old days we would have drudged in the river and got some lee," Dad said. "Now the tongers have got the best beds to themselves."

"Their votes count the same as a schoonerman's and there's a damn sight more of them," Captain Pete said.

"If the wind is still nor'west, them tongers won't be out tomorrow," Charley said. "It'll be too rough for any bateau, even in the river."

"I got bounced off the rail of a bateau once," the other schoonerman said. "Damn near drowned before I got my hip boots off. I ain't tonged since."

"Them oysters don't belong to the tongers any more than to us," Captain Pete said. "The State of Maryland ain't got no right to give them to the tongers."

"Them's the Lord's oysters," Dad said. "The good Lord put them there for those who could get them, whether it's tongers or drudgers."

"If them's the Lord's oysters, why don't we sail across them beds come tomorrow, and fill the *Kessie Price* right up to her gills?" Charley said.

"Yeh, why don't we?" the other schoonerman said. "Ain't no tongers or patrol boats coming out in that nor'west wind."

"The inspectors will be having their oysters in the bar at Annapolis," Dad said.

"I'm a religious man," Captain Pete said. "I don't aim to steal if I can help it."

"It's just like George says," Charley said. "Them's the Lord's oysters and the Lord is a cheerful giver. Don't it say that in the Bible? We'd just be taking what He wants to give us. The Lord helps those who help themselves."

"We'd better take a drink and think it over," Captain

Pete said, lifting a board in the cabin floor and finding a pint bottle. They all took big swigs.

"Does the boy ever take a drink, George?" Captain Pete said, meaning me.

"Only when he's got a stomach ache and his mother makes him a whisky toddy," Dad said. "He's too young."

"Ain't there something in the Declaration of Independence that gives us the right to take them oysters in the river, George?" Charley said.

"Sure is," Dad said. "Yes, sir, it says we all got the right to 'life, liberty and the pursuit of happiness.' And you know what Patrick Henry said. It's time us oyster drudgers do something about it. We-uns have been put on too long."

"Supposing the *Governor McLane* is snooping around and catches us," Captain Pete said.

"I'll sail the *Kessie Price* down Tangier Island way," Dad said. "I guess the Virginians still remember Patrick Henry."

"Them inspectors ain't got the stomach for rough water," Charley said. "They won't be out if the nor'wester holds."

"I'm going to take a look at the weather," Captain Pete said, going up the ladder. He didn't stay long.

"The wind's still nor'west," he said. "If she blows from that quarter come morning, what say we drudge the tonger beds, boys? What say, George?"

"I'll sail her," Dad said.

"We'll cull them," Charley said and the other culler nodded his head.

"Let's turn in, men," Captain Pete said. "We'll have to stir early." It was cold enough to keep our clothes on. We took off our shoes and slipped in between the blankets. I slept with Dad.

The first thing I heard in the morning was somebody pumping out the bilge. It woke Dad, too.

"Lord," Dad said, "listen to the cook snoring." He looked at me. "I'd better jump if I don't want to miss my cup of coffee before breakfast," he said.

The pump started to suck air and sounded almost human.

"I guess the cook must be having a bad dream," Dad said. "Sounds like he's choking to death."

We put on our shoes and went on deck. It was mostly dark with a faint rosy color toward the east. Along the shore a big heron walked, just like an old waterman looking for soft crabs. The water was still but a light breeze was coming from the northwest. Dad picked up a bucket with a line on it and tossed it overside.

"Might catch a crab for breakfast," he said, looking at me as he pulled the full bucket aboard. He washed his face and slicked his hair back.

"You're next, Noah," he said, handing me the bucket. "That'll take the sleep out of your eyes."

We went forward and joined the other men who were already drinking their coffee. They had big white cups and the coffee was black, without sugar or cream.

"Mugs up," Captain Pete said, drinking his in a couple of gulps. "This'll put a lining on our stomachs." Dad took his slower.

"Ain't you going to drink a cup of coffee, Noah?" Captain Pete asked. "You ain't been signing one of them temperance pledges, have you? That takes all the joy out of life."

"I don't need it, yet," I said, but my stomach began to feel like it needed something.

"Pretty soon you'll be getting your fill of flapjacks and molasses," Dad said. "That and scrapple." In the cook shack, the black boy was cooking flapjacks right on top of the stove.

"Cap'n and gemmens, I'se ready for the first round," he said. We all got plates and a knife and fork. The cook piled our plates and we did the rest.

"Look at the sun coming up," Captain Pete said. "It's just like one of these flapjacks smeared with apple jelly."

"The wind is coming up with the sun," Dad said. "By the time we get the hook up she'll be blowing just like she did yesterday."

"Yep," Captain Pete said, "and we are going to help ourselves to the Lord's oysters."

The schoonermen looked up when Captain Pete spoke but they didn't say anything. They walked over to the stove and filled their plates.

"You boys eat like a couple of hogs," Captain Pete said to them. "Ain't your mamas never taught you no table manners?"

"We might not get another square meal for a long time if the *Governor McLane* sees us in them tonger beds," Charley said.

"You boys ain't getting cold feet, be you?" Dad said. "Them inspectors ain't got the stomachs for this kind of a day. The Chester River's mouth is rougher than the bay in a nor'west gale. Look at the whitecaps rolling across the river."

"The mouth of the river is wider than the bay," Captain Pete said.

When I looked over the point and saw the big waves it didn't help me to finish my breakfast.

"Ain't you hungry, Noah?" Dad asked, filling his plate and pouring another mug of coffee.

"I guess not," I said. "Maybe I'll be hungry by dinner-time."

"You'd better eat when you can get it," Captain Pete said. "The boy can't cook while we're drudging. It'll be too rough."

After breakfast the men cut tobacco for their pipes and lit up. When they were drudging they only chewed. You could always spit to the leeward but the wind would blow sparks from a pipe.

"Where's your pipe, Noah?" Captain Pete said. "I bet you got one hid in the woodshed, along with cornsilk."

"He don't smoke," Dad said.

"Lord, what's wrong with the boy," Captain Pete said. "It ain't right for boys not to smoke and chew in secret."

"Well, Captain," Dad said, changing the subject, "how about pulling the hook up and getting out of here? The wind is getting stronger all of the time. And I can't sail her out with the wind where she is."

"I guess I know that," Captain Pete said. "We'll let the yawl boat kick her out and get the sails on her in the river." He led the way aft and they lowered the yawl boat. The little boat's stern and propeller were in the water but her bow was tight against the schooner and out of the water. Charley primed the one-cylinder engine several times, it started, and they went forward to get the anchor in. The schoonermen cranked the chain around the windlass drum and stuck a spike through it as the schooner slid above the anchor. The *Kessie Price* lost headway and started again with a jerk.

"She's loose," Captain Pete yelled to Dad and he started swinging the schooner toward the harbor opening.

"We'll drop the mainsail when it's time to drudge," Captain Pete said.

The schoonermen were still panting after getting the fore and main on her. I guess they didn't fancy dropping one of them so soon.

"Ain't we a pair of trained monkeys?" Charley said, taking a chew of tobacco and firing one over the leeward rail. He looked mean.

Captain Pete didn't say anything but he fired one over the rail twice as far as Charley's.

"Ain't a boat or sail in sight," Dad said, bracing himself against the wheelbox and easing her off a bit. "You're mighty pale, Noah."

"Maybe the boy needs a chew of tobacco," Charley said, sticking the plug under my nose. It must have been the smell of tobacco. Anyway, things started to come up, and I reached the leeward rail none too soon. I felt awfully lonely inside for a while and then things began to get better. The men weren't sorry for me like Mama was when I was sick and that made it easier to get well quicker. I sat down with my back to the rail and watched the schoonermen furl the mainsail. With only the foresail drawing, the schooner wasn't in such a hurry and the empty feeling in my stomach began to fill up. I stopped wishing that somehow I could get ashore.

Captain Pete tossed the lead line and fingered the twitching cord.

"We're over the beds," he said. "Let's make a haul." The schoonermen dropped the big iron basket over the side. The schooner's foresail filled again and we sailed across the oyster bar.

"Head up, George," Captain Pete called and the men cranked the basket in. It was full of oysters. They looked at their first haul.

"They're mighty fine," Captain Pete said, "better'n the bay oysters and full baskets means full pockets."

"Ain't many culls here," Charley said as he and the other fellow began to pitch the little ones back.

"You help them cull, Noah," Captain Pete said to me. Then he looked aloft. "The Lord is going to be good to us, today," he said.

"I reckon I'll get the missus a new dress when I gets my share," the other culler said.

"I'm going on a two-week drunk," Charley said. "I'm going to Baltimore and bring home a suitcase full of bottles."

"You boys really spend your money in a hurry," Captain Pete said. "Let's get the drudge aboard again." The basket was full and the culls were few.

"How much you reckon that haul is worth, Captain?" Charley said while we were culling.

"A ten-dollar bill ain't too much," Captain Pete said, "oysters being as scarce as they've been."

The other culler raked the big oysters into the schooner's hold and Captain Pete walked aft and stood with Dad at the wheel.

"You keep your eyes peeled for signs of the *Governor McLane* or any of them tongers' bateaus, George," he said. "Sound off if you see anything."

It was like that all morning, full baskets and few culls. Even the chain on the dredge sang as it went round the drum, and the cullers talked about what they could do with their share of the money. Captain Pete didn't say much but he was chewing plenty. Towards noon the forward hold was almost full and the cullers started to complain.

"I can't work much more unless I get some food," Charley said.

"My back hurts," the other culler said, "I got to rest a mite and get some warm victuals."

"Go over and get a cup of coffee," Captain Pete said. "That'll stay you for a while."

"Seems like I had four cups since breakfast," Charley said. "I've got to sit down and eat."

"How about a swig of liquor?" Captain Pete said and gave them his pint bottle. That quieted them for a while but soon they were complaining again and Captain Pete saw that he would have to give them a rest.

"All right," he said, "after the next haul we'll run into a lee and anchor. Then the boy can keep the pans on the stove long enough to cook us some grub."

It must have been about noon when we beat over to the lee shore and let the anchor go. The cook had the pork chops in the frying pan as soon as the foresail was down, and I helped to slice the potatoes which followed the chops. The cullers ate like they were starved and I had a gnawing feeling that was hard to satisfy. After everybody was full we went to the after cabin and had a little nap. I was the only one who didn't sleep. I lay and listened to the rest of them snore. But they didn't snooze long. Captain Pete woke up with a gurgling sound, like he was drowning.

"Come on, boys," he said. "Let's get some more of the Lord's oysters."

Dad stirred but the Captain had to shake the two cullers. They grunted and complained but pretty soon they had upped the anchor and foresail and we were running toward the oyster bars.

The afternoon passed slowly and it seemed to me that it wasn't as rough as it had been, maybe I was getting used to it. Mama says you can get used to anything if you have to. The *Kessie Price*'s hold was full, with oysters piled up on the deck.

"Just a couple of more hauls and we'll call it a day, boys," Captain Pete said. But we never made those two hauls for Dad yelled and pointed toward Love Point Light. When I looked I didn't see anything at first, only the big waves, then the low sun flashed on brass and I saw a long gray hull.

"My God, it's the *Governor McLane*," Captain Pete said. "Cut the drudge loose, boys."

Dad didn't need any orders. He was sailing up the river, for home. Captain Pete joined him.

"Where you going, George?" he said. "They'll catch us before we get to Morgneck."

"You want me to come about and go to meet them?" Dad said.

Captain Pete didn't say anything but he pulled out a little box and took a rub of snuff. He was already chewing so I guess he was hard put.

"You ever sail a schooner through the Narrows, George?" he said. The Narrows is a sort of a strait that divides Kent Island from the Eastern Shore. There is a channel like a creek, and a drawbridge near the center of the island.

"I ain't never done it but it could be done," Dad said, "but Old Man Peters won't open the bridge after six o'clock." They looked astern where the *Governor McLane* had rounded the point and entered the Chester River. Then they looked at the sun. It was almost down.

"That's it, George," Captain Pete said. "We'll just make it and Old Man Peters won't let the *Governor McLane* through. Do you think he would let the brass buttons through after six o'clock?"

"He wouldn't let the President of the U.S. through after six o'clock," Dad said. "He don't like nobody and he's got a book of rules to help him."

"The buoy at the mouth of the Narrows is hard to see, George," Captain Pete said. "I'll go forward and see if I can spy it for you. Do you want the mainsail up?"

"Not till we get through the Narrows," Dad said. "Then we'll put on everything and really rip across Eastern Bay.

See that high yellow bluff we are steering for? That's Stony Bar Bluff. If you run for that you'll always spot the Narrows buoy."

We looked astern. The Governor McLane was gaining on us, but she was a couple of miles away when Captain Pete saw the Narrows entrance buoy and sang out.

"Dead ahead," he yelled and there it was, so close to the shore that it was hard to see. It looked like Dad was going to beach the *Kessie Price* but the mouth opened up and we slipped inside. Captain Pete spat overside and almost hit the buoy.

"Want a swig of liquor, George?" he said.

"I thought you and the cullers had finished all of it," Dad said.

"I got a little of it hid in the cabin, for medicine," Captain Pete said.

"I need a stiff one," Dad said. "It's going to be tight going through the Narrows and if it's after six o'clock when we get to the bridge, it's going to be too bad."

Captain Pete got his pint bottle and all of the men took a long drink.

"Will they put me in jail too, Dad?" I said. "Mama won't never get over it if they do."

"They ain't caught us yet," he said. We were flying along, the current with us, so fast that the buoys were leaning close to the water. Dad ran over one of them and I heard it go bumping along the garboard but it didn't hurt the *Kessie Price*.

We passed a couple of old men in little skiffs and the smallest oyster tongs I'd ever seen. They were progging around in a slough off the channel and stopped to watch us pass.

"They're doing a little nippering," Captain Pete said. "We must be getting close to the bridge. I'll take the horn to the bow and start blowing, George." He took the fog horn from a hook beside the ship bell and joined the cullers in the bow.

"How far is it to the bridge, Dad?" I asked.

"About a mile," he said. "We'll be there in ten minutes or so."

"What will you do if the bridge won't open, Dad?" I asked. "Come about?"

"There's too much current to come about," he said. "We'd just drift sidewise into the bridge. If I have to do it, I'm going to run the bowsprit right into the creek bank. That'll stop her if it don't jar the masts out of her."

Captain Pete was blowing three long blasts, the signal for the bridge to open. We passed an old man, with a long white beard, nippering along the bank. He didn't even seem to see us. The little fiddler crabs were running for their holes in the mudbanks as we slid by. I guess they were scared, too. Captain Pete kept on blowing.

"There's the top of the draw," Dad said. "Somebody is on the draw."

Captain Pete kept blowing three long blasts and I knew the bridge tender couldn't help but see the *Kessie Price's* masts.

"There's Old Man Peters and he's putting the turning key in," Dad said. The key had a wooden bar on top to make it easier.

"She's opening, George," Captain Pete said, coming back to join us.

"Thank the good Lord," Dad said. "I guess them oysters must be His, the way He cares for us." The cullers were sitting on the deck, their backs against the cabins. They hadn't opened their mouths since Dad first saw the *Governor McLane*. "Don't thank the Lord too soon," Charley said as we slid by the draw.

Old Man Peters walked along beside us. "If you'd come along five minutes later, I wouldn't have opened her, Captain," he said. I never saw a meaner-looking man.

"The *Governor McLane* will be along in ten minutes," Captain Pete said. "Ain't you opening for her?"

Old Man Peters pulled out a big nickel watch. "In three more minutes, I wouldn't open this draw for Teddy Roosevelt," he said. He was really mean.

In ten minutes we were past Hog Island and scudding across Eastern Bay, with all sail on the *Kessie Price*. It was getting dark and I wondered if the *Governor McLane* would run hard aground, groping around in the Narrows.

"I guess we-uns are all the Lord's oysters," Dad said. "Where do you want to go from here, Captain?"

"We might anchor in the lee of Poplar Island and run into Cambridge early tomorrow," Captain Pete said. "We can sell them oysters first thing Monday morning."

"What's going to happen to me, Dad?" I said. "Mama will wonder where I am."

"You'll have to go home on the train, from Cambridge," he said.

And that's what happened, only I was late, and it was

dark, and Mama was worried. But nobody had to go to jail, and Charley got drunk for two weeks, and Mama got a new sewing machine, and I got the blue bicycle in the window of the hardware store. Dad didn't stir a hand all winter. But he did set his eel pots when the dogwood buds swelled again.